BOYS R US

A CLIQUE NOVEL BY LISI HARRISON

poppy

LITTLE, BROWN AND COMPANY
New York   Boston

Poppy

Little, Brown and Company
Hachette Book Group
237 Park Avenue, New York, NY 10017
For more of your favorite series, go to www.pickapoppy.com

First Edition: July 2009

Poppy is an imprint of Little, Brown Books for Young Readers.
The Poppy name and logo are trademarks of Hachette Book Group, Inc.

Cover design by Andrea C. Uva
Cover photos by Roger Moenks
Author photo by Gillian Crane

alloy**entertainment**

Produced by Alloy Entertainment
151 West 26th Street, New York, NY 10001

ISBN: 978-0-316-00682-8

10 9 8 7 6 5 4 3 2 1
CWO
Printed in the United States of America

To Meg Haston, a true Soul-M8.

Claire Lyons trudged across the immaculately manicured lawn of the Block estate, feeling the same way she felt after a worthy contestant got voted off *American Idol*: Technically, *she* hadn't been the one everyone text-rejected. But somehow, she felt the sting just the same.

Cam Fisher flirt-punched her shoulder. "You okay?"

"Huh?" Claire glanced up at her crush. The warmth in Cam's one blue eye and one green eye shielded her against the late-afternoon chill. She buried her hands inside the sleeves of the burgundy Briarwood Tomahawks jersey she wore over gray leggings and flirt-punched him back. "Easy!"

"Ow!" He laughed. A grape bubble gum cloud puffed from his mouth. It smelled like love.

"Worried about Massie?" Cam slipped his arm around her shoulder and left it there for approximately three Mississippis before stuffing his hand back in the pocket of his red hoodie.

Claire nodded, nibbling her Blistex-coated bottom lip to keep from purring. Now was not the time to think about how close she and Cam were standing or how he could practically read her mind. And now was definitely not the time to sneak an intoxicating noseful of Drakkar Noir. Now was the time to focus on being there for Massie, since the rest of the Pretty Committee was avoiding her the way Lindsay avoided food.

It had been less than forty-eight hours since Alicia, Dylan, and Kristen had boycotted Massie's Friday night sleepover, but to Claire, it felt longer than Lent. She'd spent most of that time fielding four-way texts and calls from her friends, having no idea how to respond. Dylan had vented about how she and Derrington could have taken their crush public a week earlier if it weren't for Massie holding her back. Alicia had bragged about how much better her cheer squad, the Heart-Nets, was going to be than Massie's, since Alicia was a superior dancer/choreographer. And Kristen had kept moaning about bad sushi.

Massie, on the other hand, hadn't reached out once since Claire and Cam had shown up to her religiously honored sleepover and found her totally alone. Her silence felt eerie, like the calm before the doors opened for a 75 percent–off sale at BCBG. Madness was sure to follow.

"Do you really think Alicia and Dylan'll stay mad forever?" Cam's gentle voice brought Claire back.

She wished she could tell Cam that the Pretty Committee would be back together before dinner. But Alicia and Dylan seemed done with Massie's rigid, Lycra-ing ways. Done with the alpha controlling everything: whom they crushed on, what they wore, and what they did with their Friday nights. Actually, Claire understood their frustration better than anybody. Before Massie, she'd been perfectly content with her non-designer wardrobe. Now she could barely walk past an Old

Navy without imagining being shot at by a round of deadly comebacks.

"Dunno," she replied honestly. She tried not to think about what could happen if her friends stayed mad. Sure, Lycra kept a tight hold on things. It could even feel suffocating. But it also held everything in its place. Without Massie, the Pretty Committee could fall apart. And where would that leave Claire?

"Sucks," he offered, obviously trying to sound sympathetic and male at the same time.

It was adorable that Cam thought he knew just how dire the situation was. But no matter how many times Claire tried to explain, he couldn't possibly understand. At this point, a reunion for the Pretty Committee seemed less likely than a five-year wedding anniversary for Spencer and Heidi.

Claire stopped in front of the French doors of the Blocks' sunroom and peered inside the canvas tote slung over her shoulder.

"Mood music?" Cam prompted her.

"Check." Claire fingered the CDs they'd burned and decorated with purple glitter earlier that day, one for each of Massie's possible states: PAYBACK PLAYLIST! (Avril, P!nk), SMILE SONGS ("Unwritten" by Natasha Bedingfield, "Party's Just Begun" by the Cheetah Girls), and MASSIE AND ME! ("True Friend" by Miley Cyrus, "My Life Would Suck Without You" by Kelly Clarkson). Claire hoped the last one would remind Massie that she wasn't totally alone.

"Gummies?"

"Check." Claire patted the small, clear plastic bag of gummies at the bottom of the bag. They were sugar free, so Massie wouldn't have to worry about the calories. And Claire had personally removed every green gummy from the bag, knowing how Massie hated them.

"Aaand, last but not least, Keds?" Cam finished.

"Check." Claire gazed longingly at the three pairs of worn sneakers—white platforms, springy polka-dotted mules, and sporty camouflage lace-ups—cowering at the bottom of the bag. Mud-stained hedge clippers stood stiffly inside the left platform, like a soldier waiting for its call to action. She shuddered at the thought of Massie transforming her beloved Keds into canvas carcasses. But there was no better target for the alpha's aggression than non-designer footwear.

"There's still time to save them." Cam hip-bumped her.

"No, I just have to be strong," Claire joked. As controlling as Massie could be, she'd ultimately made Westchester feel like home. She'd given Claire a place to belong, and friends to belong to. And that was worth all the Keds in the world.

"Okay." Claire flipped the canvas tote over so the image of Cookie Monster devouring the PBS logo was buried in her powder-fresh armpit. Massie was already upset enough.

"Let's do it." She led Cam into the sunroom and stepped out of her pink fake Uggs—or FUggs, as they were known around Octavian Country Day—and then eyed Cam's laceless brown Converse. He caught on and scraped his heels against the ivory rug until they popped off. A warm, buttery scent wafted from the three Laura Vallon Crème Brulée pillar candles flickering in the stone fireplace, masking the wet-goldendoodlesque smell of their combined footwear.

"Massie?" Claire edged past the persimmon silk–covered sofa, careful not to graze the delicate fabric with Cam's grass-stained jersey. "You home?"

Kuh-laire. Kuh-laire. As if in response to her call, Claire's cell emitted Massie's signature ring. Claire reached for her rhinestone-encrusted Motorola cell and opened the newest text in her inbox.

Massie: hlp!!! Guest bedroom closet. Hurry x 10.

Claire gasp-widened her blue eyes and sprinted into the foyer. Forgetting about Cam, she took the Pledged wooden steps two at a time, her heart slamming against her rib cage. As she hurried down the shiny hardwood straightaway and skidded into the Blocks' guest bedroom, she mentally pre-pared herself to find Massie collapsed in a tearful heap on the closet floor, wearing last year's Juicy sweats, surrounded by Sharpie-shopped photos of happier times.

"Massie?" Claire called again, diving past the toile-canopied guest bed.

"In here!" Massie's muffled voice came through the closet door.

Bracing herself, Claire gripped the ornate gold handle, pumped it once, and yanked the door open.

But instead of finding Massie curled in the fetal position on the floor, Claire found her lounging on a tufted chaise in the center of the enormous walk-in, looking like a perfectly posed storefront mannequin. Dim recessed lighting spotlighted the red YSL Raspail tote dangling from her crooked index finger. A tags-on metallic Balenciaga scarf was wrapped around her neck like a shiny boa constrictor. Claire's throat closed when she saw the four-digit number on the crisp white price tag.

"Hey." Breathless, Cam appeared in the doorway behind her.

"Took you guys long enough." Massie yawned, stretching out on the extra-long chair like she was relaxing poolside. Rotating racks of designer clothing swished around the perimeter of the walnut-paneled closet, which was easily twice the size of Claire's bedroom. Mountains of clothing, shoes, and accessories littered the gold-carpeted floor around Massie's perch.

Claire squinted at her friend, searching for signs of distress. "Um, are you okay?"

But Massie's high pony gleamed like she'd just had a blowout, and her shimmer-dusted cheeks glowed. There wasn't a mascara-smudged cheek or outdated tracksuit in sight. In fact, in an emerald cashmere minidress and espresso suede boots, she'd probably never looked better.

"Obv," Massie responded, sitting up and planting her feet on the clothing-strewn floor.

"Are you . . . sure?" Claire asked nervously. Why wasn't she devastated? Road testing her waterproof mascara while cursing Alicia and Dylan to a lifetime of flyaways and visible panty lines?

"You're not . . . upset or anything?" She took an involuntary step backward, toward Cam.

"Um, Kuh-laire, am I a Jonas Brother?" Massie blinked.

"No," Claire said, flicking her bangs away from her eyes.

"Then why are you waiting for me to lose it?" Massie grin-whipped the metallic Balenciaga scarf on the floor and stood up.

Cam snorted.

"Well . . . you said crisis . . ." Claire mumbled, a knot forming in her stomach at the sound of her crush's laugh.

"Correction." Massie paused briefly, refueling with a fresh swipe of Glossip Girl Toasted Marshmallow gloss. "CrisEEEEEEes. The first is that gawd-awful jersey you're wearing. And the second is that I can't decide which bag to donate to the homeless and which to keep." She held out both arms in the shape of a T, showcasing the two bags. On the left was a dark blue Chloé Paddington clutch and on the right a buttery, tan Kooba. "You dress like the less fortunate. Which would you like more?"

The knot in Claire's stomach tightened like a clenched fist. Being the true friend she was, she'd come to help Massie in her time of need. But Claire's definition of help didn't include getting shot down mercilessly by Massie while Cam was just inches away.

"Time's up," Massie sighed, lowering her arms. "I'm keeping both." She tossed the bags up onto a heap of clothing that almost reached the ceiling. A Bloomingdale's Big Brown Bag marked COUTURE TO KEEP was positioned in front of the pile.

Bean was asleep on top of a smaller pile marked DESIGNERS TO DONATE.

"What about my Donna Karan suit?" Kendra Block's perky voice sounded from somewhere nearby. Claire whipped her head around, searching for signs of Massie's mom.

"Spring '08 or resort '09?" Massie called back.

"Spring '08." Kendra entered the closet, holding up a cream-colored pantsuit. Her stylish dark bob gleamed under the soft track lighting. In pencil-leg jeans and a navy silk tunic, she looked like she was ready to hit the town, not clean out her old clothes. "Claire! Cam!" she exclaimed. The sweet, fruity scent of Kendra's Dolce & Gabbana Light Blue perfume chased off Cam's Drakkar Noir and claimed Claire's nostrils as its prize. Claire silently transitioned to mouth breathing.

Kendra shook the pantsuit at Massie. "Verdict?"

"Ew." Massie wrinkled her nose. "Extremely Worn."

"I only wore it twice." Kendra gazed at it sadly, as though it were an old lover.

"In public?"

Her mother nodded slowly, like she knew what was coming.

"Toss." Massie beamed, obviously marveling at her ability to instantly ID overexposed garments.

"You're right." Kendra dropped the suit on the floor next to Bean, then turned back to Claire and Cam. "I hope you came to help." She smiled expectantly. "Ever since we lost our special event chairperson to bad Botox, we've needed a few extra hands."

"Help with what?" Claire asked, only half paying attention while she surveyed Massie from the corner of her eye.

"Our clothing drive." Kendra smiled humbly. "I'm on the board of directors of the Ladies' Luncheon League." She tossed a quilted Chanel bag aside like it was an empty Starbucks cup. "I'm sure your mother's involved, Claire."

Claire nodded politely, even though she was pretty sure the only league her mom was involved in was Todd's Little League.

"I'm hosting a big fund-raising dinner here at the house. Each guest donates ten pounds of couture to the local homeless shelter." Kendra clapped her hands together in delight. "We're calling the event Ho Ho Homeless."

"Seriously?" Cam muttered under his breath. Claire elbowed him.

"My idea." Massie beamed.

The defensive knot in Claire's stomach loosened at the sight of her friend's brave smile. Massie was obviously diving headfirst into this whole charity thing to avoid the pain of fighting with her best friends. And if helping the less fortunate would get Massie through this difficult time, then Claire and Cam would work right alongside her.

"So?" Kendra prompted expectantly.

Cam coughed. "I usually have soccer practice after school, so—"

Claire glare-silenced him. "We'd love to help," she announced.

"Perf." Massie nodded. "You can start by tossing out anything gray, silver, or black."

"Why?" Cam asked, looking confused.

Massie shook her head, like it should have been obvious.

"The idea is to make the homeless stand out, Cam. Not make them blend into the pavement."

Ordinarily, Claire would have jumped to Cam's defense. But this time, she was just glad that Massie wasn't focusing on her.

"Always thinking." Kendra smiled, pulling her daughter in for a side-hug.

Massie squirmed happily under her mom's Clarins-lotioned grip. "Please. I'm just getting started." She pulled away and turned toward Claire and Cam. "Anything shimmery or metallic is a definite yes. That way, cars can see them at night."

"And she's safety conscious, too." Kendra watched her daughter proudly. She paused, tilting her head slightly to the right, the same way Massie did when she was examining her reflection in the mirror. "You really seem like you're taking to this whole philanthropic process."

"Ah-bviously," Massie confirmed, producing her white iPhone and turning it on.

"You know," Kendra continued slowly, "we have that open spot on the board—the special event chair position." She crossed her arms thoughtfully over her silk tunic. "You wouldn't be interested in chairing the event, would you? It'd be a great experience."

Claire watched a tiny smile begin to twitch at the corners of Massie's mouth. "Special event chair" was just a grown-up way of saying "party-planning alpha." And throwing parties and bossing people around were Massie's specialties.

"Depends," Massie replied nonchalantly. "What would my time commitment be?"

"Two board meetings a week, plus party-planning time after school and on weekends for the next two weeks."

"Press opportunities?"

"The local press is already scheduled."

"Put calls in to the *Times* Style section and *Vogue*," Massie advised shrewdly. "This could be way bigger than Channel Five."

As she talked, Massie's face slowly began to light up, like she'd just applied a fresh dusting of MAC Belightful highlighting powder. "They do say giving is the new getting," she pontificated, twirling her purple hair streak around her index finger.

Kendra leaned toward her daughter expectantly.

"I'm in," Massie decided grandly.

"That's my girl." Kendra glowed as her cell buzzed from the black Kate Spade holster on her hip. She reached for it and checked the screen. "Excuse me." She held her hand up, pressing the phone to her ear and bidding adieu to Claire and Cam as she sauntered out of the closet. "Olga! Tell me you've had a cancellation." She swiftly closed the closet door behind her.

"Did you hear that, Bean?" Massie scooped up her pug from the donations pile and kissed her tiny head, leaving a glossy lip print in her black fur. "I'm going to be on the board of directors for a charity!"

"Are you sure you want to give up all your afternoons and weekends?" Claire fingered a violet silk Chanel blouse as it skimmed by on the rotating rack next to her.

"Why not?" Massie shrugged. "It's for a good cause . . . and Dempsey is so going to love that I'm doing this."

That explained it. Dempsey Solomon, Massie's newest crush, had been on a mission to save the world ever since he and his parents moved back to Westchester from Africa, where they'd been doing charity work of their own. Short of showing up to school with an African orphan peeking out of her Louis handbag, getting involved with a cause was the best way for Massie to capture Dempsey's attention—and his heart.

Massie glared at the Cookie Monster tote Cam was holding. "That, by the way, is a definite no. These poor people have suffered enough already."

Claire pulled out a scuffed, camouflaged Ked and the hedge clippers. "We brought a few things to cheer you up."

"Huh?" Massie's right ear dropped toward her shoulder.

Cam placed a Patricia Underwood fedora from Massie's short-lived hat phase on his head. "Yeah. After your other friends ditched you, we thought—"

"Um, we just wanted to make sure you were okay, after everything that . . . happened," Claire finished awkwardly, dropping the shoe back in her bag.

Massie rolled her eyes. "Puh-lease." She sighed with a dismissive flick of the wrist. "I'm so over them." She pinch-lifted a hairy black sweater from the DESIGNERS TO DONATE pile like it was a pair of dirty underwear. "Those girls are like this itchy angora," she said. "Pretty, but toe-dally not worth the pain." She tossed the sweater back into the reject pile.

Claire tugged at the hem of her Tomahawks jersey. "But what about the Pretty Comm—"

"Everybody knows PCs are out," Massie said crisply. "I'm switching to MAC."

"MAC?" Cam asked.

"Massie and Crew, " she announced. "Which includes me, Claire, and Kristen."

The knot in Claire's stomach resurfaced. Massie and Crew? Could she seriously move on this quickly? Forget about the Pretty Committee like they were last season's resort wear? What if Claire didn't want to move on? What if she wanted her old group of friends back?

"What about Dylan and Alicia?" Once again, Cam practically read her mind.

"Out," Massie repeated casually, like she was Heidi Klum and Dylan and Alicia were *Project Runway* castoffs.

Claire swallowed hard. This was all happening way too fast. And she had too many questions running through her mind at once. Did being part of Massie's new group mean she couldn't be friends with Dylan and Alicia? Was Massie forcing her to pick?

Cam patted Claire's shoulder awkwardly, as if sensing her panic. His warm hand comforted her. She straightened up, looking Massie in her amber eyes. If she was going to get through this, she wanted Cam by her side. She took a deep breath. "I want Cam in too," she declared boldly, the knot in her stomach growing tighter.

"This isn't an all-you-can-eat buffet, Kuh-laire," Massie balked. "You can't just pick and choose."

Claire opened her mouth, but Massie cut her off.

"Besides, you can't have a boy-girl crew. It doesn't work." She shook her high, glossy brown pony authoritatively.

"Fine by me," Cam said, looking slightly relieved.

Claire felt her cheeks start to flush. Making mix CDs, agreeing to help with her charity . . . Cam had gone out of his way to make Massie feel better.

"But—" she started. She put her hands on her hips. Cam took a step backward toward the door.

"Kuh-laire." Massie leveled her eyes in Claire's direction. "Is Cam a fattening Girl Scout cookie layered with creamy peanut butter and a chocolate coating?"

"No," Claire snapped, knowing what was coming.

"Then don't make him a Tagalong," Massie finished triumphantly.

"So now I'm a cookie." Cam looked more confused than ever.

"All I'm saying is, maybe you could be a little more like an elastic waistband." Claire suggested, yanking at the hem of her jersey. "You know, stretch a little? Maybe if you apologized to Leesh and Dylan—"

"Eh-ma-never." Anger flickered behind Massie's amber eyes. "Alicia stole my cheerleading squad. And Dylan stole my Derrington." She scooped a large pile of silk and knit clothing from the closet floor and secured it underneath her chin. "They're dead to me. I'm moving on." Her purple hair streak suddenly lodged in her lip gloss. She spit it out ferociously. "And you have one minute to decide if you're coming with me." She brushed past Cam and stomped out of the closet, a white Chanel blouse stuck to the heel of her boot like silk toilet paper.

"But wait!" Claire called after her. "What does that mean?" She leaned against the closet wall, dizzy. Just seventy-two hours ago, the Pretty Committee had been as tight as Ben and Jerry.

"It means you're either a PC or a MAC." Massie whirled around in the doorway and turned to face her.

"Can't I be both?" Claire focused on the gold-carpeted floor to avoid Cam's disapproving glare and Massie's challenging stare.

"Im-possible. PCs and MACs are nawt compatible." Massie scraped the blouse off her heel and kicked it aside. "At some point everyone has to choose."

The knot in Claire's stomach tied its own bow. So she was being asked to pick sides. Her friends or her alpha. It wasn't a choice Claire was prepared to make.

Alicia Rivera speed-walked down the empty, locker-lined hallway toward the auditorium, silently cursing herself for being late on today of all days. She'd lost track of time trying to find the über-perfect, alpha-worthy outfit for her first post-BFF-breakup assembly entrance. She'd changed her mind more times than Jason from *The Bachelor*, but had finally settled on option number nineteen: dark, curve-hugging Blank Denim skinny jeans, a thigh-skimming turquoise silk tank to make her olive skin pop, and her new charcoal gray Theory stretch vest. Caramel-colored riding boots added an equestrian chic touch to the carefully crafted ensemble.

She slowed as she reached the assembly doors. Maybe being late wasn't such a bad thing. In fact, casually waltzing through the auditorium after assembly had started could be the perfect way to advertise just how fine she was without Massie Block breathing down her Angel perfume–spritzed neck. The perfect way to prove to BOCD, and herself, that she could capture everyone's attention without Massie by her side. To prove that she, Alicia Rivera, was an alpha in her own right.

Then her stomach did a triple pirouette. It wasn't that she doubted her ability to rock a solo entrance. Just the opposite. Years of dance training had prepared her for this very moment. She was ready for the spotlight, ready to drink in the admiration she deserved. It was just that she'd never made an assembly entrance without Massie before. Suddenly thinking about it felt strange. Like she'd forgotten to floss before a lip-kiss.

". . . if I should get Jessica Alba bangs or Vanessa Hudgens bangs, and he goes, 'What's the difference?'" huffed a honey-blond seventh-grader wearing a long black skirt, giant white sunglasses, and a floor-grazing hand-knit scarf.

"How can he nawt see the difference?" squealed her friend, whose giant black sweater coat made her look like death. "Jessica's are curtains drawn and Vanessa's are curtains open."

"I knoooow," bellowed Long Skirt.

Alicia rolled her eyes. The Mary-Kate Olsen look had just hit the seventh grade, as though it had been stuck at customs for two years and finally made it through. It was hard to believe anyone could be more behind the trends than her Spanish cousins, but hobo chic was spreading faster than strep this semester.

When Grim Reaper and Long Skirt disappeared into the auditorium, Alicia took a deep, calming breath and got ready to make a fresh start.

"And five, and six, ah-seven, eight!" she whisper-counted, bursting through the double doors.

Deafening chatter poured over her like a tsunami the second she stepped inside. Students were milling around the aisles, weaving through the rows of creaky wooden chairs as Principal Burns shuffled papers at the podium onstage. Dean Don was huddled with Mr. Myner and a few of the other teachers in the front row, whispering intently.

Alicia strategically stepped into the dusty spotlight that poured through the stained-glass windows. This was her moment.

"Heads up!" A guy's voice rose over the noise. Alicia ducked just in time, narrowly missing getting whacked in the head by a soccer cleat.

"Ehmagawd!" Straightening up, she whip-turned toward the offender. But he was too busy high-fiving his buddies to notice.

Panicked, Alicia considered ducking back through the doors and starting over. This wasn't working. She should have waited until she heard Principal Burns's voice over the microphone. But it was too late; there was no turning back now.

Scanning the auditorium for a familiar face, she spotted the Heart-Nets, the cheerleading squad she'd created last week after quitting Massie's Socc-Hers, due to irreconcilable creative differences. Namely, that Massie never accepted her suggestions, despite Alicia's superior dance ability. She had generously offered to let Massie be the alpha in life—so long as Alicia was the alpha in dance—but Massie had refused. Hence her new motto: If your alpha won't join you, beat her.

The Heart-Nets were clustered together in the fifth row of the wooden seats on the left, wearing their signature uniforms: pressed white Ralph button-downs, denim short shorts with red hearts on the pockets, and matching BCBG metallic belts. They looked ah-dorable, of course. All thanks to Alicia. But why had they shown up to school in uniform? She hadn't told them to. Had they decided on their own? Without her?

"Chug! Chug! Chug! Chug!"

In the fourth row, Dylan Marvil was pounding a can of Red Bull, her head tilted back like an open Pez dispenser. Cam, Derrington, Chris Plovert, and Josh Hotz leaned over the back of their seats in the third row, egging her on. Derrington was timing her on his iPhone and keeping one eye on the huddle of teachers in the front row, who were too busy whispering to each other to scold the students around them. With a final gulp, Dylan raised the empty can over her head in victory like it was the Olympic torch.

"Doooooooooone," she burped.

From her seat next to Dempsey Solomon, at the far end of the row in the middle section of the auditorium, Massie was busy texting, not paying the slightest bit of attention to Dylan's bodily functions. Alicia resisted the urge to catch Massie's eye before she rolled hers at Dylan.

"Seven seconds!" Derrington high-fived Dylan. "Record time!"

The guys cheered, then swiveled forward in their seats without so much as a glance at Alicia. Gleefully, Dylan tilted her can upside down and shook it as Alicia edged by her. A few drops of Red Bull landed on the toe of her caramel-colored riding boot, leaving a dark, teardrop stain.

"Dylaaaan," Alicia huffed.

"Ehmagawd," Dylan burp-breathed, her cheeks flushed

with victory. "Did you see that?" She patted the seat next to her, motioning for Alicia to sit. "Seven seconds!"

Alicia bumped the back of Josh's chair with her gunmetal Botkier Bianca satchel as she slid into her seat. Her crush turned around.

"Oh. Hey." Josh gave her a quick grin, showcasing his headshot-worthy smile. He looked beyond adorable in his red RL polo and navy Yankees cap. "Thought you weren't coming or something."

"I was just late," she explained, taking the seat next to Dylan.

"Oh. Cool." Josh pulled his cap over his eyes and slouched low in his seat.

Alicia scanned her row. Claire was sitting exactly halfway between Alicia and Massie, three empty seats on either side of her. She was gnawing at her nail beds like she hadn't eaten anything but cuticle all week.

"Kuh-laire," she called.

When Claire glanced up, Alicia slapped the empty wooden seat on her free side. "Come sit," she ordered, trying to speak just loudly enough for Claire to hear, but not loudly enough to attract Massie's attention.

Claire waved, pretending not to hear the invite.

Alicia's throat tightened. Since when did she have to recruit her friends to sit next to her? She turned to Dylan. "Where's Kristen?" she asked, nodding at the empty seat on her other side.

"Home sick from bad sushi." Dylan shrugged, extending an

open bag of caramel kettle corn in Alicia's direction. "Spicy tuuuuuuuuna rooooooooolllll."

Alicia rapid-fanned away Dylan's burp fumes, shifting in her seat. The urge to look over at Massie again was getting stronger and stronger. Was she devastated from their fight? Wishing she'd taken Alicia up on her offer to co-alpha the Heart-Nets? Finally, Alicia stole a quick glance.

Massie was staring straight ahead, her expression stoic and glassy. She wore black thigh-hugging cigarette pants tucked into Prada ankle boots. An appropriately wrinkled collared shirt peeked out from under a shrunken tuxedo blazer. Last week, Alicia would have given the outfit a solid 9.9. But this was Monday. Things were different now.

For a split second, she wondered if the fight had been a mistake. If she should have kept her glossy lips shut and let Massie run the Socc-Hers. It would have been easier. But she remembered the way she felt every time Massie tried to control her: like she was wearing a bra that was two sizes too small. Alicia shuddered at the memory. She could never go back to that constricting feeling again.

Just then, Massie looked up, locking eyes with her.

Alicia forced a laugh and whirled around in her seat, pretending one of the Heart-Nets had just said something hilarious. But a long, shrill squeal interrupted her as Principal Burns neared the mic.

"Ugggghhhh." A unanimous groan sounded over the feedback as students shifted in the creaky wooden auditorium chairs.

"Attention!" Principal Burns hunched over the podium microphone, glaring from underneath a curtain of I-just-stuck-my-finger-in-an-outlet gray hair. Her ill-fitting black polyester suit, the one she only wore on special occasions, signaled that something big was about to go down. Dean Don hovered behind her, rubbing his dark stubble with one hand. "Both Dean Don and I are pleased to welcome you to a special assembly here at Briarwood–Octavian Country Day School." She looked as pleased as someone getting an exclusive sneak peek at Ralph Lauren's spring line.

"Pssst." Dylan leaned in. "Have you talked to Massie?"

Alicia stole another quick glance to her right, then slid her gaze back to Dylan. "Who?" She blinked coolly.

Principal Burns cleared her throat, staring down at Alicia and Dylan with tiny, beady eyes that reminded Alicia of the capers in her mom's world-famous paella. "As I was saying, we have an exciting announcement to make."

"Cawwwww cawwwww," cawed a boy in the back. A swell of muffled chuckles followed.

Pretending she had no clue the birdcall was directed at her and her hawklike facial features, Principal Burns waited patiently for the laughter to subside before continuing. Dean Don coughed uncomfortably.

"Whassgoingon?" Dylan whisper-hissed as a giant white screen descended from the ceiling.

Out of the corner of her eye, Alicia noticed that Massie's glossy lips were curled as if around a secret. Did she know what the announcement was? If they were still friends, would

Alicia know too? Did the fact that she didn't know make her a bad leader? Alicia leaned forward slightly, smile-nodding like she knew exactly what was about to happen.

The auditorium lights dimmed.

"As you all are aware, an unfortunate incident at Briarwood Academy last year forced us all to . . . adapt rather quickly while the school was being repaired."

Alicia gulped.

Claire gnawed at what was left of her nail beds.

Dylan cracked open another Red Bull. Last spring, the wave pool on the roof of Briarwood had leaked, flooding the entire school. Everyone had assumed it was faulty construction, but it was actually Layne Abeley and the Pretty Committee's fault. They had sneaked into the boys' school at night to fix the secret spy cam that recorded their crushes' sensitivity training class, and ended up drilling a hole through the water pipes.

"After many, many months, we are proud to announce the completion of the new and improved . . ." Principal Burns paused dramatically. "BRIARWOOD ACAAAAADEMYYYYYY!" she yelled into the mic, like she was Oprah and Briarwood was one of her Favorite Things. Only her excitement-yell sounded more like she was pinching her nose in a stinky bathroom stall, shouting for someone to bring her more toilet paper—a mix of urgency and discomfort.

An image of Briarwood lit up the projector screen, while a recording of the boys' band playing an instrumental version of Christina Aguilera's "Keeps Gettin' Better" blared from the speakers. The school and the grounds looked brand-new and better than ever. The modern glass facade gleamed in the sunlight, wide stone steps led to a state-of-the-art atrium, and freshly sodded sports fields stretched into the distance.

Alicia's tongue felt like sandpaper. She willed Josh to turn around in his seat so they could panic-gaze at each other. The only reason she and her crush got to see each other every day was because Briarwood had been undergoing renovations. But if the renovations were finished . . .

But Josh didn't turn around. Instead, he high-fived Plovert and Cam.

"Yesssssss!" Throughout the auditorium, the Briarwood boys clapped one another on the back, grinning at the glowing image of their school on the screen. After a few seconds, the picture of the front facade melted into a shot of a sleek new Briarwood auditorium. Rows of cushy movie theater–style chairs led up to a giant, rotating stage lit by colorful spotlights.

Dean Don slid up to the mic as a gym complex popped on-screen. "The new gym floor doubles as a hockey rink and has NBA rims and an Olympic-size pool."

The boys erupted in whoops and applause. The girls looked lost and confused. Like they had been abandoned on the side of the highway with nothing but a soggy map and a Ziploc full of pennies. Dylan seemed too stricken to speak.

Out of the corner of her eye, Alicia saw Claire attempt to grin like someone who was happy for her crush. But it came off looking like she had cramps. Luckily Cam was too amped up to notice.

Alicia opened her mouth, then closed it. Why wasn't Josh upset about this? Was an in-house movie theater more important to him than she was? She was suddenly aware of the combination mothball/dusty-textbook smell that hovered over the creaky wooden non-stadium seats.

"Briarwood students will return to their school a week from today." Principal Burns nudged Dean Don out of the way and retook her place at the podium. "As a welcome-back gift, each student will be receiving a brand-new Endu(red) laptop, courtesy of Bono, who has generously donated them to Briarwood and our brother school in Kenya."

"Woooo-hoooo!" The guys were on their feet now, clapping and aisle-dancing to the beat of the music. The girls were frozen in their seats, mouths half open, stares vacant.

A back-in-business Briarwood meant only one thing.

No. More. Boys.

Which meant no more weekday flirting.

No more Briarwood Tomahawks soccer games.

And no more Briarwood Tomahawks soccer games meant . . .

A sweaty palm gripped Alicia's bony shoulder.

"Ew!" She whipped her head around to face the row of Heart-Nets, blinking in unison, as if begging her to do something.

"Does this mean no more squad?" one of the girls whisper-gasped.

"But we spent all that time rehearsing!" another whined.

Alicia's mouth parted slightly, but she had no idea what to tell her girls. Her head was spinning with too many thoughts. How could Josh be so excited to leave? What would happen to her if she lost her squad? She turned involuntarily toward Massie, who was serenely examining her fingernails as Dempsey grinned at the projector screen. She looked calm and composed. Even in tragic times like this, Massie always knew what to do.

But Alicia had never felt more powerless. Alpha was leaking out of her pores, leaving her more hollow than one of Dylan's empty Red Bull cans. To be an alpha, you had to be confident. In control. And more in charge than Visa. Alicia was none of those things. Not anymore. Not without a cheerleading squad. Not without the Briarwood boys. Not without stadium seating. She was over before she started. She was a social Zune.

"This can*nawt* happen," Dylan cried desperately. "The boys can't leave! What're we gonna do?"

Every muscle in Alicia's body tightened. Dylan needed an alpha. Someone to guide her in her time of need. And Dylan was choosing Alicia. Not because Alicia could do six pirouettes in a row without getting even a little dizzy (even though she could). Not because her hair was the shiniest in eighth, or because she was the only girl at BOCD who had a perfect chemical-free tan year-round. But because, at that moment, Dylan didn't know what to do, and she believed that Alicia did.

"Okay," she began loudly, her voice suddenly strong and clear. "Listen up."

Dylan leaned in close. From the corner of her eye, Alicia

saw Claire's gaze linger on her. They were waiting for her instruction. Depending on her to know exactly what to do, the way they used to depend on Massie.

"The boys are just excited because they think Briarwood's gonna be more fun than OCD." She rolled her eyes toward the row of seats in front of them. Cam and Josh leaped out of their seats for a chest bump as a shot of an indoor soccer field lit up the projector screen. "Right?"

"Right." Dylan crossed her legs, intentionally slamming the round toe of her Sam Edelman wedge heel into the back of Derrington's seat. He didn't notice.

Claire was tilted so far to the left to hear Alicia's words without leaving her seat that she looked like a capsized sailboat.

"So ah-bviously, all we have to do is make it ten times more fun to hang out with us," Alicia reasoned. "We can totally beat indoor soccer and stadium seating."

"Right," Dylan repeated, sounding less than convinced. "So . . .what's the plan?"

"We have to get everybody together after school today," Alicia continued without missing a beat, faking like she actually had a plan. "You, me, Kristen and Kuh-laire . . ." She sideglanced at Claire to see if she was in. Claire blinked that she was. ". . . plus the boys," Alicia finished confidently. "I'll text the time and location by lunch."

"'Kay." Dylan looked slightly relieved.

The Briarwood boys' shouts, plus the thump of the music and the flash of the slide show, all faded to the back of Alicia's mind. She felt a jolt of nervous energy, the way she did when she was waiting in the wings, about to glide onstage for a dance solo. It wasn't lost on her that being an alpha was the biggest performance she'd ever give in her life.

And choking onstage was so not an option.

The grating tick of the second hand echoing in the silent hall-way sounded like a judge's gavel rapping over and over again, sentencing Massie Block to social death. Planting one Prada in front of the other, she hurried toward her locker in a race against time, mentally thanking Mr. Myner for letting her duck out of class before the final bell.

She'd been leaving classes early all day so she wouldn't have to run into Dylan or Alicia between classes, putting on an "I'm at death's door but look how brave I am for making education a priority" face for her teachers. And she was only faking a little. Part of her really *had* died when Alicia left the Socc-Hers to start her own squad. Another part had died when Dylan and Derrington showed up together at her pool-party-slash-slumber party Friday night, only to flaunt their relationship the second she released her hold on Derrington. And an even bigger part of her had bitten the dust when Alicia didn't even bother to show up.

Being the leader of the Pretty Committee had been Massie's life. Without them, she'd practically lost her purpose. She was like Mother Teresa without the poor. Angelina without the babies. Paris without the random BFFs.

She was keeping it together for one reason, and one reason only.

Dempsey Solomon.

Crushing on Briarwood's most adorable do-gooder was the only thing that gave her life meaning now. If it weren't for Dempsey, Massie probably would have spent most of the morning's assembly wondering if her former friends were texting about her behind her back. But flirt-glancing at Dempsey and waiting for him to flirt-glance back (which he had, until he'd gotten distracted by Principal Burns's announcement about Briarwood's new solar-paneled roof) had temporarily numbed the pain of the PC breakup.

Staring into Dempsey's sea green eyes was more comforting than her 1500 thread count violet Frette sheets. Soon, she'd be able to stare into those eyes whenever she wanted. Kristen and Dempsey were next-door neighbors, and Kristen had pinky-sworn that she'd talk to him for Massie.

Kristen. When Kristen hadn't called to update her on the Dempsey situation, Massie had had Isaac drop off a get-well-soon Gossip Girl Complete Collection box set at Kristen's apartment. So why hadn't she called to thank her? Did this mean she was siding with Dylan and Alicia? And what about Claire? Massie had texted that morning, demanding Claire make a decision on MAC versus PC within twenty-four hours. And still, nothing.

Remembering her race against the final bell, Massie glanced up at the giant clock hanging at the end of the hallway. *Twenty seconds*.

Panic-stricken, she deposited her turquoise Kooba bag on the floor and zeroed in on the padlock. Her Chanel Feu de

Russie–polished fingertips flew expertly over the lock, blurring in front of her. She had to get out to the parking lot, to the safety of the Range Rover, before the halls were clogged with nosy girls whisper-gossiping about the PC's breakup. If she didn't make it, she'd be forced to face them all alone. Which would leave her more exposed than Jen Aniston on the January '09 cover of *GQ*.

Twelve seconds.

Massie yanked at the padlock. It held fast.

Ten seconds.

Frantically, she tried the combination again, tugging on the lock with all her weight. Nothing.

Seven seconds.

Puh-lease, Gawd. She tried the combination again, slower this time. The lock snapped open with ease. Ducking into her locker, she closed her eyes and inhaled deeply, breathing in the comforting smell of her Chanel No. 19 locker deodorizer. Her signature scent had been the only part of her day that felt familiar. The hints of jasmine and ylang-ylang were perfectly content to play supporting roles to the stronger green floral scent. And why shouldn't they be? Jasmine and ylang-ylang would be nothing without their green floral alpha. Just like—

Riiiiiinnnnnnnnnnnnnnnnnnnnnnnnnng.

The piercing ring of the last-period bell sent a shiver down Massie's spine like acrylic nails on a chalkboard. Just then a fresh burst of Chanel No. 19 exploded from the deodorizer, temporarily blinding her. Tears sprang to her eyes. Great.

Now BOCD would think she was nothing but a weepy LBR who couldn't survive without her friends.

Classroom doors flew open along the hallway and students spilled into the halls. Massie's stomach twisted into a jumbo pretzel at the slap of ballet flats against the shiny floor, and the metallic clanging of the boys play-shoving each other into the lockers on their way down the hall. Not wanting to face the crowd, she stayed buried in her locker, focusing on her reflection in the full-length mirror on the back of her locker door.

That morning, the pin-striped Steven Alan boyfriend shirt she'd worn under her shrunken plum Helmut Lang tuxedo jacket had seemed like the perfectly effortless complement to her cigarette pants. The hammered silver bangles on her left wrist had clinked confidently with her every step. And her conscious decision to wear only structured fabrics announced to the world that she had zero interest in incorporating elastic into her wardrobe or her friendships.

But in the harsh, fluorescent light of the hallway, things seemed different. Her shirt looked stiff and uptight, her blazer felt like a straitjacket, and her bangles gleamed like handcuffs. She was a prisoner in her own school.

"D! Go long!"

Massie froze at the sound of Derrington's voice. Slowly, she swiveled around on the heel of her black ankle boot.

Her ex-crush was holding a plastic baggie of jumbo marshmallows, and Dylan was giggle-jogging backward through the clogged hallway.

"Five seconds left on the play clock!" Derrington yelled, winding up. He was wearing the cutest Diesel jeans, brand-new forest green Pumas, and a dark blue fleece. Massie had never seen any of it before. *Was Derrington giving his wardrobe a makeover just for Dylan?* "Four, three, two!"

"No!" Dylan shriek-flirted, her sapphire-colored sweater coat billowing around her as she ran, like she was swimming underwater. Massie rolled her eyes. So now they were coordinating outfits? Who did they think they were, Posh and Becks?

"He shoots!" Derrington launched the marshmallow into the air. Dylan bobbed and weaved in the crowd, her mouth open wide. The marshmallow missed her mouth, smacking her on the forehead. She grabbed it before it hit the ground and popped it in her mouth.

"He scores!" Derrington wiggled his butt. "And the crowd goes wiiiiiild!"

Dylan chomped on her marshmallow as Derrington took a bow. A cluster of seventh-grade girls just a few feet from Massie stopped cackling long enough to envy-watch the couple as they paused at Dylan's locker. The girls were staring in the same way they used to stare at Massie as she walked down the hall. But no one was paying attention to her now.

"Ice ot," Dylan called, showcasing a mouthful of white, gooey marshmallow. She spotted Massie and her smile faded like a pair of Earnest Sewn Hefner jeans. Finally, the girls who had been watching Dylan turned to focus on Massie too.

But instead of envy, their expressions were a mixture of fear, confusion, and awe.

Eyes burning from the thick mist of Chanel, Massie stared back at them, racking her brain for the perfect thing to say or do to show them that she was still on top. But her mind was even emptier than her heart. And it didn't help when she saw Alicia and Olivia Ryan charging together down the hallway, laughing. Were they laughing at her? Racking up gossip points about *her?*

Her iPhone buzzed in her Kooba, saving her from her own thoughts, and her hand shot into her bag in record time. A text. She whirled around, turning her back to Alicia, Dylan, and Derrington, like the message was top secret.

Kristen: What r u up 2 after skl?

Massie's heart pole-vaulted over her rib cage. Kristen hadn't thanked her yet for the box set, but at least she was still talking to her. Which meant she'd chosen her over Alicia, right?

Then again, her font seemed smaller than usual. More timid. Usually it was a sign that she was nervous about something. But in this case it was probably just the bad sushi.

Massie: I have some options. Trying 2 decide. Feel better?
Kristen: Yeah. Bad sushi.
Massie: Eel made you keel?
Kristen: Tempura made me hurl-a!

Massie: Edamame hurt ur tumme?

Massie burst out laughing. Not only because their exchange was funny times ten. Or because she was glad Kristen was still talking to her. But because Alicia and Dylan were peeking at her. She could feel eyeballs searing the back of her neck. And she needed to prove that life went on without them. Even if that life felt worse than death.

Kristen: Need 2 talk 2 u about Dempsey. Meet in the locker room in 5?

Massie: I thought u were home sick.

Kristen: Soccer practice. C ya in 5.

It was official: Massie's heart was going to burst out of her intentionally two-sizes-too-small blazer at any second. Not only did Kristen want to be a MAC, but in exactly five minutes, Massie would be getting the news that her crush liked her back.

"You ready, Derrick?"

Massie looked up to see Dylan tenderly wiping marshmallow dust from the side of Derrick's mouth with her sleeve. A flash of hot anger surged through Massie's body. Dylan was rubbing her love for Derrington in Massie's face like St. Ives vanilla whipped moisturizer. And just like cheap moisturizer, it stank.

She suddenly flashed forward to the couple at ninety. Derrington would be dribbling rice pudding down his shaky lips and Dylan would wipe it away with the nubby sleeve of her puke-colored terry cloth robe. The repulsive image filled Massie with gratitude. She might have been crushless and slightly friendless, but at least her future self wasn't dabbing up Derrington's ricey dribble. And knowing that helped her get past this awkward moment.

Derrington stuffed his hands in his pockets, not looking in Massie's direction as he shuffled down the hallway. Dylan stomp-followed him. Alicia stomp-followed her. Massie's fists clenched involuntarily at her side. Then she released them, slowly. She couldn't let everyone get to her like this. It was time to move on. Dylan and Derrington were her past. And Dempsey Solomon, with his piercing green eyes, natural highlights, and eco-friendly wardrobe, was her future.

Speed-heading toward the girls' locker room, Massie kept her head held high, ignoring the whispers and pity-glances that swelled around her as she faced the seemingly endless stretch of hallway. She desperately needed to regloss. Her naked lips felt as vulnerable as she did. But that was all about to change. With Kristen, Dempsey, and Claire (she'd come around) on her side, she'd be on her way to a comeback. Dylan and Alicia would be sorry.

Finally, she reached the girls' locker room and shoved through the swinging door. The faint hiss of running showers was the only sound she could hear. Stepping over a mountain of gym bags, she hurried past the rows of sticker-covered yellow lockers. The sound of her heels clacking on the spotless cement floor echoed in her own ears. Past the locker bay, the room opened up into a small dressing area. The chocolaty smell of Bumble and Bumble's Creme de Coco shampoo flooded the steaming dressing room, reminding Massie of Alicia's cloying Angel perfume. She swatted the thought away, sending some foggy shower steam with it.

"Kristen?" she coughed, feeling her professionally straightened brown locks beginning to weaken and curl in the humidity. She squinted into the mist, making out rows of polished hardwood benches that faced a rolling chalkboard littered with dusty X's and O's.

"Guess again, Lollipop Legs." A deep, throaty voice wafted to Massie's ears, along with the shower fog.

Massie recognized the voice immediately. "Layne?" She squinted into the shower mist.

Layne Abeley was seated directly under a fluorescent light. The pale green-gray glow made her skin look even more anemic than usual.

"You talkin' tuh me?" Layne squint-glared back. "Are *you* talkin' tuh *me*?"

Massie sighed. "Layne, are you a wannabe opera singer?"

"No, why?"

"Then stop trying to be a Soprano."

Layne snorted. "Good one!"

"What are you doing here?" Massie stepped into the fog. "You're not coordinated enough to play soccer." Slowly, she lowered herself onto the edge of the bench, as far away from Layme as possible. Her social stock was down enough as it was.

"I think the better question is, what are you doing here?"

Layne yanked the hood of her yellow poly-blend hoodie away from her face, liberating tufts of dark brown hair from their synthetic prison.

Massie glared at her, making it undeniably clear just who asked whom first.

"Waiting for Kristen." Layne pulled a package of Chile Picante Corn Nuts from her hoodie pocket and ripped open the orange wrapper with her teeth.

"Oh, that's right. You guys are 'friends.'" Massie felt a shooting pain in her heart as she remembered the day Layne and Dune, Kristen's ex-crush, had let slip that Kristen and Layne had a secret, nerdy club called the Witty Committee and that Layne had recruited Kristen to help her snag Dempsey. "But Kristen has other plans. With me."

"Please, Louise," Layne said dismissively. "Her plans are with me."

"Are nawt," Massie shot back.

"Are too. She just texted and said she needed to talk about Dempsey." Layne crunched down on a cheesy nut. "She's obviously gonna tell me he likes me."

Massie's deep-conditioned ends curled slightly at the very suggestion. Dempsey couldn't *possibly* like Layne more than her, could he? Her stock was down, yes, but news like that would trigger a full-on depression.

"Kristen invited me here to tell me Dempsey likes me. She invited you here so you could start the healing process."

"The only thing heeling around here are those snobby designer boots of yours," Layne snorted. "Because Dempsey and I are perfect together." She turned to display the back of her homemade hoodie. The words DRAMA QUEEN were bedazzled in crooked script across the shoulders. "We're both actors, we're both down to earth . . . annnnnd . . . I liked him when he was fat!"

"I'm sure he'd love to know you thought he was fat!" Massie began furiously fake-texting.

"Me?" Layne grabbed Massie's white iPhone. "You're the one who called him Humpty Dempsey!"

"Give that back, chubby chaser!" Massie grabbed her hoodied arm.

"If I'm a chubby chaser, then you're a weight watcher!"

"Ohhh, good one, you gut slu—"

Puuuuuuuuuuuuuuuuuuuuuuurrrrrrrrp!

"Time. Out." Kristen was standing next to the chalkboard. She'd accessorized her chocolate brown Twisted Heart tracksuit with her soccer bag, an oversize khaki Burberry check tote. The captain's whistle she'd just used swung around her neck.

Massie resisted the urge to tell her friend she was in need of some cheek stain, stat. After all, it wasn't Kristen's fault she'd gotten food poisoning. And she had probably used her last bits of strength talking up Massie with Dempsey. So why make her feel insecure?

"Ummmm, thanksforcoming." Averting her eyes from Massie and Layne, Kristen held a stack of white note cards up to her face and cleared her throat. "What is love, really?" she began awkwardly. Her note cards were shaking so much,

Massie could feel a light breeze cross the locker room. "Webster's dictionary defines love as—" She paused, coughed again, and flipped to the next note card. "Okay. So . . . love. It's crazy, right? And when we fall in love, we do crazy things, right?"

Massie cocked her head to one side. What was going on?

"Things we don't actually want to do. But it's like we're under some magic power or something. Like we go totally insane. I think Fergie said it best when she said, 'Can't help it, you got me trippin', stumblin', flippin', flumbin', clumsy 'cause I'm falling in love.'"

"Huh?" Layne paused mid-chew, staring blankly at Kristen.

"And even though we try to fight it?" Kristen was talking faster now, gulping huge breaths of air. "We can't. We're totally powerless. It's like the Jonas Brothers say: 'Now I'm speechless, over the edge. I'm just breathless, I never thought that I'd catch this love bug.'" She was flipping through her cards at warp speed now. "So even though we never meant to hurt anybody, sometimes we do, because we're in love and we can't help it. But like Miley says, 'Nobody's perfect, you live and you learn it, and if I mess it up sometimes, nobody's perfect.'"

She exhaled, looking both relieved and like she might throw up another spicy tuna roll at any second.

Massie and Layne stared dumbly at each other, then slowly shifted their gazes to Kristen.

"English, please?" Layne prompted her.

"I talked to Dempsey." Kristen sighed.

"Aaaaaand?" Layne grinned smugly.

Massie applied an anticipatory coat of gloss. She wanted her victory smile to shine as brightly as her heart.

"Dempsey likes . . ." Kristen glanced at Massie, then at Layne.

Then back at Massie.

Then back at Layne.

The crunch of Layne's Corn Nuts sliced through the air, cutting the tension. Massie rolled her eyes.

". . . me," Kristen muttered, gnawing at her bottom lip.

"Yessssssss!" Massie victory-hissed. Wait. *What?*

Layne exhaled a cheese and lime–scented gasp.

"I said me," Kristen repeated.

"And you like him back?" Massie blurted, unable to conceal her shock.

Kristen nodded slowly, like she was admitting to cheating on a test. "I am sooooo sorry," she said weakly. "I didn't mean for this to happen." She clenched the sweaty note cards in her fist, staring down at the ground.

The girls' locker room suddenly felt hotter than a Bikram yoga studio. Massie's palms were slick with betrayal sweat, but her mouth was completely dry. How was this happening to her? One by one, each of her friends was betraying her, as if all of Rome, not just Brutus, had stabbed Caesar. Was Claire next?

"You like him?" Layne screeched, spraying chipotle crumbs at Kristen. "I can't believe this!" She leaped to her feet, her face turning beet red. "I thought we were friends!"

"We are!" Kristen yelped, her features twisting in pain.

"No," Layne spat. "We're not. Not anymore." She crossed her arms over her chest. "I almost wish it was Massie who stole him from me," she said.

Ditto, Massie thought.

"At least that way, I wouldn't be getting stabbed in the back by a friend!" Layne finished.

"I'm sorry!" Kristen started pacing in front of the benches, speed-reading through her note cards. "Butthere'smoreI wasn'tevensickfrombadsushiIjustsaidthatsoIcouldstayhome 'causeIfeltsoguilty," she heaved, pulling a purple plastic bottle of Propel from her bag and downing half of it in a single gulp. "WhichshowshowmuchIloveyouguyssinceIshouldbekeep ingmygradesupformyscholarship." She stared expectantly at Massie and Layne. "I tried not to like him. I even started to make a list of bad things about him. But I couldn't come up with anything!"

"Kristen," Massie said evenly, "is my birthday October eleventh?"

"No." Kristen lowered her eyes.

"Then stop treating me like I was born yesterday!" In under a minute, Kristen had shattered Massie's monthlong dream of adopting five to nine orphans with Dempsey Solomon. By the time he and Kristen broke up, the trend would be over. And she would have missed her chance to have a multiculti family.

"I'm nawt!" Kristen insisted. Her eyes were bright. "It's just . . . I can't help how I feel."

"Ahem*bull*ahem," Layne cough-accused.

Kristen blinked down at her last note card, her voice cracking. "'I fell so fast, can't hold myself back—'"

"Don't you dare bring the Jonas Brothers into this," Layne hissed.

Massie closed her eyes. The sweet stench of fruity bath gel and chocolaty shampoo was making her blood curdle. Or was her heart responsible?

"Try to understand," Kristen pleaded, biting her lip.

"Oh, I understand." Massie stood up and marched toward the door. "It isn't enough that you borrow my clothes, sleep at my house, and share my lattes. Now you're Apple-C'ing my crush! Gawd, too bad I didn't like Edward Cullen. Then you could have stolen him and you two would have been perfect together." Her trembling voice bounced off the sweaty tile walls.

"Why?" Kristen managed, wiping her salt-stained cheeks.

"Because you both suck!" Massie whirled around on her heel and stormed through the misty shower fog. She shoved past two girls in towels, not even caring that they were gawking at her as she passed. Hot tears filled her eyes. But this time, she couldn't blame Chanel. This time, it was Kristen's fault.

By the time she reached the parking lot, salty tears were spilling down her cheeks. She'd given everything to the Pretty Committee: fashion advice, crush advice, clothing, and every second of her free time. All to make them better alphas. And what had they done? Betrayed her, without giving it a second thought.

43

Forget the homeless. Massie Block was Westchester's new-est, saddest charity case. It would probably take years before she could get back on her feet again. And that was only if she dedicated every waking moment to her comeback.

She fired off a quick text to her mother.

Massie: Too much homework. I have to pass on the ho ho ho.

Her iPhone vibrated almost immediately.

Kendra: No no no! You made a commitment.

Massie dug her nail into the end button. Since when did the people in her life honor their commitments? Alicia and Dylan had pledged their loyalty to the Pretty Committee and they were gone. Kristen had promised to help Massie get Dempsey, and now the only thing she was committed to was Dempsey!

"I said, wait up!"

Massie whirled around to see Layne rushing toward her, her Chucks, one red and one yellow, shuffling over the pave-ment.

"What do you want?" Massie snapped, scanning the emptying parking lot for Isaac.

"Can you believe her?" Layne huffed. "That was a Shakespearian-size betrayal. We can't let her get away with this." She tilted her bag of Corn Nuts toward Massie. "You want? They're super-cheesy."

So are you, Massie wanted to say. But she held back,

hardly in the position to send away one of the only people still talking to her. Instead, as a sign of solidarity, she allowed Layne to dump a spice-dusted mound of pellets in her palm. For once, she actually agreed with the LBR. Kristen could not get away with this.

Despite the calories and the blatant grossness, Massie popped the nuts in her mouth and chewed. They were hard and salty, with a hint of sweetness.

Just like revenge.

CURRENT STATE OF THE UNION	
IN	**OUT**
Homework	Homelessness
Abeley	Gregory
Trust funds	Trust friends

"So that's four skinny half-caf lattes and four hot chocolates."
A bored-looking waitress appeared next to Alicia's table in
the very center of the Gourmet Au Lait, Westchester's newest
coffee bar, balancing a tray filled with steaming hand-painted
ceramic mugs. She raised a pierced eyebrow at the seven
empty seats around the sturdy wooden table.

"Yup, that's right." Alicia speed-nodded, hoping the waitress would think she was over-caffeinated, instead of nervous.
"Lattes on the left, hot chocolates on the right."

Customers sitting at the tiny round tables that orbited
Alicia's perch stared as the waitress deposited the drinks.
Alicia didn't bother loudly explaining that her friends would
be there any second. Or that she'd had Dean, the family driver,
drop her off a good fifteen minutes early. Admitting out loud
that she needed prep time would be the opposite of alpha.
Real alphas made it look easy. Effortless.

"I'll be back with your toppings," the waitress told her.

"'Kay," Alicia said absently, reaching for her latte immediately. She took a long, recharging sip before returning her
red polka-dotted mug to the table. Her friends hadn't even
shown up yet, and already she was starting to feel drained.
Coordinating her first big after-school social event in only a

few hours had been exhausting. First she'd had to pick a place to meet (she'd gone with the coffeehouse because one, it was the newest hot spot in Westchester, and two, the dim lighting, large wooden tables, and shelves stocked with old books and board games reminded her of her dad's study, which made her feel at home). Next she'd had to put together a witty text-vite that everyone (especially Josh) would find hilarious, and than had changed into an outfit that screamed "I'm in charge!" (dVb denim, Alexander McQueen military jacket). Plus, she'd gotten there early to scope out the best table (front and center) and order for everyone. All so her friends could show up and have everything taken care of. Just like Alicia used to be able to do, when Massie was in charge.

Alicia wasn't giving Massie credit for much these days. But she'd give her credit for one thing: Being in charge was way harder than it looked.

"I'm telling you, it's gonna be pretty sweet." Cam's voice rose above the low chatter of the café as he shoved through the front door, followed by Josh, Derrington, and Dempsey. Dylan and Claire were following close behind. "Plovert's dad's on the Briarwood board. He said the indoor soccer field's gonna be, like, one of the best in the country."

"They imported the grass from Italy," added Josh.

"Awesome." Derrington stuffed his hands in his jeans pockets.

Alicia waved to her friends, then slipped on her Juicy Couture Jessica sunglasses so she could roll her eyes behind the tinted lenses. It had been hours since Principal Burns had announced the completion of Briarwood version 2.0. How could the boys still be talking about it like it was a good thing? Like it hadn't even occurred to them that leaving OCD behind meant leaving the girls behind?

Claire and Dylan waved back as the group wove through the maze of wooden tables to get to their table.

"What's up?" Josh pulled his NY Yankees cap over his eyes when he reached the table and dropped the soccer ball he'd been carrying to the floor.

"Not much," Alicia said as casually as possible. She couldn't help the warmth that was rising to her cheeks. Josh's slightly wrinkled white collared shirt made him look like he'd just stepped off the pages of a Ralph Lauren ad. "Girls on the left, guys on the right," she said, as her friends crowded around the table.

But nobody listened. Cam and Claire collapsed into two seats next to each other, and Derrington and Dylan followed suit. Josh slid into the seat to Alicia's left, and Dempsey sat at the far end of the table.

"Toppings." The waitress appeared again, lowering her tray. She transferred tiny ceramic bowls filled with flavoring, spices, and sweets to the table. Alicia had preordered those, too.

"Yum!" Dylan's hand shot out toward the bowl of mini marshmallows, and she heaped half the bowl's contents into her latte. "Thanks for ordering, Alicia."

"Welcome." Alicia nodded like it was no big deal. She glanced at Josh, who tilted back in his chair and flashed her a thumbs-up sign. Her heart revved in her chest. And this time, it wasn't from caffeine or nerves. This time, it was pure love adrenaline.

"This place is cool." Claire dunked a cinnamon stick in her finger-painted mug and swirled it around.

Derrington chugged two sips of his hot chocolate, then slammed his mug to the table. "HOTTTT," he bellowed, sticking out his burnt tongue.

Dylan took a long latte sip. "CHOOOOCOLATE," she burp-finished, sticking out her tongue at Derrington and wiggling it like he wiggled his butt.

The guys laughed and Cam punched Derrington on the shoulder. Everyone was clearly having fun.

Point, Alicia thought to herself with satisfaction, reaching for the bowl of French vanilla whipped cream. So far, everyone was having fun, and it was all because of her. All the prep had been totally worth it.

"And we're gonna have a sundae bar in the cafeteria." Cam was back on Briarwood, talking excitedly to Claire. "None of this nonfat diet fro-yo stuff. Like real ice cream." Alicia bristled, wishing they made sunglasses for lips so she could cover her frown. After all her planning, the boys should be singing *her* praises, not the school's.

"Great." Claire sighed, blowing dejectedly on her latte.

"That's nothing, man," Dempsey chimed in. "The guys' locker rooms are gonna have flat screens, so we can watch game footage during practice and stuff."

"Uhn-uhn." Dylan's jaw dropped. "Flat screens?" She lifted her mug to her lips and drained the rest of her coffee. "No fair. Do they get cable?"

Derrington nodded.

"So jealous," Dylan huff-sighed.

"You can come over and watch, too," Derrington offered. "I mean, if you want."

Dylan flushed. "Thanks."

"Well, I heard flat screens give you cancer if you stand too close, but whatever," Alicia interrupted, annoyed. Maybe she had to accept the fact that Josh was leaving her for a better Briarwood. But she didn't have to like it. And neither did Dylan.

"Seriously?" Dylan scrunched up her nose, skeptical. "Where did you—"

Alicia kicked her under the table.

"Ooooh," Dylan said quickly. "Right. I heard that too. This month's *Vogue*."

"Really?" Claire shoved her nail beds in her mouth.

Alicia ignored her. "So isn't there anything you're gonna miss about OCD?" she asked, batting her dark lashes at Josh. But he wasn't listening anymore. None of the boys were. They were too busy running through the rumored list of Briarwood perks to pay any attention to the girls. And if there was one thing Alicia hated more than being ignored, it was the fact that their crushes didn't seem quite crushed enough about leaving OCD. In fact, they didn't seem crushed at all.

"Hey, look who's here!" Dylan was staring over Alicia's shoulder, waving frantically.

Alicia's breath caught in her chest. Was Massie behind her? Was she here to take back her friends? To stage a coup and reclaim her place as alpha? She whip-turned around, feel-

50

ing like a lioness on the National Geographic Channel, about to throw down to protect her pride.

"Hey, guys." It was just Kristen. Alicia exhaled a sigh of relief.

"You got my text." Dempsey grinned. "Cool."

"Yeah." Kristen's skin looked pasty, and her shoulders were slumped. Definitely bad sushi.

"What're you doing here?" Claire asked skeptically. "You don't look so good."

"I don't feel so good," Kristen admitted. She dumped her Burberry tote next to the empty seat by Dempsey and collapsed into it.

"Are you sure you should even be here?" Alicia wrinkled her nose and scooted her chair six inches back.

"It's not that." Kristen sighed. "I'm not sick. Long story."

"Spill." Dylan nudged a latte in Kristen's direction.

Kristen pushed it back. "Okay. But first, there's something I've gotta tell you guys." She took a deep breath. "Dempsey and I are sort of . . ." The corners of her mouth were twitching. She looked meaningfully at Alicia, Dylan, and Claire.

"Ehmagawd!" The girls screamed in unison.

Derrington blew bubbles into his hot chocolate, and Dempsey shifted uncomfortably in his seat. The guys scooted their chairs together at the other end of the table, obviously not wanting to be a part of the conversation. "So, ah, are you watching the game tonight?" Josh coughed.

"Why didn't you tell us?" Alicia demanded. This was so

51

big, she almost didn't care that Kristen was hogging everybody's attention.

"Have you lip-kissed yet?" Dylan whisper-asked in Kristen's ear, so the boys couldn't hear.

"That's nawt the point," Kristen protested. "The point is that I just told Massie." The corners of her mouth dropped instantly.

"Ohhhh." The girls' heads bobbed sympathetically as they leaned toward Kristen.

"And now she hates me," Kristen said softly. "'Cause I stole Dempsey."

"Hates me too," Dylan gnawed at her straw. "I stole Derrick."

Claire tied her bendy brown stir-straw in a knot.

Alicia's grip tightened around her mug. Why did the girls look so sad? Did they want Massie to forgive them? Did they want her to come back and be their alpha? She had to move fast. Remind them that she was just as good of an alpha as Massie was. Better, even.

"But I don't want her to hate me," Kristen said glumly. "So what am I supposed to do?"

Alicia took a long, slow sip of latte, stalling for time. It wasn't lost on her that Massie would have offered the perfect advice. She always did. Alicia had to think of something good. Fast. She sat up straight and interlaced her fingers in front of her, like her attorney dad did when he was about to approach the bench and say something super important to a judge.

"You should just . . ." she began.

Kristen and Dylan leaned forward slightly.

But Alicia's mind was as empty as a bargain bin at a Chloé sample sale. She had no clue what to say. Her friends might as well have been asking her to explain the hard science behind global warming, or the logic of the Jennifer Aniston/John Mayer hookup/breakup/hookup/breakup. It was impossible to suss out.

"You should just . . . wait," she finished. No. Wrong. Alicia's every hair follicle tightened, and her cheeks felt hot.

"Um . . . wait?" Kristen tilted her head to the side. "For what?"

Suddenly, Alicia remembered her father's number one trial tip: Say anything with enough authority, and people will believe you.

"Is it nawt obvious?" she sigh-chided her friends. "You do nothing. No apology texts, voice mails, iChats, or IMs. You didn't do anything wrong. She's the one who should be apologizing for being such a control freak. So you wait. And if she ever decides to apologize, you wait some more. Tell her you have to think about it. Make her desperate." She sat back in her chair, satisfied. Everyone knew the wait for a Massie Block apology would be longer than the wait for a Chanel Biarritz bag. Which meant her friends would need a new alpha indefinitely.

"We wait for Massie to apologize," Dylan repeated flatly. "Massie . . . Block."

"Given," Alicia said firmly.

"'Kay." Kristen didn't look convinced.

"SCOOOORE!" Josh yelled, flicking a napkin paper football

across the table and through the goal Dempsey was making with his hands.

The guys cheered. People at nearby tables looked up from their MacBooks, silently shushing the boys with their glares.

Yesterday, Alicia would have been embarrassed. But today, watching Josh go for the field goal almost made her sad. Soon he'd be flicking paper footballs all the way over at Briarwood. Without her.

"So what're we doing after this?" Dylan retrieved the paper football and wiped away her latte foam mustache with it.

"We gotta head out," Derrington said. "Practice starts at five."

"Yeah," Josh said, shoving back his chair. "Coach makes us run extra laps if we're late."

Alicia tensed. Why didn't the boys look sad to leave? Was everyone not having enough fun?

"You guys should come," Josh mumbled. Alicia silently forgave him for forgetting to pay attention to her for the past five minutes.

"Okay!" Kristen brightened.

"I don't know . . ." Alicia said loudly, nibbling her glossy bottom lip. What made Kristen think she could just decide what they were doing? After all the planning she'd already done? "What are we supposed to do while you guys practice?"

"Watch?" Cam suggested.

She shrugged and pretended to swallow a yawn, like watching the boys execute their Beckham-style scissor kicks was about as appealing as watching grass grow.

"Make you a deal . . ." Josh said. "Come to practice this afternoon, and I'll do whatever you want tomorrow."

"Mani-pedis?" Alicia tried, flashing her most irresistible smile.

Claire giggled.

"Hotz! Come on, man!" Derrington protested, his voice suddenly an octave lower than usual.

"Manicures for guys are so in," Dylan announced. "I read it in *In Style*."

"I dunnooooo," Derrington said.

"I mean . . . *GQ*," Dylan said quickly. "I read it in *GQ*."

"It's true," Alicia piped up. "Beckham gets mani-pedis before every game."

"Right." Dempsey snorted.

"If we do this, you have to swear not to tell." Derrington stabbed a mini marshmallow with his fork. "The guys will never let us hear the end of it."

"Pinky-swear." Dylan nodded.

"Deal," Josh said.

"Fine. Deal." Cam still looked skeptical. "But nobody's painting my nails."

Claire giggle-grinned and kicked her Keds back and forth under the table.

Alicia took a deep breath. She'd been waiting for this moment the entire afternoon and was *this* close to sweating with anticipation. "Deal. And since we'll be doing stuff as a group, people will definitely be talking about us," she said with authority. "And it takes *so long* to say all eight of our names. Soooo, it'll be easier for everyone if we come up with a name for ourselves."

"Like what?" Kristen asked. The color had finally seeped back into her cheeks.

The table fell silent.

"The Supreme Team!" Derrington shouted.

"The New Crew?" Kristen suggested.

"The Odd Couples?" Dylan joked.

"Wait." Alicia touched her index finger to her shellacked lip thoughtfully, as if she was coming up with an ah-mazing idea just that moment—even though she'd been thinking about it all day. Everybody turned toward her. "What about . . . the Soul-M8s? Since there are eight of us?"

"Love it!" Kristen and Claire squealed in unison.

"Brill," Dylan added. "Best idea you've ever had."

"Pretty good." When Josh smiled at her, his dark eyes flashed *I heart you*.

Alicia flashed *I heart you* right back. Finally, everything was falling into place. Finally, she had the one thing Massie Block had never had:

A boy-girl clique.

Of course, being the Soul-M8s' alpha would take a lot of time, focus, and energy. Which she had plenty of, now that the Heart-Nets were no longer necessary.

Alicia could hardly excavate her cell from her burgundy Hype Picasso bag fast enough. She'd held off on disbanding the Heart-Nets until she was sure she had something better. And now she did. She'd make the breakup quick, like ripping off a Band-Aid. And she'd put in it language that her soon-to-be-ex squad could understand.

Alicia: U had the cutest outfits
Ur kicks were super high!
Now the Tomahawks r leaving
It's time 2 say buh-bye.
Thanks a mil for being true.
But the ♥-nets r splitsville
(Population: U).

Alicia pressed send and blew on her fingertip like it was a smoking gun. Done, done, and done.

"So let's get out of here?" Dempsey emptied a packet of brown sugar into his mouth.

"You ready?" Josh asked Alicia, scooping his soccer ball from the floor.

She nodded solemnly. "Yeah."

As if on cue, her friends shoved back their chairs, slung their bags over their shoulders, and headed for the door.

"Hey." Claire gripped Alicia's arm as they exited the café. "Can I ask you something?"

"What's up?" Alicia murmured, only half listening since she was busy picturing what everyone would say tomorrow when they found out she was the leader of a new crew.

"Do you think it'll work, us hanging out with the guys all the time?" Claire asked.

"Given."

"But . . . I heard boy-girl cliques don't work."

Alicia stopped.

So did the rest of the girls.

Alicia relaxed slightly. "What are you, six?" she asked, resuming her walk. "Of *course* it will work. I'll pull a Tim Gunn."

"What?" Claire looked clueless.

"I'll *make* it work," Alicia insisted. And with that she strode ahead of her friends, taking her rightful place at the head of the group.

Kuh-laire. Kuh-laire.

Claire's Massie ringtone reverberated inside the beige metal walls of the fourth stall, where Claire had been hiding since the last bell. Trying to divide her time equally between Massie and the Soul-M8s all day had left her feeling more worn than the magnetic strip on Massie's Glossip Girl Frequent Glosser card. She'd done lunch with the Soul-M8s, then sat next to Massie during study hall, and was supposed to meet the Soul-M8s for mani-pedis in less than five. Was this what kids with divorced parents felt like all the time? It was so exhausting, she'd ducked into the second-floor bathroom to get some peace.

Kuh-laire. Kuh-laire.

Which was obviously not an option in the second-floor bathroom, or any other place with decent cell reception.

"Okay, okay." She clawed through the contents of her Anya Hindmarch for Target python satchel, bypassing a spiral notebook, an emergency sours stash, and an almost-empty tube of Sephora Sugar Cookie gloss before she found her rhinestone-encrusted Motorola.

Massie: Smoothie. Isaac can be here in 5.

Hola, chica! Hola, chica! Her phone sounded Alicia's custom ring.

Alicia: Where r u??? Etd 4 soul-m8s mani-pedi = 5 mins.

Claire closed her eyes and pressed her forehead to the cool metal of the stall door, strangling her buzzing Motorola with her sweaty grip. Why did it have to be like this? Why did she have to choose? Last year, she would have been psyched to be so in demand. But now, she felt like the old yellowed undershirts her dad used to wear when he did repairs around the house in Orlando: torn and stretched too thin.

Hola, chica! Hola, chica!

"Kuh-laire."

Claire's eyes snapped open. A pair of tan wedges tapped impatiently under her stall door.

"Massie?" The overpowering scent of sandalwood and ylang-ylang invaded her tiny sanctuary.

"Um, question for you," Massie hissed.

Claire peeked through the side-crack of the door. Massie's arms were folded across her eggplant-colored tunic, her fingertips pressed into the muslin sleeves.

"Am I piece of lint-covered cashmere?"

"No." Claire sighed, bracing her stomach for the inevitable punch.

"Then why are you brushing me off?" Massie was blocking Claire's exit, hands now glued to her hips.

"I'm not," Claire protested. "It's just . . . I sort of . . . have plans." Her fist tightened, squeezing the life out of the synthetic snakeskin handle of her satchel.

"Plans?" Massie took a step back. "With them?" She narrowed her eyes accusingly, as if she'd just caught Claire wearing white Keds with black socks.

With a deep breath, Claire unlatched the metal lock and threw the door open. "Yes," she affirmed reluctantly. "But maybe we can do something tomorrow?" she said, making a break for the sinks. She turned on the faucet to drown out her thumping heart. A rush of hot water scalded her hand. Ignoring the burn, she continued like nothing was wrong. "You know, go shopping or something. I'd love to get something new."

"Like what?" Massie jammed the slanted tip of her Glossip Girl tube against her lips. "A spine?"

Claire chewed at the inside of her cheek, speed-pumping the soap dispenser. She'd have given up sugar for a year if it meant the Pretty Committee would get back together. But in the absence of a reunion, it seemed like being friends with both Massie and the Soul-M8s was the right thing to do—not the cowardly option.

*"And I said, Romeo, take me somewhere we can be alone
I'll be waiting, all there's left to do is run."*

Claire's phone was ringing again. But this was a call she wanted to take. She rinsed her hands and reached for her phone.

"Hey, Cam," Claire whispered into the receiver, as though

saying his name softly would make their relationship less threatening to Massie.

Massie rolled her eyes.

"Hey! We're in the Riveras' limo! Out front!" Cam's voice was barely audible above Dylan's shrieking laughter and the beat of a Kanye West song thumping from the speakers. "You coming?"

Claire mashed the phone against her ear, blocking the sound of fun from Massie. She stared at the floor, not wanting to have to see the hurt on Massie's face.

"Yeah. Um, okay. I—I'll be right there," Claire blurted with the urgency of an EMT. Maybe if Massie thought someone was hurt she wouldn't feel so—

The bathroom door slammed shut. Claire looked up at the now empty bathroom. A trace of Chanel No. 19 lingered, the only proof that this whole situation was real, and not just some horrible nightmare.

When Claire reached the limo, Dylan's head popped through the open sunroof, her long red locks whipping wildly in the breeze.

"Get in!" she yelled. Then she dropped back inside the limo like a reverse jack-in-the-box.

The second Claire opened the door, Derrington bolted from the limo like a prisoner making his escape.

"Go! Go! Go!" Josh yelled.

"Save yourself!" Dempsey added, his smile curving into his dimpled cheeks.

"Ohhhhh, no you don't!" Dylan shot out after Derrington.

In seconds, she'd caught up with him and was dragging him back to his cell. "If I have to sit through soccer practice, you have to get a mani-pedi."

"Awww, man." Derrington rubbed the back of his neck, diving into the seat between Cam and Dempsey.

"Good effort." Cam elbowed him.

Claire ducked inside the limo and shut the door behind her.

"Finally!" Alicia tossed a chilled bottle of cran-grapefruit Vitamin Water in Claire's direction. "What took you so long?"

Claire eyed the tiny patch of vacant leather next to Cam. She wanted to squeeze in, but Alicia was already directing her to the spot between Dylan and Kristen.

"Sorry." Claire shrugged, without bothering to answer. After all, the question was the equivalent of "Is that what you're wearing?" It didn't actually require an answer.

Cam side-glanced at his friends, who were busy sucker-punching one another, then nudged Claire's ballet flat with his Puma. "Hey."

"Hey." Claire nudged him back. Alicia rapped on the glass divider behind her and the limo lunged forward. "These little piggies are going Chanel," she decided, rolling up the hem of her olive satin cargo pants and planting her black patent peep-toes on the edge of the leather bench across from her. "Vendetta."

"Oooh." Dylan nodded. "Good one." She took a gulp of Skinny Water and wiped her mouth with the back of her arm.

"Not me." Dempsey grinned. "Shanghai Red, all the way, baby."

"Duuuude." Derrington shook his head slowly.

Kristen looked horrified. "How do you even know that's a color?"

Dempsey's chin dropped to his 100 percent recycled IT'S NOT EASY BEING GREEN cotton tee. "My mom likes it."

"Sure she does," Josh snorted.

"You okay?" Cam asked Claire quietly, from his seat across from her.

"Yeah. Just tired." She sighed.

Cam reached into his jeans pocket and pulled out a fresh bag of sours.

"Thanks." Claire smiled, letting the stress of the day melt away like the sugar on her tongue. The vibrations from the speakers transformed the creamy leather seats into massage chairs.

"So seriously." Derrington crossed his arms over his chest, glaring out the window. "If you guys tell anybody about this—"

"Re-laaaax," Dylan said. "We won't."

"Swear," Josh insisted. "If this ever got out—"

"Pinky-swear," Alicia assured him. Claire caught Cam's green eye and smirked. Once she'd drawn a little heart on his big toe with her red Sharpie. He widened his blue eye, as if embarrassed at the memory. But Claire knew for a fact that he'd worn the heart on his toe for over a week. She turned to nudge Massie, the only person she'd told about the Sharpie session, then remembered the alpha was too far away—in all senses of the word—for an inside joke.

All around her the limo was full of life and giggles and chatter. But for some reason, Claire just felt empty.

"We're here!" Alicia announced when they arrived at the spa ten minutes later.

Dean opened the limo door. "Just text when you're ready," he instructed Alicia, his furry brow knitting together like a caterpillar inching its way across his forehead.

"'Kay." Alicia marched to the head of the line, narrowing her eyes at the boys as they huddled close the limo, not wanting to go inside. "Come awn," she ordered, leading their dragging feet to the frosted glass door.

Inside, giant crystal chandeliers cast a shimmering light over the all-white decor. Customers sat at large white marble cubes, their hands outstretched toward their aestheticians. Even though the spa was packed, the only sound came from the rush of the indoor waterfall that spilled over the glass wall at the back of the spa. It was chic times ten. Alicia mentally applauded her choice of venue.

"Miss Rivera!" A striking woman wearing black skinny pants and a ruffled black button-down sashayed across the slick marble floors to greet them. She air-kissed Alicia on both cheeks. "*Cómo estás?*"

"*Muy bien.*" Alicia beamed. She turned to the group for introductions. "Soul-M8s, this is Estée. Estée, meet the Soul-M8s."

Estée smile-nodded, the soft white light from the chandeliers illuminating her perfectly chiseled cheekbones. "Hello, ladies," she said, before her eyes fell on the boys. "And gentlemen?" she said, her voice lifting in surprise.

Alicia smile-nodded proudly.

The boys reddened.

"There. Are. No. Other. Dudes. Here," Derrington hissed. Dylan elbowed him playfully.

"Estée, as in Lauder?" Claire marveled.

"Yeah," Kristen said under her breath. "Estée Lauder's got nothing better to do than pumice your feet."

"I want paraffin treatments for the boys," Alicia announced, pacing back and forth in front of the group. The staccato click-clack of her heels punctured the silence of the spa.

"Parawhat?" Cam whispered in Claire's ear.

"Hot wax," Claire whispered back. "I think it's French for 'waste of money.'"

Alicia jabbed Claire with her elbow.

Dempsey hitched up his cargo pants. "Will the wax make the soccer ball stick to my feet?"

"No!" Kristen giggled.

"I can't believe this," Josh muttered. "Least they have snacks." He reached for the crystal bowl sitting on a side table in the waiting area. Plunging his hand into it, he stuffed the contents into his mouth.

Claire's hand flew to her mouth. "Josh!" she whispered. "I think that's—"

"Gross!" Josh yelled, spitting out a dried rosebud.

"No waaaay!" Cam, Derrington, and Dempsey doubled over laughing while Josh spewed potpourri like a leaf blower.

Estée pursed her plumped lips. A stooped dowager furrowed her goo-covered brows. A technician tapped her French-manied nails on her white workstation and glared.

Alicia turned bright purple but pretended not to notice.

"And for the girls . . ." Alicia paused briefly in front of Claire, letting her eyes run from the green silk Tea and Honey blouse to the violet ballet flats. "We'll go with Essie," she decided. "Cloud Nine."

"Excellent choice." Estée nodded her approval as Alicia moved on to Kristen and Dylan, relishing the feeling of being in charge and taken seriously.

"I'm sure you'll find everything to your satisfaction." Estée led the Soul-M8s past the marble cubes when Alicia finished making her color choices. The boys sashayed behind Estée, mimicking her hip-swinging walk. Alicia swallowed a reprimand as the old lady customers sharpened their glares.

At the back of the spa, in front of the waterfall, a line of eight white leather massage chairs and eight all-black-wearing pedicurists were waiting. Nestled in the left armrest of each chair was a champagne flute filled with sparkling cider and topped with dark chocolate shavings that looked like confetti. Each glass had different initials gold-stamped on the base.

"Just like I wanted," Alicia proclaimed with a satisfied nod.

Dylan swiped a truffle off a tray and popped it in her mouth. "Mmm, peanut butter," she mumbled.

"Sweet!" Derrington held up a pair of white earbuds that had been plugged into the side of the chair. "We can listen to the regional finals!"

"ADD is gonna clean up," Dempsey said. "Their team is sick this year."

The guys high-fived, clearly relieved to have a manly activity to distract them from their para*fem* pedicures.

Alicia found her glass, stamped with the initials AR, and settled between Dylan and Kristen. Dunking her feet into the lavender-scented water, she tilted back her chair and sipped her cider. The moment was perfect. Everything had gone according to plan. Everyone was here, having fun. And, once again, it was all because of her.

"Claire. Cam. Get together." Alicia pulled a tiny digital camera out of her handbag. The only way to make this moment more perfect was to capture it forever.

"New camera?" Claire asked through her frozen smile.

"Yep." Alicia lowered her index finger. The camera emitted a tiny click. "I got it for making good grades this year."

"Puh-lease," Kristen said into copy of *Shape* magazine. "We've been in school for like a month. You don't have any grades."

"Well, I've 'demonstrated exceptional academic promise,'" Alicia air-quoted. "Now do me." She tossed the camera to Claire and lifted her champagne flute in the air. "I propose a toast," she announced, pausing long enough to narrow her eyes at the camera.

Claire took the shot, then raised her glass.

"To the Soul-M8s!" Alicia announced.

"To the Soul-M8s!" the girls echoed.

"Cotton bomb!" Derrington lunged forward suddenly, launching a handful of cotton balls in the girls' direction.

"Ahhhhhhhhh!" the girls scream-ducked.

A collective, sharp inhale from the customers around them did nothing to stop Kristen from picking up a giant loofah. She waved it menacingly.

"You wouldn't dare," Dempsey challenged.

"I would!" Dylan flicked a nail file down the row, pegging Derrington in the chest.

Claire laughed out loud and chucked a foam toe separator at Cam, as if she didn't care what the customers in Estée's fancy spa thought about her or her friends. Alicia's cheeks burned, and not from the rubbing alcohol–laden cotton ball that had just hit her cheek. A little voice in the back of her head told her this never would have happened if Massie were around. She wouldn't have allowed it. She'd be too concerned with her reputation and how people wouldn't regard her as a serious patron of the pampering arts. And the Pretty Committee would have been too scared to cross her. But how could Alicia stop it without seeming uptight and unfun?

Derrington reached for the tray of chocolates. He palmed a dark chocolate truffle and wound up.

"Miss Rivera!" Estée faced all eight chairs, her toned arms crossed over her chest. A wet cotton ball whizzed past her elbow and landed with a splat on the marble floor.

The boys snort-snickered.

Dylan bit her lower lip.

Kristen buried her face in *Shape*.

Alicia could feel her dark skin fade to a yellowish gray. "Yes?" She blinked rapidly, like it was Morse code for "Please don't tell my mom."

"I'm going to have to ask you and your friends to control yourselves, or you will be asked to leave."

Again, a little tiny disloyal voice popped up in the back of Alicia's head, and she couldn't help but wonder how Massie would respond to Estée's threat. Would she bust out a snappy comeback? Something like "Um, Est, are you Steven Spielberg? Then why are you telling me how to act?" Or would she flat-out deny everything, making Estée think she was having a delusional episode. It was hard to predict. But one thing Alicia knew for sure was that Massie would never, ever—

"I'm sorry," Alicia mumbled the words before she could stop herself.

Apologize.

Claire, Kristen, and Dylan exchanged a look. Suddenly the smell of lavender was overpowering. Alicia's eyes burned and she couldn't get enough air. Her friends' looks confirmed what Alicia instantly knew to be true: that in the OCDictionary, "I'm sorry" was just another way to say "I'm a beta."

An hour later, Claire waddled awkwardly into her bedroom in the spongy flip-flops provided by the spa, her ballet flats dangling from her fingertips. She stepped over the pile of Keds next to her door and tossed her shoes into her open walk-in closet. A tiny yelp escaped from inside, and Bean trotted out, chewing a green Kate Spade sandal that had been a Massie hand-me-down.

"Bean! No!" Claire knelt down and wrestled the soggy shoe away from the puppy, careful not to smudge her nails.

"She has ah-mazing taste." Massie's voice leaked from inside the closet.

"Hey!" Claire inhaled sharply, her heart thumping in her chest. "I didn't know you were here." She yanked the closet door open wide. Massie was standing inside, Claire's favorite jeans and a yellow silk top Claire still hadn't worn draped over her arm.

"I needed more clothes for the homeless." Massie shrugged, scooping Bean from the floor. "Your mom let me in." She glare-nodded at Claire's flip-flops. "How were your plans?"

"They were"—Claire started carefully—"okay." She sat on the edge of the bed and gingerly removed her foam shoes. Her feet were still slick with sweet almond massage oil. She wiped her smooth soles on the floor, as if trying to destroy the evidence of her fun afternoon.

Claire studied Massie for a second. Her lips were practically reflective, like they had a protective shell.

"I missed you. We all did." Okay, so maybe that wasn't exactly true. But Claire had to believe that deep, deep, deeeeeeeep down, the other girls missed Massie too.

Massie's face seemed to soften slightly.

"You know, it's not too late to—"

"I already told you." Massie's features hardened faster than quick-drying nail polish. "Elastic is for Lululemon." She reglossed. Claire could almost see her reflection in Massie's lips. "It's time to choose."

"Choose?" Claire squawked.

Massie nodded slowly. "PC or MAC?"

Bean barked once.

"Um, what's MAC again?" Claire stalled.

"Massie and Claire," she said flatly.

"What about Kristen? And, you know, the crew?"

"What's it gonna be?" Massie hissed at Claire's pearly toes, ignoring the question.

"Neither!" Claire collapsed back onto her duvet and stared up at the glow-in-the dark stars plastered to her ceiling. "I mean, I'm not choosing. I can be friends with you both."

"Won't work," Massie retorted. "Do you think Courtney Cox Arquette is friends with Brad and Angie?" She dropped Bean to the floor.

Alicia's voice echoed in Claire's head. She bolted upright.

"I'll pull a Tim Gunn," Claire insisted. "I'll make it work."

"Trust me. You can't." Without even looking in Claire's direction, she headed for the door. "Don't say I didn't warn you. And don't come crying to me when your PC crashes." She stormed out.

Bean lifted her tiny nose in the air and followed.

Claire tasted pennies. She couldn't let Massie walk out on her twice in one day. "Wait!" she said desperately, rushing toward the door. She tripped over her Keds, jamming her big toe into the doorframe.

"Owwww!" she yelped, hopping up and down on one foot. Downstairs, the slam of the front door told her Massie was gone. Pain shot through Claire's toe, all the way to her heart.

Collapsing in defeat on the floor, she examined the wound. Her toe was red and throbbing, and her pedicure was ruined. Just like her afternoon.

"Et maintenant, le subjonctif," Madame Vallon wheezed from the front of the classroom, gripping the sides of the wooden podium like it was a walker. Massie took a break from the *Teen Vogue* quiz on her desk to indulge in a quick wrist sniff. The Bengay-slash-mothballs-slash-stale-peppermint smell that hovered within a ten-foot radius of OCD's ancient French department head was making her feel light-headed.

Or maybe it was the faint combination of spicy chocolate, crisp green apple, fresh grapefruit, and cheap drugstore vanilla that was making her ill. Reminding her that Alicia, Kristin, Dylan, and Claire were all sitting in the back row, speed-texting, while her iPhone sat eerily cold and silent in her lap.

"We'll begin with the verb *avoir,*" Madame Vallon trilled, sending her face wrinkles into vibrating spasms. She pressed her giant putty-colored hearing aid into her left ear, then turned to the board, leaving her deaf ear exposed to the class.

"To haaaaave," Dylan burped from the back of the room. The class exploded into giggles. Massie pinched the skin between her index finger and thumb until it hurt.

"Répétez: que j'ai, que tu aies, qu'il/elle ait." Madame Vallon turned back toward the class, oblivious. The wrinkly neck-

skin that spilled over the top button of her shapeless oatmeal cardigan swung slowly back and forth as she spoke.

While the rest of the class chanted in monotone voices that suggested hypnosis by neck fat, Massie pulled her Nutella gloss from the pocket of her charcoal wide-leg Yaya Aflalo trousers. Nutella was the newest flavor from Glossip Girl's international collection, and the rich chocolate gloss tinged with hints of hazelnut and espresso made her feel like she was somewhere way more exotic than room G-16 of Octavian Country Day. Somewhere she could start fresh. Where she'd be appreciated for her fashion-forward style, her ability to move in a four-inch-plus heel, and most of all, her talent for taking charge. Paris, *peut-être*.

". . . *que nous ayons, que vous ayez, qu'ils/elles aient*," Madame Vallon continued.

Realistically speaking, Paris was out of the question, especially given Massie's strict policy against horizontal stripes and simple carbs.

Usually, when she needed a change, she made a beeline for Jakkob's salon. But the kind of change she needed now was bigger than fresh highlights and a bang trim. It was bigger than a new wardrobe from Barneys or a day at the spa. She was going to have to start from scratch. With a whole new group of friends.

Wasn't Kendra always telling her to quote-unquote "learn from her mistakes"? Well, the only mistake she'd made recently was in whom she hung out with. She was done, done, and done with alpha-wannabes, food-obsessed ex-snatchers with an excess of gas, sporty crush-stealers, and neutral Switzerlands. Her new friends had to be more alpha than her old ones, in every way.

Staring at the mag quiz in front of her, Massie nibbled her lower lip. The chocolaty flavor sent a sugar rush through her veins. It cleared her head and renewed her confidence, giving her an idea that was beyond genius.

Flipping open her notebook, she got to work on a quiz of her own.

ARE YOU MAC MATERIAL?

1. You leave the house looking hawter than hawt in your new black lace Miu Miu cami and BCBG wide-leg pants. You open the door of the Range Rover. Massie is wearing the exact same cami! EHMAGAWD! No worries, you know exactly what to do. You:

    A. Do nuh-thing. You know you look hawt, so why should it matter?
    B. Take a bad sushi day. The cami was ah-briously Massie's idea first.
    C. Trick question! You would cuh-learly never buy anything without consulting with your alpha beforehand.
    D. Trick question! Underwear-as-outerwear is so last year. You'd sooner wear acid-wash denim.

Answer: C & D. Obv. ♥

2. An ak-dorable Briarwood boy moves into your building. He's mature, stylish, and tanned. You just know he'd be perfect for Massie. Even though she needs zero help with boys, you offer to see if he's into her. What's your first move?

    A. Give Massie 72 hours notice, then plan an "accidental run-in" with Massie and Briarwood Boy. Follow up with a *casual* text to determine Briarwood boy's level of interest. Make sure there's nothing in the text to make the boy like you instead of Massie. Also, make sure there's nothing that would make him think *you* like him. Double-check before sending.

    B. First move? You have a jillion ideas, and they're all fantastic. So you prepare a short PowerPoint presentation and let Massie choose. After all, who knows more about anything than she does?

    C. Plan an "accidental run-in" with Massie and Briarwood boy. Forget to warn her.

    D. Plot ways to get him to like you instead. Then, when she least expects it, tell her he's just not that into you. Pretend to be sorry.

    Answer: A & B are both acceptable options. Check in with Massie and proceed accordingly. ♥

3. If you were a celebrity, you'd be:

    A. Angelina Jolie. You and your C-cups are nawt to be trusted.

B. Oprah. Fine, everybody likes you. But you've got major eating issues and seriously? We're all sick of hearing about it.

C. Hayden Panettiere. So you're sporty, have a hawt bod, and can hang with the guys. Big. Deal.

D. Anne Hathaway. You're a sweetheart who's come a long way, fashion-wise. But your super-sugary ways are starting to rot my smile.

Answer: EW-ma-gawd! None of the above! If I were a celeb, I'd be: _____. ♥

INSERT CELEB NAME HERE.

As Madame Vallon switched to the conjugation of *être*, Massie folded the quiz and dropped it into her purple metallic Rebecca Minkoff bag, satisfied. She'd distribute it to people at school who showed potential and use it as a screening device for new friends. She'd have a hawt new crew in no time.

Massie scanned the room for quiz-worthy girls. But everyone around her had at least one major flaw. Mascara boogers, mismatched fabrics, unbleached teeth . . . it was like a parade of *Glamour* "don'ts" had invaded G-16. Massie felt her heart sinking fast. Was it possible that Alicia, Dylan, Kristen, and Claire were the best OCD had to offer?

"And now, the verb *faire*." Madame Vallon turned back toward the board.

"Psssssssst."

Massie smelled corn. She swiveled around slowly.

Layne Abeley was leaning over the desk behind her, handing her a folded piece of Chococat notepaper.

Massie tilted her head toward the iPhone on her desk, indicating that she only accepted texts. Then she quickly turned back around, resisting the urge to stare down Kristen, who was whispering to Alicia behind her *Allons-y!* workbook. Were they talking about her? Or did Kristen have gossip? And if so, would Alicia know how many points to give? The uncertainty made Massie's head throb.

The bell rang, and Madame Vallon spit-muttered something about copying conjugations for homework, but the sound of scraping chairs and screeching backpack zippers drowned her out.

"Remember the look on Estée's face?" Alicia said loudly from her seat across the room.

"I know, right?" Dylan giggled. The girls got up and started to make their way to the door.

Massie sniffed her wrist again, this time for courage. The girls would be passing her desk in seconds. They couldn't know she hadn't found new friends yet. Pretending to be engrossed in her iPhone, she laughed out loud as Alicia, Dylan, Kristen, and Claire slid by.

"Ehmagawd, too funny," she murmured to herself, staring at her text message inbox.

It read 0 MSGS.

It might as well have read 1 LBR.

When she heard her exes disappear down the hall, she slung her bag over her shoulder and headed for the door.

"Hey." Layne grabbed Massie's arm the second she hit the hallway. "I hafta talk to you."

Massie rolled her eyes but slowed so Layne could catch up with her. Secretly, she was glad to have the company. But she'd rather have box-dyed her hair than told Layne that.

"About what?" She sighed, even though she already knew.

"You know . . ." Layne said with a meaningful nod. Flecks of orange glitter from her obviously homemade headband went flying everywhere. "Revenge."

Massie pinch-plucked a piece of glitter from the shoulder of her Lela Rose cropped shrug, feeling like she was caught in a tacky snow globe. Stopping in front of her locker, she reached for the padlock.

"Look." Layne jumped between Massie and the locker. "Are we gonna do this or what?" She sounded shady, like they were a couple'a street thugs meeting in a dark alley.

"Did you come up with a plan?" Massie tapped her foot, wondering if she actually needed Layne to pull off Massie and Crew. Did she *really* want her right-hand woman to be a glitter headband–wearing thrift store junkie with barbecue breath? Then again, they were bonded in revenge, and Massie had to admit, Layne wanted to burn Kristen as badly as Massie wanted to burn the ex-NPC. And with Layne at her side, at least Massie wouldn't have to stage a comeback on her own.

"Eh. Not really." Layne shrugged. "We'll come up with something." She pulled a half-empty bag of barbecue Corn

Nuts from her backpack and shook the dusty pellets into her cupped hand. "We just have to find the perfect scenario." She slapped her palm to her mouth and tilted back her head.

Massie inhaled sharply as an eighth grader wearing a too-tight Cheetah Girls T-shirt and tapered jeans sidled up to a locker nearby. "Well, we're not gonna find perfection within a five-mile radius of that shirt."

Layne's eyes followed Massie's. She stared at the ensemble with a mixture of admiration and disgust. "That outfit takes some serious bawls." She nod-approved.

"Focus, Layne," Massie snapped. Suddenly, the hallway seemed packed with ill-fitting jeans, dull hair, and Lohan-orange foundation. "I need alphas. And there obviously aren't any here."

Layne shoveled another handful of Corn Nuts into her mouth, staring into space. "See, this is why I love the thea-tahhhh," she said. A nut was stuck on her eyetooth. "You can create a whole new world, and everything goes exactly the way you want it to. Same with Sims."

Massie shuddered at the word *theater*. It reminded her of Dempsey. "I'm so done with actors."

Layne's head snapped back to position. Nuts clattered to the ground as she gripped Massie's shoulders with both hands.

"Ow!" Massie yelped.

"Actors!" Layne said excitedly. She released her grip, tiny bits of red salt clinging to Massie's shrug like colorful dandruff. "Gimme your iPhone."

"No way." Massie took a cautious step back. Layne's eyes looked wild. It was probably the cheap glitter liner, but Massie wasn't taking any chances.

"Come awn," Layne begged. "My aunt runs a talent agency in the city. We could borrow some of her actors and use them to get back at that Dempsey-stealing dirtbag." She glanced meaningfully at the iPhone in Massie's hand. "Just take a look at some of the headshots."

Massie hesitated, the idea blooming in her mind. If she hired actors, she could get them to be whatever she wanted them to be. And what she wanted them to be was pure alpha. She felt an instant surge of hope.

"Fine," she whispered to Layne. "But not here." She speed-scanned the hall, searching for signs that Layne had been overheard. If anyone found out she was considering hiring best friends, she'd have to transfer to another hemisphere.

Layne's eyes flashed with excitement. "So where?"

Massie nodded sharply, signaling for Layne to follow her. It was lunchtime, and the crowds in the hall were starting to thin. "In here." She ducked back into the now-empty G-16 and shut the door behind them.

"What's the name?" Massie asked, unlocking her iPhone.

"Shooting Stars Talent Agency," Layne whispered.

Massie connected to the Web site. The headshots page was filled with black-and-white thumbnails. Massie clicked on the slide show setting, waiting for the girl parade to begin.

"Lemme see." Layne loomed over the iPhone, fogging up the screen with her hot nut breath.

"Layne!" Massie barked, wiping the screen with the back of her arm. "Two steps back." She held the phone at arm's length, the way Kendra did when she was trying to read the *New York Times* Sunday Style section without glasses. As pictures began fading from one to another, she surveyed the girls for flyaways, chapped lips, or recklessly applied highlighter. But each was more perfect than the next.

"She looks good." Layne pointed to a shot of a willowy girl with flawless, translucent skin and an edgy dark pixie cut. Her large, light blue eyes were the only pop of color in the photograph. She stared directly into the camera, like she was daring Massie to pass on her. "Check her stats."

"Lilah Poole. Five-seven, black hair, blue eyes," Massie read aloud. "Broadway debut in *Chicago* . . . plus a couple of indie films . . . and a guest appearance on *Law and Order*." Massie fought the smile starting to twitch at the corners of her mouth.

"So?" Layne tugged at her faded I ♥ ME T-shirt. "Whaddaya think?"

"I think," Massie said slowly, "whoever I hire has to be the complete opposite of the Pretty Committee."

"So . . . you want girls who're . . . nice," Layne said drily.

Massie didn't really care about defending the PC anymore, so she chose to ignore the jab. "I'd need at least four," she said decisively, twirling her purple hair streak around her index finger. She felt excitement starting to bubble up inside of her like fizzy bath salts. "Let's make the call."

"No deal, Lucille. I'll call my aunt, but only if I'm in the crew too."

Massie's hyper-glossed lips dropped open. "You?"

"Yeah," Layne said brandishing her cell like a weapon. "If I make the call, you let me in. That means sleepovers, parties, and a guaranteed lunch table spot. No tricks."

"But you hate cliques, re-mem-ber?" Massie tried to steady her voice. Adding Layne to her new crew was a guaranteed way to drag the alpha average lower than the rise on a pair of J Brand Boyfriend jeans. "And how will it help you get back at Kristen?"

"I'm not sure yet," Layne admitted. "And even though I hate cliques, I like a good ensemble cast, and I *love* revenge." She extended her right pinky. "Deal?"

Suddenly, the PA system crackled to life.

"Good afternoon, OCD, I'm Alicia Rivera and this is your lunchtime update."

Massie's stomach clenched at the sound of Alicia's voice. Her polished, peppy newscaster voice used to make Massie proud to be friends with Alicia. But now it just felt fake. Like their friendship must have been.

"Great," she muttered to Layne. "It's Meredith Vi-*ew*-a."

Layne snorted.

"Just a reminder that this Friday is the Briarwood boys' last day," Alicia chirped.

"Yeaaaaaaaahhhhhhhh!" The boys could be heard all the way from the New Café.

"So let's spend the rest of the week making them all sorry they have to leave." The sound of rustling papers echoed over the speakers.

"And now for a new segment I like to call Couples Update."
A brief pause was followed by a prolonged kissing sound.
"Which Briarwood thespian is now playing opposite OCD's
cutest soccer star? And are rumors of a steamy all-night
textathon really true?"

Massie clenched her iPhone in her fist. This was a total
abuse of journalistic power.

"Plus, which four alphas and their crushes were spotted
in a white limo yesterday afternoon? And is it true things
really got hot when AR and JH"—Alicia giggle-paused—"got
a couples foot massage together? Tune in next time to find
out. Till then, this is Alicia Rivera for OCD saying, I heart
you."

Layne made a gagging sound. "I don't know how you ever
hung out with her," she said, shaking her head.

Massie closed her eyes, the sound of Alicia's voice pounding inside her brain. She swallowed the growing lump in her
throat, recalling the one piece of useful information she'd
learned in world history last year: In times of war, people
did unthinkable things. It was unthinkable to let Alicia
think she had what it took to be an alpha. Unthinkable
to let Kristen think she could steal Dempsey. Unthinkable
for Dylan and Derrington to be so ah-nnoyingly perfect for
each other. Unthinkable for Claire to think she didn't have
to choose sides. Unthinkable for Massie to conspire with
Layne. Unthinkable for them to hire actresses as friends.
The only thing more unthinkable than any of that was to sit
around and do nothing.

Opening her eyes, Massie linked pinkies with her new partner in crime and shook.

"To the Fraud-Squad," Layne whisper-giggled.

"To the Fraud-Squad," Massie allowed herself to whisper-giggle back.

CURRENT STATE OF THE UNION

IN	OUT
Headshots	Latte shots
Actress	Drama
Hiring friends	Firing friends

"'Scuuuuze me." Alicia speed-walked into the New Café, balancing a teetering pyramid of gold tissue–stuffed gift bags with the skill of an Olympic gymnast. The inaugural gifts she'd had overnighted for the Soul-M8s had arrived that morning, and it had taken every ounce of self-control not to spoil the surprise before lunch.

She walked slowly to her table, using the opportunity to show off the new ensemble she'd bought for the boys' last day: black pencil-leg jeans paired with a black silk Elizabeth and James racer-back tank. Classic black Louboutin flats and a stack of bangles finished the outfit. The all-black was meant to subtly indicate that while Alicia Rivera might be suffering, her sense of style wasn't.

Even though she knew the outfit was at least a 9.8, she almost wished Massie could have confirmed her suspicions. But since that wasn't an option anymore, Alicia had had to settle for having her dad rate her before she left the house. He gave her an 11 out of 10. As always.

"Prezzies!" Dylan squeal-clapped when Alicia reached the table, temporarily forgetting that she was supposed to be in mourning. The black half-veil spilling from the comb lodged in her side-part fluttered as she jumped up and shoved the trays of soy cheese veggie burgers and tofu stir-fry out of the way to make room for the gifts.

Alicia tilted forward and dumped the overstuffed bags at the head of table thirty-six, like she was barfing generosity. "It wouldn't be a going-away party without presents."

"'S no big deal." Derrington shrugged, elbow-nudging Dylan. "We're just going back to Briarwood."

"Yeah," Josh added from his place at the boys' end of the table. "It's like five minutes away."

The girls were suddenly silent. Alicia's smile morphed into a tight line. Why couldn't Josh at least *pretend* he didn't want to leave?

"I guess," Dylan sniffed, producing a tube of DiorShow waterproof mascara and shellacking her lashes with it.

Kristen shrugged, yanking the zipper of her black Puma hoodie up to her chin.

Claire just stared down at her untouched soy cheeseburger, looking sadder than her faded black Old Navy henley.

"Okay!" Alicia said brightly. Just because the boys were leaving didn't mean her party had to be a funeral. "Let's get this party started!" She eyed Cam and Dempsey, who were hunched over their end of the table, working on their paper football goal kicks.

After a few seconds of silence, the boys finally took the hint and settled down. Alicia distributed the bags according to the gold glitter–scripted initials on each tag. "The boys can go first," she announced, taking her seat at the head of the table.

Derrington held up his bag and shook it. "Ugh," he said, wrinkling his nose at the tissue paper. "What's that smell?"

"Wellareyougonnaopenitornawt?" Alicia said quickly. Maybe she'd been a *little* heavy-handed with the perfume. But the extra spritzes of Angel ensured that they'd remember her long after they left OCD.

"Harrington!" Ben Wright, a seventh grader and the Tomahawks' second-string goalie, came up behind Derrington's seat. "Careful not to mess up those naaaaiilllllls." He wiggled all ten fingers in front of his face.

The boys flushed.

"Heard you guys got mani-pedis," Ben's friend Topher Bank added, using a squeaky girl voice. "Was it just to diiiie for?"

"Shut up, Bank," Josh mumbled, whipping a roll at the boy's head.

"Who cares?" Dylan said through a mouthful of fries. "I saw you guys last weekend getting spray tans at Sun of a Beach."

Ben and Topher's bronzed cheeks turned purple. Derrington stared at the table, looking like he couldn't tell whether Dylan had just saved him or doomed him.

"Whatever, mani-prettys," Ben spat, storming off.

"Okay, seriously," Alicia groaned, annoyed that the focus had shifted from her. "Open the presents."

"Hey, is this made from recycled paper?" Dempsey asked, pointing to the gold tissue.

Kristen kick-nudged Alicia with a black Puma.

Alicia bounced impatiently in her seat. "Just open it."

Dempsey's forearm disappeared into the bag. When it

reappeared, a key chain attached to a small, square LED screen was dangling from the crook of his finger.

"It's a digital photo key chain," Alicia chattered nervously, searching the boys' faces for their reactions. "So you'll remember OCD. It has pictures of us from the last few days. Like from the spa and stuff."

"Ehmagawd, that's too sweet." Dylan dabbed at her eyes with a napkin. Her "waterproof" mascara left a dark football player smudge under her left eye.

"You've got proof?" Derrington screeched, slumping back in his chair.

"If those things ever get out . . ." Dempsey shook his head, his green eyes wide.

Alicia froze. Was her idea totally lame? Should she have gone with the monogrammed iPod shuffles instead? "Plus it has 'Soul-M8s' engraved on the back," she said quickly, trying to reel them back in. "Annnnd it's an MP3 player."

"Cool!" Cam smiled reassuringly. "Did you load music onto them already?"

Alicia's cheeks burned. Should she have? Would Massie have thought of that? She shook her head no, but Cam grinned anyway.

"Thanks." He scooted his chair closer to Claire and started scrolling through pictures of them eating gummies together. Claire smiled sadly down at the screen, as if the photos were the last memories of Cam she'd ever have.

Derrington jumped up and wiggled his butt.

"Yeah, thanks." Josh leaned across the table and lifted his

palm for a high five. His dark brown eyes flickered like he meant it.

Relieved, Alicia met his hand midair. A jolt of electricity shot through her palm and zipped down to her stomach the instant their fingers touched. She realized it had been ten days since their last lip kiss. Who knew how long it would be before their next one, now that they wouldn't see each other every day.

"Yeah, really cool," Dempsey echoed, immediately gathering the crumpled tissue paper. He smoothed it out over the table before folding it up, probably to save and reuse it later.

"Girls' turn!" Alicia nod-signaled the girls.

"Thought the girls just had their turn," cracked a trio of passing lacrosse guys.

Embarrassed, the boys stuffed their key chains in their pockets. They might as well have stabbed Alicia in the heart with their cleats.

Claire, Dylan, and Kristen tabled their grief long enough to fish soft velvet boxes from their gift bags. Their excitement fueled Alicia like a triple-shot macchiato. The boys might not have appreciated all the trouble she'd gone to, but the girls did. And come Monday, when BOCD went back to OCD, they'd be the only ones who mattered. Alicia stole a glance at table eighteen. It was empty. Where could Massie possibly be?

"Ehmagawd!" Dylan tilted her Bulgari jewelry box toward Derrington, showcasing the delicate platinum chain nestled inside. Two tiny charms hung from the necklace: a soccer cleat and a spa slipper.

"To remember this week," Alicia explained. "We'll add a new charm for everything we do together."

"Awwwwwww," the girls synchro-gushed.

"Love it!" Kristen fumbled with the clasp on her chain. "Sort of like the bracelets we got for the boy fa—" She stopped herself just in time. "I mean, the last presents we got together."

"But better," Dylan insisted, stabbing her tofu stir-fry with a plastic fork.

"They're really great, Leesh," Claire added.

Satisfied, Alicia slipped her chain around her neck. She was growing into her role as the Soul-M8s' alpha. And the fit was practically custom-made. She sipped her Borba water while scanning the café over the top of the bottle, surveying her kingdom. Suddenly she spat the light pink liquid back into the bottle and gasped. "LBR U serious?"

"What?" Dylan whipped around in her chair, following Alicia's gaze. Massie was gliding through the frosted glass doors with none other than Layne Abeley in tow.

"Ehmagawd."

Kristen and Claire turned to look. So did the boys.

"What are they doing together?" Alicia slammed down her bottle, sending a few skin-replenishing drops toward the greenhouse ceiling.

Massie and Layne made a beeline for the do-it-yourself tofu bar while the Soul-M8s watched. They whisper-giggled as they spooned steaming spoonfuls of brown rice, tofu, and veggies into biodegradable to-go boxes. Alicia was dying to dispatch Claire and have her follow them. But what if they were doing something more fun? Claire might defect. And the M7s sounded like a mass transit bus line.

Kristen squinted. "But those two hate each other!"

"Maybe they're friends now?" Claire hoped.

"Doubt it." Dylan's mouth lolled open slightly.

The boys lost interest and went back to paper football.

Alicia eyed the tiny smile playing across Massie's lips. Alicia knew that smile. It was the kind of smile Massie had when she was about to pull something off. Something big. The same smile she'd had in the days before she'd announced her boy-girl Halloween party last year.

"Well, I opposite of care," Alicia lied, rapid-glossing her parched lips.

But the girls kept staring. Without even trying, Massie was stealing the focus. When she and Layne finished at the bar, they hurried back toward the smoky glass doors, not even bothering to sit. Or look in Alicia's direction.

Then again, none of the Soul-M8s were bothering to look in her direction, either. The girls were too busy staring at Massie, and the boys were too busy flicking paper triangles at one another's heads. It was time for The Announcement. Alicia had practiced it seventeen times in front of the vanity mirror in her bathroom. She was ready.

"Breaking news." Alicia slammed her elbows against the table, her clinking bangles announcing that table thirty-six was back in session. "I'm having a party next Friday night, and I want everybody there."

"What kind of party?" Josh was refolding the football.

"A dinner party." Alicia's nose lifted slightly.

"Oh." Josh raised his dark eyebrows, as if trying to look psyched.

Dempsey, Cam, and Derrington scrunched their noses, looking like they'd just stepped in a giant heap of dog poo.

"Text me any food preferences–slash–allergies no later than Monday at midnight," Alicia instructed, trying to ignore the boys' poo faces. "Joyce likes ample time to shop."

"No sushi," Kristen groaned.

"Sounds fun!" Claire smiled for the first time that lunch period. "What can we bring?"

"I'll explain it all tonight," Alicia replied. "My house. Eight p.m. Sleepover."

Dylan froze mid-chew.

Claire nibbled her cuticles. "Tonight?"

"What?" Alicia snapped.

Her table was silent. Alicia jerked her head toward the glass doors. "It's nawt like she invented the sleepover. We're allowed to do whatever we want now. Our Friday nights are open."

"True," Claire said nervously. "But—"

"Butts are for shaking, Kuh-laire."

The boys burst out laughing. But Alicia didn't even notice.

Claire flushed. "I sort of told her I'd go to her sleepover tonight."

Alicia took three long sips of Borba water to calm herself down. Was this it? Was Claire siding with Massie?

Claire picked at her soy burger, leaving crater-size holes

in the seven-grain bun. "Maybe I could stop by her place for a couple hours and then come over?"

Alicia shook her head slowly, whipping her sleek, deep-conditioned locks from side to side. How was Massie still having her sleepover without the PC? Who could possibly show up? She was dying to ask Claire if she knew, but she stopped herself.

"Nawt possible," she said, leveling her gaze at Claire. "It's either hers or mine." She smiled knowingly at Dylan and Kristen, like she knew exactly what Claire would decide. Choosing the Soul-M8s over Massie was a serious no-brainer. It was like choosing LC over Heidi. LC over Audrina. LC over anyone. "You have to pick."

Dylan and Kristen chewed anxiously, exchanging glances. But Alicia couldn't take her eyes off Claire, who was staring down at her lap. Every second she didn't choose the Soul-M8s left Alicia feeling less and less in control, like she was trying to run across a just-mopped parquet floor in slick-soled stilettos. And, if she'd learned anything from Massie, it was that any alpha worth her weigh in diamonds never lost control, or her reign as alpha was over.

Alicia clutched her water bottle, waiting for Claire to definitively pick the Soul-M8s, to pick Alicia as her leader. But Claire just clutched her stomach, yelled, "Bad sushi!" and ran out of the café.

Claire stood outside the Blocks' spa, shivering in the chilly night air. Holding her sleeping bag and pillow, she adjusted the canvas overnight bag on her shoulder. After holing up in the second-floor bathroom for the rest of lunch, she'd ultimately decided to go to Massie's sleepover this weekend and do Alicia's dinner party next weekend. What used to be a fun sleepover now felt like Friday night visitation. Divorce really *was* hardest on the kids.

Claire sighed and lifted her knuckles to the door, but the heavy wooden door to the spa swung open before she had the chance to knock. Massie stood in the doorway, wearing a fluffy white terry cloth robe and spa slippers. Her wet tresses had been swept back into an adorably disheveled twist.

"Heyyyy!" Massie's avocado-honey face mask cracked around the eyes and mouth when she spoke. She looked Benjamin Button chic. "Better seventeen minutes late than never."

Claire, ignoring the dis, slip-kicked off her pink Uggs and corralled them by the door. "Wouldn't miss it." And the second she released her bag to the floor and surveyed the spa, she knew she meant it.

Sort of.

Massie's Friday night sleepovers were a Pretty Committee tradition, like rating one another's outfits, fashionably late assembly entrances, and uncomfortable footwear. And with all the changes in the past week, the familiar sights and smells of the spa were more comforting than the loose gray sweats she was wearing. Even if things weren't exactly the way they used to be, the trickle of the limestone Zen fountain and faint smell of polished leather and lavender were reminders of the good old days. And in times of crisis, fond memories were the bridge that helped her get to the other side.

"Bean!" Claire exclaimed as the pug scampered into the room, wearing a robe identical to Massie's and tiny purple spa flip-flops. She raced figure eights around the marble-topped coffee table and zebra-print ottoman, then collapsed in a panting heap by Claire's pedicured feet.

The puppy's heavy panting seemed strangely loud. With a twinge of sadness, Claire realized that the sound of the PC's laughter no longer drowned out the sound of Bean's breathing. She bent over to scratch the puppy's head, wondering if the dog's unusual display of enthusiasm was a cry for help. Was Bean lonely too?

"Ehmagawd, what is *that?*" Massie winced, pointing at Claire's neck.

OMG, another one of those brutal chest-zits? Was it time to switch soaps again?

Her hand flew to her neck, and her fingers collided with cool metal. She realized her charm necklace had slipped out from under her apple green fleece. And was now swinging back and forth to the rhythm of the playground tune "neh

neh neh neh nehhhhhna," mocking Massie's very existence. Why hadn't she taken it off before she left the house? Oh. Right. Because she'd sworn to herself that she wasn't going to choose sides. She wasn't going to get sucked into the drama. She wasn't going to change.

It was times like these when Claire really couldn't stand herself.

Stuffing it back under her jacket, she dragged the zipper to her chin in record time. Claire was searching for an explanation but, thankfully, Massie had already moved on.

"Inez didn't know what kinds of gummies you liked best," she said, pulling her wet purple streak out of her bun and twirling it around her finger. "So I asked her to get them all." She smile-nodded at the snacks arranged on the coffee table. Where the evenly spaced crystal bowls had once overflowed with chocolate-covered popcorn (Dylan), cinnamon-sugar-dusted pretzels (Kristen and Dylan), gourmet trail mix (Alicia and Dylan), and gummies (Claire and Dylan), now an assortment of gummies filled each one.

"Yum! Thanks." Kneeling in front of the flickering fireplace, Claire smoothed out her sleeping bag so it was head-to-head with Massie's.

It looked lonely without Alicia's, Dylan's, and Kristen's to complete the circle. But she shook the depressing thought from her head. She'd pinky-sworn to herself that she would Tim Gunn it tonight even if it killed her. It shouldn't be too hard, right? Alicia's dinner party next Friday night, then back to Massie's the Friday after that, and so on. The MTV Video

Music Awards had successfully switched from New York to L.A. a billion times. And that was a much bigger deal.

"Kuh-laire!" Massie crossed her arms over her robe. "Just pick one already!"

"Huh?" Claire pushed herself to her feet. Sometimes she wondered if Massie had special mind-reading powers.

Massie exhaled slowly. "What. Would. You. Rather?" she said, like she was repeating the question for the millionth time. Maybe she was. "Have a crush who totally ah-dores you and no friends, or have tons of friends and a crush who hates you?"

Claire wrinkled her nose. "Neither."

"You can't pick neither." Massie sat on the edge of the espresso-colored leather love seat.

"Yes, I can!" Claire insisted, tightening her fists to squash her frustration. She wanted to tell Massie to get over it, but even in her weakened state, the alpha's teeth were sharp.

"Your turn." Massie frowned.

"Fine." Claire's words were clipped. But she almost didn't care. Let Massie see how annoyed Claire was starting to get with her control issues. Let her see how her Lycra-ing ways had driven the Pretty Committee away. Stalking over to the coffee table, Claire dug into the center gummy bowl and scooped out a handful. But instead of being comforting, the gummies tasted cold and waxy on her tongue.

"Kuh-laaaaiiire." Massie tapped her naked left wrist. "Time's up."

Claire chewed slowly, wondering if she was brave enough to ask Massie the question that was on her mind. Maybe Massie's teeth were sharp. But without the rest of the Pretty Committee to back her up, maybe her bite would be reduced to a bark.

Claire took a deep breath, like she was standing at the edge of a cliff and about to dive into choppy, shark-infested waters. And then she jumped.

"Okay, what would you rather?" She swallowed the taste of pennies and continued. "Friends who love you but don't always do what you say?"

A single, tiny fissure appeared in Massie's mask, next to her eye. It cracked all the way down to her lips, like a silent green tear.

"Or friends who always do what you say but don't really like you?"

Massie was as still as a moss-covered statue. Claire bit the inside of her cheek.

"Both."

"Huh?"

"Friends who love me and always do what I say." Massie smirked.

"That's not realistic," Claire managed.

"Yes, it is." Massie crossed her arms over her chest and looked Claire straight in the eye. Like she had seen the future and knew it was good. "You'll see."

Claire opened her mouth to ask what Massie meant, but she was cut off.

Hola, chica! Hola, chica! Alicia's voice rang from the pocket of Claire's fleece.

Claire's stomach plummeted. Alicia knew she was at

Massie's. Was she calling just to interrupt? Did she need Claire's input on the dinner party? Did she want intel?

Massie's nails dug into the leather armrest, leaving sad-frown imprints.

"Sorry." Claire yanked her phone from her pocket and hit ignore. "Where were we?"

Pick uuuuuuuuuuuuuuup! Dylan's digitalized belch ripped through the air.

"I've got a question," Massie snapped, her yellowish-green mask cracking like punctured crème brûlée. "Which would you rather? Hang here, with me and Bean?"

Bean let out a gentle sigh.

"Or hang with them?" Massie's head whipped toward the phone in Claire's lap.

Claire felt face-lift tight. She was sick of tiptoeing around her friend. *I'd rather be here with everyone. Giving out gossip points, laughing until I puke sours, and crush-texting. I don't want to stuff jewelry down my shirt to keep you from getting upset. I don't want to feel torn. I want the real Massie back. The Massie who couldn't care less what kind of gummies I like. The one who makes everything fun.*

That's what Claire *wanted* to say, at least. But all that came out was, "Here. I'd rather be here."

Pick uuuuuu—

Claire flipped open her phone, silencing Dylan mid-burp.

Massie touched her cheeks lightly. "I've gotta wash off this mask. You can check your precious messages now." She huffed, like message-checking was no less deplorable than reading someone's diary or strangling their cat.

Claire waited until Massie was completely gone before checking her screen.

3 TXT MSGS.

Claire's finger hovered over the power button, telling herself she should shut off her phone for the rest of the night. It was only fair. But her heart wanted to know what the other girls were doing without her. Were they calling their crushes? Doling out gossip points? Making new inside jokes?

Or maybe there was some kind of emergency. She *had* gotten three texts in less than a minute.

Bean lifted her head from her purple velvet daybed long enough to snort at Claire. Had she been thinking out loud? Or could the dog sense human insanity?

Claire turned her back on the pug and hit read.

Bean yipped once and stalked out of the room.

Alicia: I just got 500 gossip pts! Hint: it involves Cam. 2 bad ur not here. I'm sworn to secrecy.

Dylan: Planning the seating for A's dinner party. Should we sit across from our crushes or beside them? K says across. A says beside. Try to secretly ask Massie what she would do. This is getting annoying.

Dylan: P.S. Did M say anything about me yet?

Claire's thumbs hovered over the keypad. How was she supposed to respond? Part of her was annoyed with Dylan for asking her to go undercover. Staying friends with both sides didn't mean Claire had any interest in playing double agent. And the other part of her was just glad Dylan was asking about Massie at all. Maybe it meant she missed her. Maybe it meant there was hope.

Claire stared blankly at her new manicure, wishing the answers would appear in two-point font across her Cloud Nine polish. But all that appeared was her own warped reflection.

In the distance, the water faucet shut off. Massie's slippered feet began shuffling toward her, followed by Bean's clacking nails. Claire snapped her phone shut and reached for another handful of gummies to keep herself busy. Maybe she wouldn't respond to the texts at all. Why not let the girls think she was having too much fun to check her messages? After all, she probably would be. Any minute now . . .

Two loud thuds against the wooden spa door made Claire jump. A second later, the door creaked open. Claire whipped around, ready to yell at her younger brother, Todd, for lurking.

"I'm heeeere." Layne was holding her Hello Kitty sleeping bag in one hand and her ratty old pillow in the other. "Tell me you didn't start without me!"

Claire almost choked on a red gummy. "Layne!" she cough-stared as Layne kicked off her Sharpie-grafittied Converse sneakers. "Is everything okay?"

"Everything's great," Layne said happily, wiggling her toes inside her rainbow toe socks. "Just here for the partaaaay." She ditched her gear at the door and shut it behind her. "Where's—"

Just then, Massie padded back into the main room. Her still-damp skin glistened, looking healthy and fresh. But the second she saw Layne, her features rehardened. Claire waited for Massie to demand what Layne was doing here, but she just crossed her hands over her silk robe.

Layne threw her sleeping bag in front of the fireplace. "So wha'd I miss?" she asked, collapsing next to Claire on the leather sofa as if Massie had spread her arms wide and told her to make herself at home.

Claire glanced at Massie, who was refusing to meet her gaze. Then back at Layne, who looked happier than a chocaholic at Dylan's Candy Bar. Then back to Massie. And Layne.

How many times had Claire dreamed about this scenario, of having her two best friends together, without any problems? But now that she was actually sitting with Layne in Massie's spa, it felt strange. The way she imagined sitting with Cam in her parents' bedroom might feel. Something just seemed . . . wrong.

As Massie opened her mouth, Claire expected a flurry of insults to fly off the alpha's tongue. But all she said was, "Nothing."

"Good." Layne lunged forward, grabbing a handful of gummies. "BTW, I made the call," she said. "She's expecting us tomorrow at ten."

Claire's head was starting to spin from all the uncertainty. "Who's expecting you where?" she asked.

"No one," Massie replied sharply.

At the same time, Layne said, "The city."

All three girls paused, staring silently at one another. Massie's mouth flattened into a straight line. Layne raised her eyebrows.

Suddenly Massie wilted against the stone fireplace, looking pale and weak.

"You okay?" Claire asked, concerned.

"I don't think so," Massie said, her voice ten times softer than it had been just seconds ago. She glanced forlornly at Layne, then Claire. "I think I'm sick. Bad sushi. You both should probably go."

Bean whimpered in the corner, as if to echo the sentiment.

"Sushi?" Layne raised her left eyebrow. "But you had grilled chicken over field greens for dinner."

"But we had sushi to start," Massie snapped.

"Wait." Claire held her hands up. "How did you know what she had for dinner?" she asked Layne, suspicious.

"She told me on the—"

"Okay, seriously, I think I might vom," Massie barked. "Both of you. Out." With impressive force, she marched over to the door and threw it open.

"But—" Claire started. Massie handed Claire her sleeping bag and gingerly kicked her Uggs through the open door.

"Geez, Louise." Layne shoved her feet into her sneakers as she joined Claire outside. "I hope you're over this by tomorrow morn—"

"G'night." And with that, Massie slammed the door behind them.

It was cold outside, and the sky was pitch-black, without a star in sight, which was appropriate, since Claire felt totally in the dark.

Massie examined her Onyx Stila Kajal eyeliner in her Sephora compact. It was perfect, and the true black with just the slightest hint of sparkle conveyed that she was edgy and uncompromising.

"Did I tell you my aunt almost signed Sienna Miller?" Layne announced, springing forward in her seat as Isaac steered the Range Rover along the bumpy cobblestone streets of the Meatpacking District. "She was *this* close." She held her thumb and index finger millimeters apart to illustrate. Both were tinged an unnatural orange color and smelled like barbecue.

Massie glared at Layne's neon fingertips, a gesture that Layne obviously mistook for interest. But Massie simply didn't want that neon sludge anywhere near her teal Castle Starr leather jacket. She was about to embark on stage one of her comeback, and the last things she needed staining her image were Layne's fingertips.

"When she started the agency, none of these stores or restaurants were here yet." She adjusted the faux–diamond studded cat eye glasses she wore without the lenses in them. "It was all slaughterhouses," she said proudly. "She was a total pioneer."

Massie opened her mouth, then closed it when she saw Isaac giving her a half-amused, half-warning look in the rearview mirror. She stared out the window, remembering the last time she'd been here, shopping for the perfect outfit for her *Teen Vogue* shoot. She'd been in a fight with Alicia then, too.

That time was different, though. That time, she'd known deep down inside that they would make up eventually. But if Alicia couldn't accept that Massie always had been and always would be OCD's one true alpha, they were through. It was time to face the sad truth: Their friendship was more over than Paris Hilton's film career. And it was time to move on.

"Right here, Isaac," Layne instructed loudly. "On your right."

"Have a nice lunch, girls." Isaac pulled to the curb, idling behind a moped. "Should I pick you up at Pastis?"

"Wha—" Layne started.

"Uh, no thanks." Massie slid across the backseat and onto the street before Isaac had the chance to ask any more questions or get suspicious. She slammed the car door a little harder than usual. But the slam was more of an announcement. Like the clap of the skateboard on a movie set. This was Massie Finds Best Friends: take two!

The dilapidated building in front of her put the "crime scene" in *CSI*. Steel awnings stretched over the sidewalk, and graffiti covered the brick exterior. As a police siren pierced the chilly air, Massie took a step back. Should she make a break for it? Sprint for the familiarity of the snotty salesgirls just blocks away? Too risky. She'd never make it in her Marc Jacobs boots. The cracks between the cobblestones would nip at her heels and take her down faster than a pit bull. Besides, Layne was already pressing the buzzer for suite 207.

Massie eyed Layne's furry black thrift store coat, jeans, and sneakers with disdain. Thank Gawd she wasn't a celebrity, and there were no paparazzi here to document this momentous-slash-desperate occasion. She couldn't believe she was actually buying friends, and not in the old-fashioned way (with expensive jewelry). Instead she was buying them with her AmEx.

Then again, many BFFs had started out working together. Jessica Simpson and Ken Paves. Zac and Vanessa. The entire cast of *Gossip Girl*. The more Massie thought about it, the more she realized that hiring a best friend was the same as buying a puppy. She'd do with these girls exactly what she'd done with Bean: charge it and take her new BFF home. After a few days of intense behavior training and positive reinforcement using treats (or in this case, accessories), the girls would come to learn that Massie was their alpha. Since she'd groomed them that way, they'd never question her. It was perfect.

A loud buzzing noise sounded, and Layne gripped the rusty door handle. "Did you e-mail my aunt your character descriptions?" Layne yanked open the door and ducked inside. "She said she has some really out-of-the-box ideas."

Out of the box? Massie imagined herself shopping with a

troupe of Cirque du Soleil contortionists and a juggling monkey. "The only thing I want out of the box is a new pair of Golden Goose riding boots." As she stepped onto the elevator, Massie wondered if hiring Layne's LBR^2 (Loser Beyond Repair Relative) was a bigger mistake than her bright yellow skinny jeans from Patricia Field. What Massie needed, now more than ever, was someone who spoke fluent alpha. Someone who understood the importance of appearances. Nawt some casting renegade with a soft spot for carnies.

Closing the heavy door behind her, Massie blinked, her eyes adjusting to the dimly lit waiting area. A giant theater marquis with the words SHOOTING STARS TALENT hung over the curved receptionist desk positioned against the far wall. A flock of nervous-looking girls were perched on the edges of vintage theater seats bolted to the exposed-brick floor. Some were speed-flipping through scripts while others were nibbling at the corners of Luna bars. One was staring lovingly at the headshot in her lap.

"Those seats are originals from the Lyceum here in Manhattan," Layne said with pride. Tilting her head back, she nodded at the framed antique movie posters that covered every inch of wall space. "Did you know my aunt went on a date with Paul Newman? She said his breath smelled like classic Caesar salad dressing, and that was way before he even made salad dressing."

Massie stared up at the metal pipes that snaked across the ceiling several stories above them. Before she could beg Layne to stop gushing, a fiftysomething woman with jet-black, Dita von Teese—styled, finger-waved hair, and perfectly applied red lipstick swooshed though the red velvet curtain hanging at the far corner of the waiting area.

"L-Boogie!" the woman rasped, throwing her arms wide as she hurried toward Layne. The waiting wannabes straightened instantly, sucking in their nonexistent stomachs and reaching for headshots.

"P!" Layne yelled back, bouncing in her sneakers.

Massie was trying not to stare at Layne's aunt. And failing. Her perfectly fitted Chanel suit accentuated her hourglass figure. Black Louboutin peep-toes showcased scarlet-polished toes that matched her fingernails and lipstick. A sparkling cocktail ring glowed on her right hand. And the tiny black cocktail hat perched on top of her head added a quirky twist.

She was vintage alpha, all the way. Massie silently apologized for judging her based on the building's dingy exterior. And the fact that she was related to Layne.

"So glad you're here!" P enveloped L-Boogie in a giant hug.

"Ditto." Layne beamed. She pulled away. "Love the hat."

"It's from the set of *Casablanca*," Layne's aunt said proudly, reaching up to touch the hat gingerly. "I got it on eBay."

"Sweet." Layne turned toward Massie. "This is my aunt."

"Peace." The casting director shot her a wide, perfectly straight smile.

"Uh . . . you know it." Massie flashed a Miley Cyrus peace sign.

"No," Layne snorted. "That's her name. Peace."

"But everyone calls me P." Layne's aunt winked, showcasing the purple shooting stars tattoo that arched over her left eye. "And you must be Maysee."

Layne giggled.

"It's Maa-ssee actually," Massie said politely. "You know, rhymes with cl—"

"Assy," Layne blurted.

"Oh, you are so baaaaad." Peace playfully slapped Layne's shoulder.

Massie reddened. "So can we talk business, or what?" She leveled her eyes at Peace, fighting for control.

"Thought you'd never ask, Cookie. Come on back." Peace led the girls across the waiting room floor, throwing her hips from side to side as she walked. The wannabes leaned forward in their seats, hate-glaring at Massie for cutting ahead of them in line. Their jealousy recharged her like a postworkout ginseng smoothie. She scooted past Layne and took the spot next to P.

"This place is great," she said coolly, like she hadn't really decided if it was or not.

"Isn't it? I've been in this neighborhood forever. It's like de Niro always says—there's no place like New York." Peace pushed through the curtain, leading them into an enormous warehouse that had been transformed to look like an old theater. Rows of purple velvet seats faced a sprawling stage framed by heavy tasseled curtains. Overhead, in the box seats and balcony area, agency employees paced in front of their desks, pressing

Bluetooths into their ears and typing furiously on slim silver MacBooks. Massie's heart revved. P was into Mac! It was a sign from Gawd that she'd come to the right place.

"My staff has been working twenty-four-seven to pull together your cast," P announced, ushering Massie and Layne into the front row. "These girls are exactly what you asked for. But if you see anything you don't like, jot it down and we'll find someone better." She handed Massie a Shooting Stars Talent note pad, then turned and gave a sharp nod toward the balcony.

Immediately, the theater darkened to AmEx black.

"Ahhhhhh," Layne and Peace yelled together.

"What?" Massie jumped. The chalky soy milk from her latte crept up the back of her throat. "What happened?"

They burst out laughing.

"We always do that when the lights turn off," Layne managed once her hysteria calmed to a goofy giggle.

Massie elbowed Layne in the ribs.

"Oof!"

"Well, *I* always do *that*." Massie smirked.

A platinum spotlight hit the stage as the willowy girl with light blue eyes and a pixie cut from the Web site slouch-walked from the wings. She was wearing wide-leg trousers, a white ribbed tank, and a shrunken menswear-inspired vest. She paused in front of Massie, jutting her hip to one side and planting her palm on it.

"Nominated for a Spirit Award for her first silver screen performance last year, Lilah is America's next indie queen,"

P announced as the girl narrowed her eyes at the spotlight. "She's also worked on the stage, recently wrapping a six-month run with the ensemble cast of *Chicago*."

Massie leaned forward in her seat, nibbling her lower lip thoughtfully. So the girl had an impressive résumé. But did she meet the real requirements?

P must have read Massie's mind. "Most importantly, Lilah never speaks above a murmur. She counts eating in public as one of the seven deadly sins. And she has never burped. Ever."

Lilah agree-stared into the spotlight.

"She's perfect!" Layne elbowed Massie in the ribs.

Massie nodded her approval, scribbling Lilah's name with a giant smiley face next to it on the pad.

P clapped once, and Lilah slouched downstage right. On cue, a petite blonde in a purple silk minidress and gold stilettos hit the stage. Her platinum hair was parted down the center and cascaded down to her boobs in soft, mussed waves. Dark roots peeked out along her part, and her charcoal gray eyeliner was slightly smudged, both in a totally deliberate way. She walked toward center stage with total alpha confidence, planting one stiletto loudly in front of the other.

"Mia loves the spotlight," P announced. "When she's not out partying with Rumer, she's working on some of the hottest young television sets out there, including *Friday Night Lights* and MTV's *The City*. She's currently in negotiations to star in her own reality spin-off for the network."

"Yay-uhhhh." Layne raised her arms over her head and rocked out, obviously impressed.

"And?" Massie turned toward P and raised her right eyebrow.

P smiled, crossing her toned arms over her vintage tee. "And per your request, Mia speaks zero Spanish."

Mia smirk-nodded.

Massie felt a smile spreading across her face. Finally. A second-in-command who knew how to get attention, and when to keep her shiny lips shut.

P clapped again, and Mia clacked over to her spot next to Lilah. Next, a petite brunette in a tracksuit leaped across the stage, cradling a soccer ball under one arm. Her high pony swung in rhythm behind her.

"Jasmin is our highest-paid commercial actor," P explained. "She's portrayed a soccer player in commercials for products such as Powerade and Tampax Sport."

"Ew," Massie blurted. Her blood pressure was starting to rise. Seeing that soccer ball made her think of Kristen, which made her think of Dempsey, which made her think of Kristen and Dempsey, which made her want to stiletto-stab something.

"Cut!" she yelled, jamming her pen onto the pad.

P held up one finger. "But in real life . . ." She paused dramatically, and Jasmin ripped off her jumpsuit, revealing a tailored Stella McCartney ensemble. The soccer ball rolled off the stage and under Layne's seat. "Jasmin prefers Stella to soccer any day of the week."

Massie exhaled a sigh of relief, her heart slowing to normal speed.

"She doesn't own a single tracksuit, turtleneck, or hoodie," P continued. "And her parents are legally prohibited from monitoring her school outfits."

"Emancipated minor," Jasmin clarified.

"In addition to commercial work, Jasmin has appeared as an extra in several box office hits, including—"

"Background actor," Jasmin interrupted. "We prefer the term 'background actor.'"

P shot her a look. Jasmin gulped and took her place next to Mia.

"And last but not least . . ." P drumrolled her armrest. "Kaitlyn."

An African-American girl with dewy skin, intense gray eyes, and a short, angular bob entered. She walked in towering YSL peep-toes with as much ease as if they were bedroom slippers.

"Kaitlyn hails from Los Angeles," P said proudly. "She's a West Coast girl with East Coast style. She hasn't worn Keds since she was five."

Mia wrinkled her nose, as if the animal guts/garbage smell from the street had leaked its way into the theater.

"Which, coincidentally, was the same year she swore off candy and homemade jewelry. Plus, she wears a size six shoe and her favorite hobby is sharing her killer boot collection," P continued.

Layne nudged Massie, who smile-nodded.

"So?" P smiled her close-lipped scarlet smile. "Thoughts?"

Massie was speechless. These girls were better than she

ever could have hoped. No insecurities, fashion faux pas, or annoying habits. Best of all, they were there for her. To do, say, and be whatever she wanted.

"I'll take them all," Massie said happily. She reached for her Coach wallet.

P lifted a finger, stopping Massie mid-grab.

"Ground rules first, Cookie," she rasped. "You're hiring these girls on a week-to-week basis. Since they're minors, they have to be tutored for a minimum of twenty hours per week, they can only work eight hours per day, and they must be fed and walked regularly."

Massie concealed a smirk. They were like puppies, after all. "Done."

Peace winked. "Massie, I think this is the beginning of some beautiful friendships," she said, doing a spot-on Bogart impression. Massie couldn't have agreed more.

CURRENT STATE OF THE UNION

IN	OUT
MAC	PC
Peace	War
Scene stealers	Crush stealers

"Do it," Alicia instructed, yanking her ponytail to maximum tightness.

"I mean it," Claire insisted, flicking the soft tassel hanging from the tangerine silk pillow in her lap. "There's nothing to tell."

"Kuh-laire," Alicia snapped. She nudged the thick issue of *Vogue España* across the jewel-toned rug on her bedroom floor. Her Spanish cousins had sent her a subscription for her birthday last year. But since she could only read a few words of the six-hundred-page fashion encyclopedia, she'd had to find creative ways to put the magazine to use. "Swear." She was starting to get impatient. What good was it to lure Claire to her house with promises of sweets and a *The Hills* DVD marathon if Claire wasn't going to hold up her end of the bargain?

Sighing, Claire lowered her right palm onto the glossy cover. "I, Claire Lyons," she muttered.

"Do solemnly swear." Alicia straightened up, rolling back her shoulders and smoothing her midnight blue curve-hugging sweater.

"Do solemnly swear."

"To tell the truth, the whole truth, and nothing but the

truth, so help me Gawd," Alicia finished in her most official newscaster voice.

Claire repeated the oath, then collapsed back onto the mountain of brightly colored pillows in the corner.

"Now spill." Alicia leaned forward, her heart beating faster. Letting Claire go to Massie's sleepover the night before had been a genius move. Now Claire could report back everything she'd seen and heard.

"Um . . ." Claire wiped her palm on the worn thigh of her root beer bottle–brown cords. "When I got there, she was doing a face mask, and—"

"Color?"

"Green."

"Seaweed or avocado-honey?" Alicia pressed, using her father's interrogating-a-witness tone.

"What difference does it make?" Claire shifted uncomfortably on the couch.

"Seaweed means Massie's stressed. Avocado-honey means she was on the verge of breaking out, which means she was stressed times ten."

"Um, avocado-honey, I think?"

Alicia nodded, satisfied. "Go awn."

"We played What Would You Rather? And then . . ." Claire paused, her blue eyes darting back and forth, like they were scanning her brain for the right thing to say. "And then we went for a walk outside and I, uh, went to bed."

"Outside? For a walk?" Okay, something was definitely up. *Did Bean have diarrhea? Was there a lunar eclipse? Was the spa on fire?* Alicia knew for a fact that Massie wouldn't walk outside between October and May until global warming hit Westchester. She'd told Alicia that once. A sadness-pinch gripped Alicia's intestines. It was weird knowing so much about someone you no longer considered a friend. It was like having all the Ralph Lauren clothes in world, only three sizes too small. All you could do was hand them down to someone else and hope they appreciated them as much as you did.

"Yep, a walk." Sunlight poured through the enormous bay window, making Claire squint. Or was that her "I'm lying" face? Because they kind of looked alike.

Alicia eyed the magazine between them. A sweaty palm print still glistened on the cover. Claire was definitely hiding something.

Pushing herself to her feet, Alicia glided over to the mini fridge and pulled out a small glass bottle of Diet Coke. Alphas were supposed to know everything about the betas in their pride. And if Claire was keeping something from her . . . Were Claire and Massie planning a takeover? What if Dylan and Kristen were in on it? Alicia was starting to feel light-headed, like she'd gone an entire dance class without water. She gripped the edge of her desk to steady herself.

"Leesh?" Claire nibbled on her thumbnail. "You okay?" She sounded concerned but looked guilty.

"Given." Alicia closed her eyes and took a long swig of soda. The fizz invigorated her senses, while the sting of cold bubbles rushing down her throat made her feel protected, like an army of tiny spirited soldiers was entering her body to help her fight. Her lids snapped open. "So, that's every-thing?"

"Yup." Claire's head bobbed up and down so fast, Alicia thought it might snap off. "That's it. So tell me about the planning party last—"

Alicia shook her head slowly, her shiny ponytail swishing accusingly from side to side. Why Claire was still being so loyal to Massie, after everything she'd done, was beyond Alicia. But Alicia had had a feeling this might happen. She reached for the yellow legal pad on her desk, and a black Sharpie.

"What's that?" Claire asked.

"Oh, nothing," Alicia said casually, popping off the Sharpie cap. "Just the guest list for my dinner party." The Sharpie hovered over the pad. "BTW, I could really use your help on this."

"My help?" Claire repeated warily.

"It's just that I really only have room for seven," Alicia said, widening her large brown eyes. "I'm thinking about cut-ting someone. And since everybody else's crushes are gonna be there, I would really hate to have to cut Ca—"

"Okay, okay!" Claire cracked like an antique vase, just like Alicia knew she would. "There's one more thing. But she made me pinky-swear not to tell."

"You can trust me," Alicia giggle-grinned, kneeling grace-fully on the pillows next to Claire.

"She was going into the city today." Claire exhaled.

"So?" Alicia's shoulders dropped. Nothing unusual about that.

"With Layne."

Alicia burped Diet Coke through her nose. The burn—or was it rage?—made her feel like a fire-breathing dragon. "You mean *Layme*?" she sputtered. Oh yeah, something was *definitely* up.

Claire nodded, and Alicia's heart thumped behind the low neckline of her midnight blue curve-hugging sweater. It was the best gossip Alicia had heard since the Dempsey-Kristen hookup hit Twitter last week.

No matter how hard she tried, Alicia couldn't mask the giddiness she felt when she imagined Layne and Massie sharing a bite of the Big Apple. What would they possibly do? Plastic bead shop in the fluorescent-lit DIY jewelry stores between Thirty-second and Thirty-eighth streets? Dumpster dive for used clothing? Beef jerky buy at every Duane Reade from Battery Park to Harlem?

The corners of Alicia's glossy lips curled into a Cheshire cat grin.

It seemed as though her absence had forced Massie to friend Layne, like a crab doomed to bottom-feed for survival. Finally, Alicia had something Massie Block wanted. Status.

Correction.

Alpha status.

And she was determined to rub it in Massie's face like an avocado-honey mask until she turned green.

Exactly fifty-seven minutes later, Dean, Alicia's driver, rolled through the Blocks' open gate. The red brake lights of the

Range Rover were just ahead of them, coasting smoothly up the drive. Perfect timing.

"Thanks for the ride, Dean," Claire called.

Dean smile-nodded his thanks in the rearview mirror.

"Just park next to Isaac," Alicia instructed, tightening the sash on her trench. She slipped her hand into the bag at her side, feeling around for her legal pad for the eighth time. It was still there. "I want to say hey to Massie."

Claire snorted. "Um?"

Alicia batted her mascara-lengthened lashes and checked her ponytail for bumps. "Calm down, this won't take long." She gripped the door handle with a slightly trembling hand and reminded herself that she could pull this off. That there was no reason to be nervous. So why did she feel like she'd just had one too many lattes?

She opened the door and stepped onto the Blocks' drive-way, Claire at her heels. It felt like she was stepping onto enemy soil. Massie opened her door too, slamming it loudly when she saw the girls.

"Um, is your name Hue?" Massie asked with detached disinterest.

Alicia nodded disappointedly, like she was so over this childish routine.

"Then why are you stocking me?" Massie cocked her head.

Alicia might have laughed if they were still friends, but instead, she cocked her head right back and matched Massie's cool tone. "I was just dropping off Kuh-laire." She paused for dramatic purposes. "But now that I'm here, I'd like to make you an offer." She lowered her white Tom Ford shades, even though it was starting to get cloudy.

Claire chewed at her nails, glancing back and forth between the girls.

Massie lowered her mirrored Prada aviators. "Unless you're offering to leave, I'm not interested."

Alicia felt a twinge of pity for her ex. She was obviously too proud to admit defeat.

"I heard about your little field trip with Layne," Alicia said, reaching into her bag. Her fingers closed around the crisp edges of her legal pad.

"And?" Massie folded her arms across her buttery soft leather jacket.

"Aaaaand I have a solution to your problem." Alicia waved the pad under Massie's sharp chin.

"What problem?" Massie smacked the pad.

"Your FATS problem?"

Claire gasped.

"What?" Massie snapped. "I don't have Fallen Alpha Trauma Syndrome."

"Ahhh, denial." Alicia sighed. "It's the first symptom of FATS." She re-shoved the pad in Massie's airspace, this time with added force. "Read this. It will help." The contract her dad had helped her draw up would speak for itself.

Massie peered over the top of her sunglasses. "'From the desk of Alicia Rivera,'" she read in a monotone voice. "'Hear ye, hear ye. The alpha of the second part—'"

"That's you," Alicia clarified.

"'Agrees that the alpha of the first part—'"

"Me."

Massie rolled her eyes. "'Is heretofore the sole alpha of the Soul-M8s, hereafter referred to as quote-unquote "the pride."'" She slapped the legal pad to her side. "What is this?" she demanded.

"Keep reading," Alicia said evenly.

"'The alpha of the second part is hereby invited to join quote-unquote "the pride," providing that said alpha pledges allegiance to the alpha of the first—'" Massie stopped cold. "Wait. You want me to join something called the Soul-M8s?" A small smile twitched at the corners of her mouth. "Alicia, do I look like I dance with a crew?"

"It's not a dance crew." Alicia rolled her eyes. "It's *my* crew," she announced, liking—no, luh-ving—the way that sounded. "And I'll let you in pursuant to the terms of the agreement, ah-bviously," she added, to avoid sounding eager. She reached inside her bag for the glitter pen. "You're as good as in, so long as you agree that I'm the alpha. Nawt you." She handed Massie the pen but avoided her eyes. This was probably a humiliating moment for her, and she didn't want to make it any harder. Besides, there would be plenty of time to gush once the contract was signed.

"Take it." Alicia waved the pen. "It's okay. It's over." She grinned warmly, preparing herself for the hug that always followed one of their fights. For the flurry of "I'm sorry"s and "I didn't mean it"s and "I heart you"s.

Until she realized Massie wasn't taking the pen.

"Um, Alicia?" Massie asked sweetly.

What was happening?

"Is my name Helen Keller?"

Alicia braced herself. "No."

"Then why would I sign?"

Massie opened the back door of the Range Rover. Four girls slid out, each one looking like she had stepped directly off the runway and onto the driveway.

"Ehmagawd." Claire's palm flew to her mouth.

"Meet Massie and Crew." Massie smirked, oozing confidence and control. "Or MAC, as we like to call ourselves."

Alicia felt like she'd just gotten socked in the stomach with *Vogue España*. She whip-turned toward Claire, shock and rage clouding her features. How could Claire's intel have been so wrong? For one thing, Layne wasn't even here. And second, Massie didn't look like she was suffering at all.

"Come awn, girls," Massie ordered. Silently, the model lineup turned in perfect sync, following their alpha toward the house.

And even though Claire was standing right next to her, Alicia had never felt more alone in her entire life.

Shampoo-yellow sunlight spilled over Massie the second she stepped out of the Range Rover. Eyes closed, she tilted her face slightly toward the sky and let the warm beams ignite her shimmer-dusted cheeks. The fall air was crisp, invigorating, and, most important, boy free. She applied a generous of coat of Mango Magawd Glossip Girl and grinned, feeling like her old self again.

For one thing, Alicia wanting her back made her feel in demand. And for another, now that the boys were safely at Briarwood, the Soul-M8s had been cut in half and were now just 4-Squares. Plus their alpha, *Ew*-licia, was probably still reeling from Massie's rejection, and *that* made them weaker than knock-off perfume. The girls of Octavian Country Day needed guidance more than ever. And Massie and Crew were ready to give it to them, effective immediately.

After a final check in the side-view mirror, Massie couldn't decide which sparkled more: her future, or her cheekbones.

Hoooooooooooooooooooooooooooooonk!

A line of luxury SUVs was starting to form behind her.

"Puh-lease." She rolled her eyes and saunter-stepped across the pavement, smoothing the pleated ivory sweater dress she wore over textured olive DKNY tights. When the light caught the shimmering Lurex threads in the soft cash-mere, her outfit literally glowed. She felt like an animated fairy. If she were sprinkling golden glitter-dust with every step, Walt Disney would have risen from the dead and handed her a contract.

"Heyyyyyy!" Layne was waiting for her on the curb, bouncing in her sneakers and flapping her long arms like a hyperactive chimp. "Hurry up! They're waiting!"

Massie slowed slightly. Last Friday she'd rented the old overflow trailers from the school, saying she needed a "pri-vate study zone" and had them revamped over the weekend. Even though she was dying to see how her new friends looked in their trailers, taking orders from Layne Abeley was like borrowing Claire's Keds: It just wasn't going to happen.

Just then, two girls in long black skirts ambled by, the hems collecting leaves and dirt as they trailed across the ground. Massie had to swerve to avoid a head-on LBR collision.

"Ehmagross." She winced. "FOOD!"

"Huh?" Layne asked, rolling up the sleeves of her navy plaid men's shirt.

"Fashion Opposite Of Do!" Massie gasped. "They're every-where."

The outfits were bad, but the unwashed hair and makeup-free faces were unacceptable. The girls did less for OCD's curb appeal than a barbed-wire fence jammed with Taco Bell wrappers and bird feathers. Looking around, Massie noticed that slumped shoulders, glossless lips, and dull hair plagued every student in sight. OCD had been transformed into one big "before" picture, and Massie was the lone "after." "What's going awn?"

Layne unwrapped a brick of neon green gum and popped it in her mouth. "The Briarwood guys are gone. 'Dress to impress' is just for weekends again." A girl in SpongeBob pajama pants lumbered toward the main building. "I think it's liberating," Layne announced, chomping smugly on her gum.

"I think it's nauseating." Massie fought the urge to vom.

"Well, you're not gonna believe how great our girls look," Layne gushed as they walked to the back parking lot. She yanked the brim of her navy baseball cap low over her eyes. The phrase DIRECT TO DVD was printed in gray block letters across the foam forehead. "We've been rehearsing your talking points and strut formation all morning."

She and Layne passed the towering, leafy trees that shaded the trailers, and Massie's stomach flip-flopped.

"Ehmagawd." Massie gripped Layne's wrist at the sight of the trailer. The dingy gray rectangular box that loomed in front of them looked like it had been power-sprayed with milky-white pigeon poo. Dents cratered the walls like unsightly acne scars, and rust surrounded the windows and doors.

It was beyond disgusting.

Which made it the beyond perfect hideout. No one in the entire school would think to come anywhere near this poo-encrusted, tetanus-inducing sardine can.

"Isn't it great?" Layne sprinted up the carpeted stairs and threw the door open.

"Totes." Massie hurried after her, careful not to touch anything.

The inside of the trailer looked exactly like the blueprints she'd drawn up for Willem Rowe, Westchester's premier set designer. The floor had been carpeted in crimson velvet to make the MAC girls feel like they were walking the red carpet when they stepped inside. Silk-covered director's chairs were arranged against the far left wall, each girl's name embroidered in rhinestones on the back, and four rectangular dressing room mirrors hung in front, surrounded by glowing heart-shaped bulbs. Beneath them were four shelves stocked with makeup and hair products to complement each girl's coloring and hair type. The very back of the trailer served as the costume department: Four clothing racks were filled with items Massie had preapproved and had overnighted from Neiman's. Behind the racks was a *Project Runway*–style accessories wall lined with shoes, handbags, and chunky necklaces.

The trailer was perfect. Only one thing was missing: the actors.

"Okay!" Massie whisper-barked. "Coast's clear. You can come out."

One by one, the MAC girls popped up from inside their dressing room cubbies.

"Excuuuse me," Lilah said, smoothing her pixie cut. "My call time was, like, forty minutes ago. Even Cameron Crowe didn't make me wait around this long."

Jasmin, aka Tampax Sport, widened her chocolate brown eyes. "You worked with Cameron Crowe?"

The tiny hairs on the back of Massie's neck bristled, but before she could put the actresses in their places, Layne interrupted.

"This was how you wanted it, right?" Layne tapped the white dry-erase board at the front of the room, which had been transformed into a storyboard. She had used colorful markers—lavender for Lilah, magenta for Mia, jet-black for Jasmin, and kale green for Kaitlyn—to chart each girl's story line, blocking, and call times for the day. On Saturday morning, Massie had e-mailed Layne GABs—General Areas of BSing—so the girls would know the following "facts:"

A) The crew of MAC attends the International
   Billionaires' School
B) Went to awesome high school party on Saturday
C) Gossip points awarded for best intel

"Yes." Massie nodded briskly, then quickly scanned over the actresses' outfits to make sure they were costumed according to her specifications. She pulled out her iPhone and cross-referenced her list against her new A-list friends. "Mia, step forward."

Mia gave her Fergie-inspired center-parted locks a shake. "This trailer is bananas." She wore a belted black DVF maxidress and giant Bulgari sunglasses.

"Check," Massie said, accepting the compliment with a satisfied smile. "Kaitlyn?"

She stepped forward, spinning around to show off the

cream-colored Nanette Lepore minidress. It popped beautifully against her dark, glowing skin. Massie nodded at her approvingly, then quickly checked off Jasmin's Stella voile shirtdress and Lilah's bronze Miu Miu shorts and crème Dodo + Angelika knit top.

Satisfied that the MAC girls looked better than acceptable, she allowed herself a full five seconds to bask in the glory of her accomplishment. Finally, she had friends who went along with exactly what she wanted. It was more refreshing than Pinkberry pomegranate fro-yo. And then she got to work.

"Listen up!" she said crisply, basking in the warmth of all the eyes on her. "We have exactly four minutes before you make your OCD entrance. I can*nawt* stress this enough: This first scene is cuh-*rucial*. It sets the tone and establishes the mood. And if the mood isn't total envy, we—by which I mean *you*—have failed." She pinched a piece of platinum hair off Mia's shoulder and flicked it to the ground. "Visible foundation lines, static cling, or frizz will get you cut faster than a dangling nose hair. So I suggest you start acting like best friends and check over each other's outfits before we go public."

Layne jumped down from her director's chair and stood next to Massie, digging a Hello Kitty clipboard into her fleshy hip. "Should I prep them for the walk?"

Massie nodded and turned back to her new friends. "You'll be synchronizing your walk to the beat of Beyoncé's 'Upgrade U.'"

Layne lifted the bullhorn to her lips. "Places!" she whisper-bellowed. "And action!"

Checking out the window to make sure no one was around,

Massie led MAC out of the trailer to the back door of OCD's main building, where they gathered in the practiced formation. She took a deep breath. It was time to show her school she was back.

"Ah five, six, seven, eight!" she murmur-counted, throwing open the doors. The halls were overrun with sloppily dressed, uneven-skinned girls. As painful as it was to look at them, Massie was glad they were there. The more witnesses she had, the better. She strutted one pace ahead of Lilah, Mia, Jasmin, and Kaitlyn, whose heels clacked in perfect rhythm behind her as they made their way down the main hall. The mini hand-fans inside their open handbags tousle-blew their hair, making them look like they were a living, breathing photo shoot. The crowd parted around them, and pre-homeroom chatter was replaced with silent envy-stares.

And then the moment she had been waiting for arrived.

Alicia, Kristen, and Dylan turned the corner, heading straight for her. Alicia was wearing chocolate brown leather pants and a slouchy gray off-the-shoulder sweater. To be fair, the outfit rated a 9.2, or at least it had back when she debuted it the third week in September. But now that it was in reruns, it was a 7 at best. Massie didn't even bother checking out Dylan and Kristen's outfits. After all, a girl's outfit was only as good as her alpha's.

A few steps more and MAC and the Soul-M8s met in the middle of the hallway, both groups screeching to a halt. The hall went dead silent. Nervous-seeming onlookers pretended to search for their cell phones inside their bags, like they weren't waiting for a *Flavor of Love*–style throwdown in the middle of the hall.

Dylan chewed her bottom lip while Kristen yanked her hair out of its high pony, then re-tied it. Claire was MIA, probably trying her hardest to stay clear of the drama. Or, since she'd refused to ride with Massie or Alicia in the morning in order to stay "neutral," lying in a ditch under the spinning wheels of her Bratz bike.

Massie smile-blinked at Alicia, feeling more in control than Spanx. "Um, would you like your egg sunny-side up?"

"No," Alicia snapped, surveying the MAC girls warily.

"Then beat it!" Massie finished triumphantly. Seeing her ex-besties nervous and knowing the MAC girls were just inches behind her made her feel safe.

But when they stayed silent, she whip-turned toward them.

"Line!" she whisper-hissed from the corner of her mouth.

"Oh. Yeah." Mia giggled, then snapped into character. "I have gossip from the high school paaaartyyyyyyyy we went to!" she bellowed like Oprah, finger combing her blond waves.

Alicia gasped.

"How many points?" Lilah asked eagerly, blinking her wide blue eyes.

"Seven-fifty," Mia announced. "And I don't mean seven dollars and fifty cents. I mean seven *hundred* and fifty."

Massie bit the inside of her cheeks and forced herself to let out a *that inside joke gets me every time* laugh. "Ehmagawd, I forgot he said that!" Massie shook her head at the fake memory. "Now, what's the gossip?"

Mia's face went blank. So did Lilah, Jasmin, and Kaitlyn's faces.

"Whenever you're ready," Massie whisper-snapped.

But the girls remained silent, their blank stares suddenly melting into wide-eyed panic. They glanced at each other, then at Massie.

"Juuuuiiicy," Dylan burped. Kristen and Alicia giggled.

Massie's palms were starting to sweat. What was happening? Why weren't they answering? Was it time for their walk?

"*Ohhhhh.*" She drew the word out, nod-hinting for them to follow her lead. "I get it." She forced a conspiratorial smile. "The gossip's so hawt, you have to tell me in private. Riiiiight?" Tossing her bag over her shoulder, Massie resisted the urge to tote-smack every single one of them right there in the hallway.

Riiiiiiiing.

The first-period bell never sounded so good.

"I better go," she announced. "Have a good morning at International Billionaires' School, 'kay?"

The girls stood firmly amidst the swirling frenzy of girls, bags, slamming lockers, and last minute sips of latte.

"I want that gossip, so try to sneak out and come back for lunch," Massie tried. Still they stood there.

All of a sudden Layne appeared, waving scissors over her head like the town psycho. "Cut!" she called, snipping the

134

air. Massie blushed for Layne and her beyond-embarrassing existence. "Cut, cut, cut!" she call-snipped.

Thankfully, the hallway was too hectic for anyone but Massie to notice. The MKO look-alikes had resumed polishing the hardwood with their skirts as they hurried to their classrooms.

"Cutttttttttt," Layne offered one final snip before slipping into her Spanish class.

The actresses finally got the hint and hurried away. Massie smile-waved, pretending not to notice her ex-friends darting side-looks from Layne to Massie to the retreating backs of her crew.

"Nice meeting your new . . . *friends,*" Alicia said suspiciously. The she turned, linking arms with Dylan and Kristen. They headed down the hall, their feet in step, like a choreographed routine. Knowing Alicia, it probably was.

Massie watched them go: The sound of heels on the parquet felt like gunshots piercing the air, invisible bullets killing her reputation. Slumping against a locker, Massie played a silent-solo round of What Would You Rather? Option 1: Have people know she was in cahoots with Layne. Option 2: Have people know she'd hired (stupid times ten) friends.

After some serious thought Massie chose option 3. She had no clue what it was but knew it couldn't possibly be worse.

When the bell rang, signaling the end of first period, Massie sprint-walked toward the actor trailer. She'd spent most of French class seething over the fact that her girls had botched their very first scene. What was she paying for if they couldn't get it right on the first take? Throwing open the trailer door, Massie ducked inside and slammed the door behind her.

The MAC girls were hunched over their desks as their tutor, a frumpily dressed woman wearing bifocals and a stretched-out cardigan, stood in front of them. Layne was slouched in her director's chair, doing the OCD crossword.

Massie clapped her hands loudly, and everyone's heads snapped up. "Girls! What happened out there?"

The tutor narrowed her eyes at Massie. "I'm going to have to ask you to allow the girls to finish their homewo—"

"Mia," Massie said, cutting the t-*ew*-ter off. "Have you been swallowing chicken bones?"

"No?" Mia squeaked.

The other girls stared down at the open textbooks in front of them.

"Then why did you choke?" Massie screeched.

Lilah snorted. Jasmin and Kaitlyn leaned even closer to their books, their noses almost touching the pages.

"You asked what the gossip was," Mia said defiantly, her voice gravelly and bored. "I didn't have lines for that, so I didn't say anything."

"I told you to prepare for a gossip question." Layne smacked her palm against her forehead.

Jasmin stood. "In Mia's defense, we never got a script and we're not trained in improv, so—"

"Plug it, Tampax," Massie barked, pacing the width of the trailer.

Layne yanked off her baseball cap and ran her hands through her frizzy brown hair. "Massie, if we expect the crew to know their lines, we need to write them." She noted something down on her clipboard that looked like a squiggle, then pierced it with a sharp dot. "I have a close friend I like to call Shakespeare"—Layne's accent turned vaguely British—"and she can help me—"

"No friends!" Massie snapped.

"Fine." Layne shrugged. "I'll do it myself. We'll do a table read after school."

Massie hesitated. On one hand, she didn't need Layne thinking she was running the show. On the other hand, she didn't actually *want* to write a script. And when in doubt, delegate.

"Fine," she told Layne, just as the bell rang, signaling the start of second period. "But I have final approval."

Glaring at Mia, she stomped toward the trailer door. She gripped its cool metal handle hoping for a dramatic exit, but it slipped from her sweaty palm. After a quick wipe on her sweater dresss, she tried again. "It better be e-mailed to me by lunch, or you're all fired." She pulled the door open, praying to Gawd it wouldn't come to that. Because when you couldn't even *buy* good friends, what hope was there?

Massie straightened the glitter-swirled *RESERVED* placard in the very center of table eighteen, then licked the tip of her index finger and pressed it into the tiny mound of fallen violet sparkle.

"So who are all these new girls I've been hearing about?" Claire asked as Massie sprinkled the excess glitter on the floor. Even though it was an Alicia day, she'd walked to lunch with Massie and had obviously stayed at the table to ask this particular question.

"They go to the International Billionaires' School," Massie replied. At the next table over, Kori Gedman and Strawberry McAdams and bunch of seventh graders were hover-whispering about who would be sitting at table eighteen. Massie tried not to smile smugly. She was back where she belonged. "I met them when I was interviewing to transfer there last week and we just clicked."

"International Billionaires' School?" Claire put her elbows on the table, leaving Jergens-scented smears on the perfectly buffed bamboo table. "Never heard of it."

"I'm nawt surprised," Massie said, adjusting the plates of fresh sushi and seaweed salad, interspersed with individual servings of bright pink pickled ginger and low-sodium soy sauce, so they were evenly spaced. "IBS is super exclusive. They only ask a few girls to interview there every year. And only one of those girls gets picked to attend."

Just then her cell buzzed with a text.

Layne: Script done & Oscar-wrthy. Run-thru went gr8. Just say "action" and we'll roll like Pillsbury.

"Who's that?" Claire asked, leaning forward.

Frantically, Massie dropped the cell in her lap. The less Claire knew, the better. "Just Jasmin, one of my new friends." She surreptitiously texted Layne back.

Massie: I need to read 1st.

Layne: I swear. You will luv. Theme = crushes. Totally inspired.

Massie: e-mail 2 me & i'll txt my decision

After this morning, lunch had to be nothing short of perfection. One more public slip-up and she'd be forced to enter the LBR protection program and go into hiding. Which meant she wouldn't get the chance to debut the new Tory Burch Anamarte wedge sandals she'd ordered last week. Just thinking about banishing the sandals to a life of obscurity made Massie's blemish-free forehead bead with sweat.

"You're not seriously thinking of leaving OCD for IBS, are you?" Claire tugged at her uneven bangs. At the tables around them, girls picked at their food, looking bored and directionless. The café was quieter than usual since the boys weren't there to raise the noise level with their alphabet burping and food-fighting.

Massie's iPhone buzzed again, this time with a new e-mail from Layne, subject: SCREENPLOY. Massie shrugged, wishing IBS were a real place, with real alphas who didn't need scripts to tell them exactly what to say.

"So are you?" Claire urged. Just then, Alicia, Dylan, and Kristen strolled into the café and settled at their new table. They hunched together, whispering intently. Suddenly, Alicia's head jerked toward table eighteen. Massie plastered a giant smiled on her face and pretended not to notice.

"Am I *what?*" Massie said, wondering if there was a way to angle her phone so Claire couldn't see. She was desperate to read the script and make changes before the show went live.

"Transferring?"

"Maybe." She shrugged. "I have a few days to think about it."

"Do I get a vote?" Claire asked shyly.

Massie smiled involuntarily. At least Claire sometimes knew the right thing to say. She looked up, glancing into Claire's light blue eyes. Her expression said: If you leave, how will I know what to wear?

Massie allowed herself to blink back: You won't. Her heart filled with warmth as she and Claire stare-gazed at each other. For a split second, Massie remembered the way it used to be, before the PC split.

A burst of laughter exploded from the Soul-M8s' table.

Claire glanced nervously back and forth between Alicia's table and Massie's table, and the moment between them vanished into the soy cheese–scented air. The neck-swivel was simply another reminder that Claire hadn't chosen Massie. Yet. A twinge of uncertainty buzzed behind her navel. Now *would* be the perfect time to show up the 4-Squares in front of the entire school. But could she trust Layne's script? Either way, she had to get Claire out of here. Two minutes with MAC and she'd realize Massie's new friends were more artificial than Sweet'N Low.

"Anyway, the MAC girls'll be at my sleepover Friday night, so you can hang with them then."

"This Friday? Isn't your mom's charity thing this Friday?"

Massie froze. She'd been so focused on her actors that she'd completely forgotten about Ho Ho Homeless.

"Uh, yeah," she said quickly. "They'll ah-bviously be there for the event, and then they're sleeping over."

"Oh. Okay." Claire nodded. "Sounds fun. Cam and I are going to Alicia's couples' dinner party that night, but maybe—"

"Couples' *what?*" Massie blurted, then mentally smacked herself for acting like she cared.

Claire reddened slightly. "It'snothingbigjustadinnerparty withIdunnoafewcouplesorsomethingactuallyI'mnotreallysure."

Massie's scented body cream instantly evaporated from her skin, leaving her feeling dry and exposed. In its place, a dark Chanel No. 19–scented cloud hung over her head. If it was nothing, then why wasn't Claire jumping at the chance to come to her event instead? Since when did alpha status expire like milk and credit cards? Fingers flying over her iPhone keypad, she texted Layne.

Massie: Action.

Who cared if she hadn't read the script? It was time to show OCD who the *real* alphas were. And if Layne was telling the truth, and the script really was about crushes (probably high school crushes, from the quote-unquote "party" MAC had quote-unquote "gone to" Saturday night), then there'd be no contest. MAC and high school boys were way more alpha than the Soul-M8s and their lame party.

"Anyway, I could come over when we're done," Claire offered, like she was doing Massie a favor.

"Whatever." Massie shrugged. She didn't have any more time to waste on Claire. On top of coordinating MAC's OCD lunch debut, she now had to plan the most ah-mazing charity function Westchester had ever seen. Ho Ho Homeless would have to be bigger, better, and more Twitter-worthy than Alicia Rivera's wannabe couples' dinner party. Times ten. Besides, didn't "dinner" imply eating and "couples" mean in front of boys? And didn't Alicia firmly believe the two should never mix?

Suddenly, the frosted glass doors of the New Café flew open, revealing Massie's army of alphas. The entire café quieted, as if sensing they were in for a show. Massie's heart surged with excitement. It was Massie and Crew: take two.

With all eyes on them, Lilah, Mia, Jasmin, Kaitlyn, and Layne swished into their scene with perfectly choreographed synchronicity, heading straight for Massie's table.

Correction: Lilah, Mia, Jasmin, and Kaitlyn swished in perfectly choreographed synchronicity. Layne just sort of ambled alongside them, moving to a beat that was much more Killers than Beyoncé. She stuck out like a clearance-rack sweater that had accidentally been hung with spring's newest tanks.

The entire student body was staring openmouthed, following the girls' every move with glazed-over stares. Massie pulled her Guerlain pressed-powder compact from her bag and positioned the mirror so she had a perfect view of the Soul-M8s' table. Even Alicia's glossy mouth was slightly open.

As the girls neared her table, Massie side-glanced at Claire. She was leaning forward and squinting hard at the alphas, like she was at the eye doctor and they were the tiny letters marching across the bottom of the sight chart on the wall.

"The brunette," Claire murmur-squinted.

"Who, Jasmin?" Massie said proudly. "Isn't she ah-dorable?"

"She looks familiar," Claire said. "Like I've met her before, or something?"

"Probably 'cause she has one of those faces you've always dreamed of having," Massie snapped quickly. With a single, swift move, she swept Claire's imitation handbag from the pristine surface of table eighteen, sending it to the floor with a crash-clang that sounded like breaking technology.

"Hey!" Claire ducked under the table to retrieve her knocked-off knockoff.

"Oops." Massie shrugged innocently. She hadn't counted on anyone recognizing any of the girls. She never should have hired Tampax Sport. What would happen when Claire pegged Jasmin as the goalie who gave 100 percent even on her heavy flow days?

"Heyyyyyyy," MAC purred when they reached the table. The glittery lavender *Guests of Massie Block* pins they wore were not only adorable but also functional. They announced to the student body that these alphas belonged to Massie. In case there was ever any question about who was in charge.

"'Sup," Layne said, ruining the perfectly coordinated moment.

"Hey!" Claire emerged from under the table, looking almost shy. Layne grinned back.

"Sit," Massie said crisply, motioning toward the empty seats around her.

The girls sat. Except for Jasmin who glanced meaningfully between Claire and Massie.

Claire cocked her head. "Do I look familiar, because you totally—"

"You're in her seat, Kuh-laire," Massie panic-barked. "That's why she's looking at you."

"Oh, right." Claire stood. "Sorry." She kept her gaze fixed on Jasmin as she backed away from the table. "Okay, well, have a good lunch, guys. I should go anyway, since today's technically an Alicia day. But I'll be back here every other Tuesday and the third Friday of every mon—"

"'Kay, see ya," Massie cut her off again, and with one last glance at Jasmin, Claire slunk away to table eighteen.

Massie shifted her attention back to her girls and took a long, cooling sip of her frosty green-tea smoothie. "Great entrance," she whisper-congratulated. "Don't look, but everyone is very intrigued. This is exactly where we want them."

The girls turned.

"I said don't look!" Massie snapped.

"Chill, dude." Mia, appearing slightly bored, reached for the chopsticks next to her plate and maneuvered them expertly around a giant spicy tuna roll.

"Did you read the scene?" Layne whisper-asked hopefully as Massie glared at Mia.

"Not yet." Massie pushed her smoothie aside. "Before we start the scene," she said in a low voice, "we have to talk about this party I'm chairing Friday night." She speed-opened a to-do list on her iPhone. "I want you all there dressed in—"

"Okay." Layne pulled a squat orange mini-golf pencil out of her bra and began scribbling on her napkin. "We're gonna need wardrobe, hair, makeup, a new script, call times, a brief synopsis of the event, attending VIPs, and—"

"Giveita," Massie interrupted.

"Giveita?" Layne lifted her pencil.

"Yeah." Massie reached for the napkin and crumpled it into a ball. "Giveitarest!"

The MAC girls glanced at Massie, then burst out laughing. Even Layne smiled.

Massie's insides flooded with warmth. So her new girls *were* capable of acting like normal friends, even without a script. They just needed time to grow into their roles as MAC girls. Massie felt the last bit of uncertainty melt away.

Layne gnawed at a pungent rope of beef jerky while the other girls dipped their chopsticks daintily into their seaweed salad sides. Except for Lilah, who reglossed while her food sat untouched.

"Moving awn," Massie said, deciding the party could wait. MAC needed to strike now, while they had a captive audience. She leaned in close. "Layne says you guys are ready to do the lunch scene."

The MAC girls nodded.

"And you get that screwing this scene up in front of the entire café is nawt an option?" she said, eyeing Mia pointedly.

The girls nodded again, looking like perfectly made-up bobbleheads.

"Okay." Massie exhaled. "Layne? Any last minute notes?"

Layne shook her head, slipping on the lensless glasses she'd worn in the city. "Nope. All set."

Massie glanced one last time at the Soul-M8s' table. Alicia, Kristen, Dylan, and Claire were all still staring. Perfect.

"Action!" Layne whispered. Then, as Massie looked on aghast, Layne collapsed into a heap on top of the bamboo table. "I JUST DON'T GET IT," she faux-sobbed-yelled. "I THOUGHT DEMPSEY LIKED ME FOR ME! WHAT HAP-PENED?" Whipping her head around so her face was visible to the entire café, she screwed up her eyes, letting a tiny tear slip down her cheek.

The entire café fell silent.

"I KNOW, RIGHT?" Lilah slap-patted Layne's shaking shoulders. "IT JUST DOESN'T MAKE SENSE! WHY WOULDN'T DEMPSEY GO FOR YOU?"

Massie's spicy tuna roll made a beeline from her stomach to the back of her throat. "Cut!" she ordered. This scene was supposed to be about MAC and their high school crushes, not Layne and her Dempsey obsession! But somehow, the scene kept rolling.

"AH-GREED." Kaitlyn broadcasted a sympathetic pout across the room. "YOU'RE TOTALLY UNIQUE. YOU'RE LIKE A BREATH OF FRESH AIR COMPARED TO EVERYONE ELSE AROUND HERE."

Kori and Strawberry were starting to snicker. Massie stole a panicked glance at Alicia, who was giggling behind a Smartwater bottle and elbowing Dylan. Claire was still staring at Jasmin. Massie had to put a stop to this. Now.

Layne took a deep, shuddering breath. "I KNOOOOOOO—"

"CUT!" Massie snapped again, careful to keep her voice low. Her grip tightened around her smoothie glass.

"What?" Layne looked up, sounding irritated.

"You were great." Lilah patted Layne's hand.

"You really went deep," Jasmin added.

"I almost cried," Mia deadpanned.

"Seriously?" Layne beamed. "You should hear my monologue on page—"

"Layne," Massie barked as, thank Gawd, the noise level in the café rose to normal again and everyone returned to their gossip sessions and tofu.

"What?" Layne exhaled an indignant corn-scented protest.

"I'm hiring a new writer," Massie announced.

"Who?" Layne's hazel eyes bulged in horror.

"Me." Massie folded her arms across her chest and leaned back in her chair. "I'll send it out tonight."

"But—" Layne started.

"The rest of you, start learning your lines as soon as you get the script," she whisper-instructed. "We'll do a run-through after school tomorrow." She paused, making brief eye contact with every girl at the table. "Screw this up and you'll be doing community theater until you're old enough for adult diaper commercials."

The MAC girls gasped.

"Um . . ." Mia blinked as she tucked a strand of wavy hair behind her ear. "Isn't *this* community theater?"

The table went silent.

Massie felt her pores tighten. She lifted her smoothie to her forehead in a desperate attempt to freeze her angry thoughts until they broke off like icicles and fell away. But the chill just gave her even more brain pain. Mia obviously wasn't MAC material. And Massie, with a script to write, a charity event to plan, and a dinner party to ignore, simply didn't have time to mold her.

"Mia, are you Madonna's arms?" Massie asked.

"No."

"Then why are you so cut?" Massie slammed her smoothie glass on the table.

"What?" Mia's gold shimmer–glossed lower lip dropped.

"You're fiy-ered," Massie said slowly, like she was speaking to a two-year-old. "And don't try to stuff anything from wardrobe in your two-seasons-ago purse on your way out."

As the rest of the table stared wide-eyed at her, Massie shoved her chair back and threw her bag over her shoulder. Rehearsals were over. It was time to act.

CURRENT STATE OF THE UNION	
IN	**OUT**
IBS	OCD
Block parties	Dinner parties
M.I.A.	Mia

Once inside the radio booth, Alicia leaned against the sound-proof steel door with all her weight, forcing it to close faster. She was desperate for the dim, recessed lighting, flickering control panel, and nubby gray-carpeted walls. The space was hers, and nothing from the outside world could take that away.

Everywhere Massie and her new friends went these days, people stared. And without Josh and the boys around to distract her, she had nothing to do but watch MAC steal her spotlight.

But inside the radio booth, at exactly 12:05 p.m., Alicia was the star.

"*Ehhhhhhmagawd.*" She sighed when the door finally closed. She locked it, the *click* soothing her like Norah Jones. Then she reached for the yellow folder that held the day's news brief and speed-fanned herself with it, resisting the urge to sneak a peek. She never read the announcements until she was on the air. It was good practice for her career as a live television journalist. It taught her how to think on her heels.

At 12:04, she slipped on the giant headphones, pulled the announcements from their paper sleeve, and got ready to do what she did best. Her fingers flew across the glittery panel of lights, flipping switches and turning dials. Soon, the ON THE AIR sign flashed red overhead.

"Good afternoon, OCD, and welcome to your lunchtime update." Alicia's signature opener rolled smoothly off her tongue. "Next week marks the start of Yes, We Canned!, OCD's first annual canned food drive." Alicia rolled her eyes to the ceiling at the sound of the corny name that had obviously been Principal Burns's idea. "Remember to bring two unopened canned goods to school by next Friday."

After a brief, transitional pause, she continued. "And now onto other, more important news," she read from her script. "For a limited time, tickets are on sale for Ho Ho Homeless, a beyond fabulous charity event to be held this Friday at 8 p.m." She wrinkled her nose, wondering who would choose to waste their Friday night on charity work. "The catered, circus-themed event of the season will include a fashion show featuring today's most popular model-slash-actresses, plus a VIP after-party with a band too hot to even mention."

Alicia's journalistic curiosity was starting to get the best of her. She read faster. "The ultra-exclusive platinum ticket package comes with backstage passes, plus the chance to be a guest model in the fashion show."

Alicia's heart was starting to race under her Robert Rodriguez embellished tank. How could OCD's most trusted journalist and gossip not know about an event like this? How could she be so in the dark? Steadying her voice, she finished the announcement. "For more information, contact head board member Massie Blo—"

Suddenly, the air in the booth seem stale and hard to swallow. Somehow, Massie had managed to invade the only sacred space she had left. "ThisisAliciaRiverasigningoffand sayingIheartyou," she gasp-finished. Ripping off her headphones, she swirled around in her chair and yanked the door open. Her mind flooded with a million thoughts at once, each worse than the next. Had Claire known about this all along? What else was she keeping from Alicia? What if the rest of the Soul-M8s would rather go to Massie's party than hers? And what if no one showed up but Josh, and he decided she was nothing but an LBR whose only redeeming qualities were an amazing wardrobe and the trays of mini crab cakes she'd have left over from her no-show dinner party? *Why not donate them to the homeless, along with the rest of her friends?*

Alicia speed-walked down the hall toward the New Café. Her heart was thundering in her ears. The muffled sound reminded her of her visits to Spain and her cousin's stereo blasting through the thin walls. She could barely hear herself think.

When she reached the entrance, she stopped to finger-comb her hair. She'd never give Massie Block the satisfaction of seeing her this disheveled. Pressing her sweaty forehead against the smoky glass doors, she squinted hard, trying to figure out what was happening on the other side. But she couldn't see a thing. She was totally clueless. For all she knew, Dylan could be charging three tickets to Massie's bash on Merri-Lee's AmEx black.

Alicia shook the thought from her head, her glossy black hair whipping over her shoulders. Reaching into her slouchy Prada Mordore bag, she gripped the worn pink New York Yankees cap Josh had given her at the beginning of the year. Ever since Josh had left for Briarwood, she'd carried it everywhere. She even slept with it under her pillow. It reminded her that there was more to life than Massie Block. And she needed that reminder now more than ever.

With a deep breath, Alicia threw open the doors . . . and slammed right into Massie, who was bolting through from the other side.

"Hey!" Alicia smile-blurted, forgetting for a split second that they were in a fight. "Oh," she quickly corrected, her expression and stomach sinking at the same time.

Massie rolled her eyes, adjusting her purple Envi drape top. "Thanks for the advertising." She smirked. "But I hope you're not here for tickets. We just sold out."

Alicia ignored her, stuffing her hands in her pockets to keep them from shaking. "I wouldn't go to your fund-raiser if you paid me," she said, looking Massie directly in the eye.

"What are you trying to say?" Massie squinted her amber eyes.

"I'm saying I already have plans."

"I heard." Massie pursed her lips. "Dinner. In your dining room. With your parents in the next room."

Tiny beads of sweat were starting to form beneath the underwire of Alicia's bra. How did Massie know about her party?

"Maybe I don't have a band or models," Alicia finally managed, knowing her face was turning a deeper shade of crimson by the second, "but I have something you won't have."

"What?" Massie sneered. "Tapas?"

"No!" Alicia shouted, not caring that half the New Café had stopped mid-chew to watch them. "A date with an ah-dorable eighth-grade boy!" She plunged her hand into her purse, gripping the Yankees cap so tight it made her fingers tingle.

"You're right." Massie blinked but didn't miss a beat. "I won't have an eighth-grade boy. I'll have a high school one. So will all the models, because they'll be escorting us down the runway."

Alicia's throat tightened, and she ducked into the hallway, slamming the frosted door in Massie's face. That was it. No more letting Massie make her look like an LBR in front of the whole school. If Massie was throwing the party of the season, Alicia would throw the party of the year. She had no idea how she was going to beat models and high school boys, but she'd Tim Gunn it somehow. And if that didn't work, she'd consider transferring to IBS. Wherever *that* was.

Massie crossed her arms over her black silk tank and tapped her foot rapidly on the red-carpeted floor. "Lah-ane!"

"For the last time, I don't know anything!" Layne jabbed at the air with her empty Powerade bottle for emphasis. Blue liquid dribbled down her wrist. "All Peace said was that she's sending one of her top clients." She launched the bottle toward the white plastic trash can next to the door. It dropped neatly into the can.

"Score!" Kaitlyn pouted as her makeup artist, a wiry redhead with smoky eyes and a slicked-back ponytail, hovered over her with a lip brush. Each of the MAC girls was perched in her makeup chair, going through a hair and makeup dry run so Massie could approve or reject possible runway looks before the big show.

"Close 'em," the makeup artist instructed. Kaitlyn pursed her lips dutifully.

"One of her top clients?" Massie settled into the director's chair next to Layne's.

Layne threw her arms in the air. She had a hole in the pit of her SAVE A TREE, EAT A BEAVER T-shirt. "One of her top clients, her top client—what's the difference?"

Massie glared at Layne in disbelief. The difference was

beyond obvious. Having the very best models strut her runway on Friday night would mean two things: one, that she'd pulled off yet another amazing event, and two, that she'd outdone Alicia. The party had to be over-the-top, which was why she'd decided on a circus theme.

"Anyway, I have no idea who it is. Swearsville." Layne wiped her sticky Mountain Blast fingers on her camo leggings. "But if my aunt is handpicking her, she'll be good."

"Your aunt picked Mia, re-mem-ber?" Massie reminded her. "And look how that turned out."

"*You* picked Mia," Layne snorted good-naturedly. "Re-*mem*-ber?"

Opening the chunky script in her lap, Massie flipped to the last pages and pretended she hadn't heard Layne. She hated when LBRs were right. She cranked up her lip pencil and held it menacingly over the page. Cruella was the perfect shade of crimson for last-minute script revisions, like axing the "Layne and Dempsey slo-mo reconcile montage" Layne had sneaked into Massie's rewrite during lunch.

"If I were you, I wouldn't worry about the new girl," Layne advised. She pulled a tube of Hello Kitty gloss from her pocket. Slathering the wand recklessly, she left two shiny magenta stripes where her mouth had been. "We've got a bigger prob, Bob."

"Like your lips?" Massie mutter-asked. The neon purple was less flattering than Jessica Simpson's high-waisted jeans.

"Like the fact that you told Alicia we'd have high school

boys at the party Friday night," Layne retorted, adjusting the volume on her director's bullhorn.

"How is that a problem?" Massie asked. "Isn't Chris Abeley in high school?"

"Chris Abeley, like, my brother Chris Abeley?" Layne wrinkled her nose.

Massie speed-nodded.

"Yeah, but—"

"Butts are for slapping," Massie interrupted. "Make Chris bring his hawtest friends. Make sure they know they'll be walking the runway. So no shorties."

"Ninth-grade boys?" Kaitlyn whipped around in her chair, flashing a devious smile. Her gray eyes glowed under thick, dark lashes. "This is seriously the best job ever." Her stylist click-snapped her flatiron together three times like lobster claws, but Kaitlyn ignored her. Instead, she rested her chin on the silk back of her chair, beaming at Massie.

"I'm five nine," breathed Lilah, smiling close-lipped at Massie and Layne in her mirror while her hairstylist finger-combed shine serum through her dark, boy-short locks. "I'll need a model over six feet."

"Done." Massie nodded.

"But—" Layne started.

"Thanks!" Lilah beamed at Massie. "This is going to be awesome."

"Given." Massie smiled back, her heart skipping a beat. Finally—girls who appreciated her.

Jasmin coughed. "Um, isn't it almost time for our break?"

she asked. "We've been on for like six hours, and I promised my friends back home I'd check in after school."

Massie's stomach clenched at the reminder that the MAC girls had other lives. Other friends. She tried to block the thought from her mind, but it kept creeping back in. Before she could tell Tampax Sport that if she wanted a break, she could take a permanent one, the trailer door flew open.

"Sorry I'm late," breathed the silhouette standing in the doorway.

Kaitlyn squinted at the door. Lilah and Jasmin swivel-whipped around in their chairs, shooing away the fluffy brushes hovering around their faces like pesky mosquitoes. Layne gnawed at her magenta lower lip. Massie leaned forward in her chair. Sunlight poured in behind the stranger and shaded her face, making it impossible to see her.

The silhouette shut the trailer door and stood proudly before them. The newest MAC girl had thick dark chocolate locks that fell just below her shoulders and glistened under the trailer's track lights. The golden flecks in her hazel eyes matched the sheen of her dusted cheekbones. And her outfit was pure fashinspiration: a pomegranate boyfriend cardigan-turned-minidress cinched with a tangle of skinny metallic foil belts, worn over herringbone tights and slate gray over-the-knee suede boots.

Nine point two.

Massie gripped the smooth wooden armrests of her chair and casually crossed her dark denim–slicked legs. She wished she had been wearing sunglasses so she could stare.

Nine Point Two dropped her slouchy shoulder bag on one of the slate board desks. "I'm Cassidy. Your new actress."

"I'm Massie. Your new best bend."

Cassidy crinkled her thin brows in confusion. "Best bend?"

"Boss-friend," Jasmin explained patiently, as if being a paid BFF was completely legit, like a career in sales or marketing.

Massie hugged her script to her chest. "Just don't screw up your lines like the last girl did, and you'll be fine." She nodded toward the empty makeup chair at the end of the row, next to Kaitlyn. "Have a seat."

"Great boots," Kaitlyn remarked as Cassidy settled in next to her. Jakkob rubbed his scruff thoughtfully as he stared at his new client. Then he looked to Massie, waiting for instruction.

"We're going platinum," Massie decided quickly. "And short. Don't be afraid to experiment."

"Awesome." Jakkob began rifling through the contents of the shelves in front of him, whipping bottles, combs, and bowls from the shelf.

"Woah," Layne muttered. "Risky."

"Totally." Lilah stared at her reflection in the mirror, looking jealous.

Cassidy turned around, her elbow hanging over the back of her chair. "Platinum?" she asked skeptically, patting her dark locks. "Um, I've read the script and I'm pretty sure my character wouldn't go platinum. What's my motivation?"

"Let's see." Massie tapped her chin lightly, breathing through the irritation churning in the pit of her stomach.

"Your character is a D-level actress. She is out of work and desperately needs a job, especially since the economy is tanking and unemployment is at an all-time high. She finally lands a well-paying gig in Westchester, where all she has to do is learn a few lines and act like a friend. If she wants to keep said job, she will listen to her new bend and dye her hair. If she doesn't, she is free to hop the Metro-North back to Grand Central and admire her natural hair color in the reflection of the train window."

"Oh," Cassidy said, turning around in her seat. "That motivation. Right." She stared longingly in the mirror at her hair, as if she was saying goodbye to a crush she knew she'd never see again.

"Now. On to business." Massie hopped off her director's chair and crossed the trailer, pacing behind the row of makeup chairs. "We have exactly three days to get you ready for the fashion show."

"Peace told you I don't do dresses, right?" Lilah asked, turning around again in her chair. "Girly doesn't really go with my look."

"Amen, sister," Layne called through the bullhorn.

Massie lifted her palm, silencing Layne. "That means," she continued, "that we're all gonna be working overtime."

Jasmin raised her hand. "But our contract says we only work for eight hours a day."

Kaitlyn nodded. Her hairstylist firmly grabbed her head. "Stop moving!" she hissed, running another strand through the flatiron.

"Your contract also says you won't screw up a scene in front of the entire school. And you've already done that. Twice," Massie retorted. A knot formed in her stomach that felt suspiciously like loneliness. She'd supplied makeup, killer clothes, and money, but the MAC girls were approaching their kick-butt jobbies like it was MACDonald's and she was forcing them to ask, Would you like fries with that? What was wrong with them? "Any more questions?" she sigh-asked.

The MAC girls were silent.

"Good." She tossed a script to Cassidy, who had her eyes squeezed shut as Jakkob painted bluish-white streaks into her hair. The script smacked her in the thigh. "I have some calls to make. Run lines for five. When I get back, we'll start the table read."

"TAKE FIVE, PEOPLE," Layne squawked into the bullhorn.

The girls opened their scripts.

"Time to party plan." Massie turned back to Layne, whose camo leggings–clad legs were slung over the armrest of her director's chair.

"You haven't done that yet?" Layne's magenta lips dropped open. Her tongue was tinged blue from the sports drink. "The party is Friday!"

Massie twirled her purple hair steak. The exclusive all-access pass was like shopping with limit-free plastic. Nothing was off limits. "Three days is more than enough time. Just get me the high school hawties, okay?"

"Fine." Layne sighed. She slid out of the chair and headed for the leather couch in the middle of the trailer and collapsed into it. She laid a hand over her eyes, like her life was too much to handle.

Massie finger-searched her iPhone for the necessary cell numbers. Justin Timberlake would get the crowd pumped for the fashion show. The Pussycat Dolls would be the main event, followed by the Jonas Brothers to wind things down.

It was the perfect lineup. Massie giggled to herself, thinking of the dizzying salsa music the Riveras always played at dinner parties. Poor Claire. Someday she'd realize that neutral was a nail polish color, nawt a way of life.

Massie composed a quick text for Justin's manager.

Massie: JT—ASAP. Block Estate by 7 this Friday ready to perform for charity. P.S. Leave 7th Heaven at home.

After writing drafts to the Dolls and JBros, Massie reglossed and held her iPhone out at arm's length. Making sure her purple streak was visible, she smiled at the camera and took the shot.

"Done, done, and done." She attached the photo to the texts and sent them.

Massie's iPhone buzzed back instantly.

She opened the text with one hand and stroke-thanked her streak with the other. Ever since Massie had, ahem, borrowed the purple streaking pen from Anastasia Brees, founder of Be Pretty cosmetics, as a reward for all her hard work selling cosmetics to LBRs over the summer, she'd been more VIP than the entire cast of *Gossip Girl* combined.

Massie opened the text. A single word glowed on the screen.

Expired.

Her stomach plummeted to the floor. "Expired?" she said out loud. It was a mistake. It had to be. Anastasia Brees hadn't said *anything* about an expiration date for the purple streak. Massie read the text again.

Expired.

Her phone buzzed twice more.

Expired.
Expired.

Layne was saying something, but Massie couldn't hear over the sound of her world crashing down around her. Her iPhone slipped from her sweaty hands and fell to the floor. Losing her streak meant losing her power. Without it, she was like Diane von Furstenberg without the wrap dress. Scientology without Tom Cruise. Tyra without her forehead.

The MAC girls blurred into one well-styled blob, and she couldn't feel her toes in her maroon riding boots. Beneath her tank, her heart beat out a staccato rhythm and her ears whirled like the ocean inside a conch shell. Was this what dying felt like?

"MASSIE!" Layne had turned the bullhorn up to maximum volume. It sliced her through thoughts like an ax through sashimi.

"E-nuff!" Massie yanked the bullhorn away from Layne's mouth and pitched it across the trailer.

The MAC girls gasped, but Massie didn't care. Maybe now they'd get that this wasn't just another gig. This was the performance of a lifetime. A public statement. A lesson in biting the manicured hand that feeds you. It was MAC versus the Soul-M8s. And there was no *way* she would to lose to a bunch of crush stealing ex-friends with a wannabe vanity license plate name.

"You work with the actresses. I'll get the boys and the band," Layne said calmly, as though she were talking to a young child mid-tantrum.

Massie swallowed the panic lump in her throat, hating how Layne tried to take over at every turn. She was starting to act just like the ex-PC. Like she didn't think Massie could handle the situation on her own. Massie promised herself that as soon as her social stock was on the rise, she'd drop Layne faster than an online dater in a wireless dead zone.

"I'll take care of it," Massie insisted, even though she had no idea how.

"You don't trust me?" Layne blinked, looking hurt.

The truth was, Massie *didn't* trust Layne's taste in boys. The only girls whose cute guy–dar she trusted were the ex-PC.

But they were gone, and Layne was all she had. "Fine." She sighed. Admitting that she needed Layne's help made her feel lamer than a three-legged dog. But what else was she supposed to do?"

"Really?" Layne's hazel eyes widened in disbelief.

"As long as you book the opposite of what you like," Massie clarified. "Which means no boys with eyeliner and no bands with car show experience."

"Promise, Thomas." Layne grinned.

"And no confirming until I ah-pprove."

Layne nodded her consent. "Don't worry, I'll deliver like Domino's."

"You better, or I'll fry you like KFC." Massie narrowed her amber eyes, insisting she meant it. Which she did.

Because if Layne screwed this up, Massie's alpha status would end up like her purple streak.

Expired.

Claire bit her nails as she checked out the flavors at the brand-new Pinkberry in the Westchester Mall.

"Pomegranate with Cocoa Pebbles!" Dylan borderline shouted at the wide-eyed girl behind the counter. "Wait! No! Green tea with coconut." She hovered over the glass case that displayed a colorful array of exotic fro-yo toppings. "No! Original. With—"

"Ehmagawd, Dylaaaannnnn." Kristen sighed behind her.

"Fine," Dylan huffed, crossing her arms over her Haute Hippie sweater poncho. "I'll have a smoothie."

"And can I get another sample of original?" Alicia asked sweetly, leaning against the sea green wall next to the cash register.

Claire sneaked a glance at the door. Cam and the rest of the boys should be here any second, since today was an off day for soccer. She couldn't wait to finally get some time in with her crush. Since the boys had been shipped back to Briarwood, she hadn't seen Cam in four whole days, which felt like forever. Oddly, Claire had seen even less of Cam than she had back in the Pretty Committee days. It was almost like they couldn't hang out unless Alicia had something planned.

Was Massie right? Were boy-girl cliques impossible? Did being a Soul-M8 leave Claire a No-M8?

The Pinkberry girl cleared her throat.

"Oh. Sorry." Claire flushed slightly. "Um, I'll have original with cookies 'n' cream. Please."

"And that sample, whenever you get a chance." Alicia narrowed her eyes, sounding miffed.

The Pinkberry girl eyed the teetering stack of empty sample cups piled on Alicia's tray.

Alicia stared right back, daring Pinkberry to comment.

Pinkberry sighed and reached for a fresh sample cup.

"Point," Alicia said under her breath. She was stocking up on samples, so she wouldn't have to eat in front of Josh.

After they'd gotten their fro-yo, the girls claimed the white table at the very front of the store. From their post at the giant window overlooking the mall, they watched couples walking hand in hand into Godiva, hipsters in skinny jeans bobbing their heads to their iPods, and goths stomping into Hot Topic.

Finally, their crushes appeared at the very end of the hallway, laughing and shoving one another as they maneuvered the after-school rush.

Dylan sucked in her stomach and buttoned her jeans. Alicia arm-swiped her empty sample cups into her YSL tote. Kristen wiped off her MAC Lipglass and replaced it with a swipe of environmentally friendly PlantLove gloss.

Claire straightened up in her chair, her heart vibrating louder than the Taboo buzzer on the Lyons family game night.

Cam Fisher, his piercing one blue and one green eye, and his backpack full of sours were just seconds away.

"Quick! Pretend I just said something hilarious," Alicia whisper-hissed, tossing her black hair.

The girls burst out laughing.

Derrington waved, walking straight toward the table like he didn't see the giant window that separated the boys from the girls.

BAM!

At the last second, he'd turned his cheek and his entire body smacked into the partition like a bird flying into freshly cleaned glass. He slid slowly down the giant glass pane, making squeaking noises as he slumped to the floor.

Dylan's faux laugh turned into a real one, complete with a snort.

Alicia rolled her eyes, reached into her YSL tote, and pulled out her pink Yankees cap. "Do you hawnestly think he's funny?"

"Do you hawnestly think that hat goes with anything?" Dylan blurted, eyeing the cap with disdain. "Twitter update: It's PinkScary."

"You're PinkHairy," Alicia retorted, tossing a coconut shaving at Dylan's red ponytail.

"I'm PinkClaire-y," Claire chimed in.

The girls cracked up. Not so much because it was funny but because the boys had entered Pinkberry and were standing over them, looking nerve-wrackingly cute.

A dizzying combination of Drakkar Noir, fresh grass, and

boy sweat found Claire like Cupid's arrow. She wished she could bottle the scent, even though Massie would probably call it *Ew* de Cam. Claire felt a twinge of sadness cut through her excitement. As weird as it sounded to want Massie here to insult her . . . she did.

"Coulda warned me about that window," Derrington said as he plopped down in the seat next to Dylan and rubbed the side of his face where he'd hit the glass.

She swatted his arm.

Alicia beamed at Josh, who was wearing a crimson RL fleece hoodie.

"Nice hat," he said, chin-nodding at the Yankees cap on the table.

Alicia blushed, then eyed the cap like she couldn't decide whether to stuff it back in her bag or wear it.

"What's up?" Kristen glanced up at Dempsey, swirling her green tea yogurt with her spoon.

"Um, the sky?" Dempsey said, flashing his dimpled smile. He sat down across from her, and they grinned at each other, nervous crush waves shooting back and forth between them.

"Hey," Cam said, but the way he squinted his blue eye told Claire he'd missed her.

Her head nod said hi but her grin screamed, *Let's lip-kiss.*

He dragged a chair next to Claire's and plopped down into it. His smile was warm enough to melt Claire's fro-yo. And her heart. Her mind spun with all the things she'd wanted to tell Cam since they'd seen each other last. They'd texted the night before about Massie and her new billionaire friends, but he didn't know how Mara Hill from seventh had discovered Principal Burns's MySpace page and set it as the home page for every computer at OCD. Or how Claire had aced her last French test without even having to crack a book. And how that was mostly because Madame Vallon had accidentally given the same test she gave the week before.

Cam stuck his finger in Claire's ice cream. "What flavor'd you get?" What he was obviously saying was, *School sucks without you there.*

"Original." Claire smiled. Same. The soft glow from the giant white orbs that swung overhead made Cam's eyes sparkle even more than usual. She couldn't tell if it was the frosty fro-yo making her teeth chatter or her crush.

"—that corner kick with like five seconds left?" Dempsey was saying to Kristen while the boys eyed the menu at the front of the store.

"I know!" Kristen plucked a soggy piece of granola from her cup and popped it into her mouth. "I DVR'd it and played it back a billion times."

"AC Milan's team is sick this year," Dempsey said. "Who's your favorite player?"

"Who's yours?" Kristen shot back.

"On three?" Dempsey's dimple deepened.

Kristen nodded happily. "One . . . two . . ."

"BECKHAM!" they shouted in unison, high-fiving. Kristen's cheeks flushed pinker than her fro-yo.

"So have you guys seen Massie's new friends?" Alicia said loudly, obviously bored with the soccer talk.

Claire sighed. She was getting sick of talking about, hearing about, and seeing Massie's new friends. Couldn't they talk about something else?

She turned toward Cam. "So how was prac—"

"You know the one with the short haircut?" Dylan said. "I heard her family invented graham crackers. That's how they made their first billion."

"Lame," Alicia decided. "But not as lame as the little get-together Massie's having Friday night. Her sleepovers have gone downhill fast." She turned toward Josh. "Apparently, since we're not available, she's inviting lots of homeless people."

"No way." Josh's eyes gleamed like they did whenever Alicia had juicy gossip.

Alicia nodded. "Sooo sad." She pouted happily.

Claire gripped her plastic spoon so hard she thought it might crack. What was Alicia talking about? Claire had seen the way she'd reacted at lunch yesterday, shouting and storming out of the café after Massie had tricked her into announcing the event. Why couldn't Alicia just admit that she was freaked out that Massie's party would be better than hers? For that matter, why couldn't Massie admit that having billionaire friends just wasn't the same as having the old millionaire ones?

"Hey." She nudged Cam's thigh with hers. "Wanna go to Sharper Image?"

"Ooohhh! Lyons and Fisher need some alone time," Derrington teased. He turned his back to the table and wrapped his arms around his body, making kissing noises.

"Ehmagawd." Dylan giggled.

"Gimme a break," Cam said, turning red. But he avoided Claire's insistent stare.

Claire's heart was starting to race again. This time it was definitely not in that "I just can't wait to see my boy-friend" kind of way. Why didn't Cam want to spend any time with her?

"I'm starving," Cam announced, shoving back his chair. "Do they have real food here?"

"We can go to the food court," Claire stood quickly. She remembered a CosmoGirl.com article she'd read last week about how boys didn't know how to take a hint. You had to tell them exactly what you wanted, or they didn't get it. She followed Cam up to the register. Despite the cool, stainless steel counters, the calming green walls, and the soft lighting, her stress level was definitely on the rise.

"Cam," she started. "I want to get our own table." There. She said it.

"Green tea with Fruity Pebbles," Cam told the girl behind the counter. "Large." He turned toward Claire.

"You mean ditch everybody else?" he said over a sticky green mouthful. "That's not cool."

"Never mind," Claire snapped, stalking back to the table. She yanked her chair out so hard it almost toppled over.

"Easy, Lyons," Josh joked. His eyes slid back and forth between Claire and Cam, who had slumped into his seat and was poking silently at his Fruity Pebbles.

"Don't mind her," Alicia said, batting her thick lashes.

"She's just mad because Cam wants to hang out with us and she doesn't."

Claire clenched her jaw.

Alicia didn't let up. "Or is it that you'd rather be hanging out with Massie and *her* crew?" she challenged, pointing her spoon at Claire. "'Cause if that's the case, don't let us stop you." She motioned grandly toward the door.

Dylan and Kristen stared down at their empty cups.

The boys looked totally clueless.

And Cam did absolutely nothing to stand up for her.

"This is crazy," Claire muttered, jumping up from her chair. She wove through the maze of tables and chairs, heading for the bathroom. She should have been mad, but she was just sad. She missed her friends being together. Missed hanging out with Cam alone. Missed seeing Alicia eat. Having two groups to hang out with was like having two crushes: great in theory but way too complicated in real life.

Shoving through the bathroom door, she leaned against the cool, shiny steel of one of the stall doors. It was time to admit it. No matter how hard she tried, she couldn't pull a Tim Gunn. This just wasn't working. If she wanted to stay friends with Massie and the Soul-M8s, there was only one option: Somehow, she had to get everybody back together.

And unless she wanted to spend the rest of her life hiding out in public bathrooms, she had to do it fast.

Alicia hovered over the dark wood podium at the front of her house's home theater, reviewing her PowerPoint slides one last time. Accidentally announcing the details of Massie's event had forced her to get seriously serious about her dinner party. Everything had to be perfect.

"Popcorn!" Dylan said gleefully, lifting the individual red-and-white striped snack bag Alicia had personalized for each of her friends. "With peanut M&M's!" She cracked open the chilled Perrier in her armrest. It fizzed over, soaking her black Design History turtleneck. "Aww, man!" she groaned. "I just changed twenty minutes ago."

"Mine has gummies!" Claire was rapidly finger-tapping her armrest and fidgeting in her seat, like she had major gossip and couldn't wait to spill. Before Alicia could ask her what was up, Kristen interrupted.

"Carob chips!" Kristen dug into her bag. "My fave. Thanks!"

Alicia graciously accepted their praise with a modest bow. "Okay, girls. Time to focus." She clapped twice, accidentally activating the surround-sound system. One of her mom's Spanish drum CDs blasted from the speakers.

"Ahhhhhhhhh!"

Kristen scrunched her nose and Dylan dropped her popcorn and covered her ears.

Alicia triple-clapped the music off. "Oops. Sorry."

"Tell us that's not for the party." Dylan ate the spilled popcorn off her lap, combining it with peanut M&M's.

"Given." Alicia tightened the skinny back patent leather belt that she wore over a silver silk blouse.

"Phew." Dylan sank back in her love seat, looking relieved. "I don't want Derrick thinking I listen to that cr—"

"Let's get started." Alicia cut her off, resting her hands on her hips. She had fifty-two hours until her guests arrived, and there was tons to do. "First, I have an announcement to make. Friday night is no longer just a regular couples' dinner party." She paused, drinking in the girls' curiosity like fresh cucumber water. "It's . . . a paparazzi party!" A broad smile spread across her face. She'd stayed up half the night coming up with a theme better than Massie's. Not that "homeless people" was a tough one to beat.

The girls were silent.

"You mean, like, we're supposed to dress up as paparazzi?" Kristen tilted her head to the side, looking confused.

"Don't they wear camo so they can hide in the bushes outside celebs' houses?" Dylan asked, her mouth full.

"You're not supposed to *dress* like the paparazzi." Alicia sighed, her excitement leaking slowly. "You're supposed to dress *up* like you're going to a red-carpet event, and there'll be paparazzi *there.*"

"Camo makes my hips looks wide," Dylan pointed out.

"Dylan. Nobody but you said anything about camo," Alicia snapped.

"So it's like a red-carpet party?" Claire grinned, still tapping her armrest. She pushed her overgrown white blond bangs behind her ear. They slipped immediately back over her eye.

"Fine. It's a red-carpet party." Had Alicia just let Claire rename her party theme? "So we'll dress up like we're going to an awards show with our crushes."

"Can we make it a green-carpet party?" Kristen piped up. "Dempsey'll definitely show if it has an eco-friendly theme."

"Opposite of yes," Alicia snapped.

"Hey, Leesh? I dunno if Derrick's gonna be down for Friday night dress-up." Dylan stretched out on her love seat, a shower of popcorn kernels falling from her lap to the floor. "But I can check." She reached for her cell.

"It's *nawt* dress-up," Alicia insisted. Wait a minute. *Check? Green carpet?* Why were her friends treating the theme like it was negotiable? They'd never questioned any of Massie's party ideas before. And besides, this wasn't a democracy. It was a cliquetatorship! Suddenly, her belt felt too tight. She loosened it to give herself some air.

"Sounds fun," Claire called out supportively.

Ehmagawd. That was a pity shout-out if ever she'd heard one. And from Claire, of all people.

"I love that this is Derrick and my first party as a couple," Dylan said, slapping her feet excitedly against the leather love seat.

"Same for me and Dempsey!" Kristen squealed. "Ehmagawd, maybe we'll lip-kiss at the end of the night."

"Us too!" Dylan screeched.

"Moving on," Alicia yell-announced. "In your party planning packets, you'll find your assignments, plus personalized to-do lists."

The girls reached for the thick spiral-bound packets propped up against their seats.

"Dylan. Refreshment duty." Alicia reached for a tiny electronic remote in the back pocket of her jeans and pressed a button. A white screen descended from the ceiling, and a picture of Dylan in the New Café, laughing with her mouth full of food, lit up the screen. The phrase REFRESHMENT COMMITTEE glowed above Dylan's red curls. "I tried to give you a job you'd actually be into."

"Wait, isn't your housekeeper handling the food?" Dylan tilted back her head, funneling the remainder of her popcorn bag straight into her mouth.

Alicia sighed. "I thought you could approve it since, you know, you'll probably be the only one eating."

"Oh. Right." Dylan flushed.

Claire raised her hand from her seat in the back.

"Yes, Claire?" Alicia said warily.

"Are we sure we want Joyce there?" Claire asked. "I mean, what if she keeps bringing new dishes in and interrupting our time with our crushes?"

"My lip-kiss!" Dylan gasped. "What if she walks in right when Derrick is about to—"

"Joyce knows to stay in the kitchen," Alicia said. "Now, Kristen, your job is to—"

"And what about your parents?" Claire interrupted. "What if they keep peeking in to check on us?" The corners of her mouth were twitching.

"My parents will be at the Blocks' house." Alicia sighed, wishing she could go upstairs and take a hot bath to melt the stress away. Why did Claire look like she was up to something? Alicia resolved to keep an eye on her for the rest of the meeting. "Now, back to—"

"What about those security cameras your parents just had put in?" Claire continued, leaning forward in her chair. Her cheeks were flushed, the way they always got when she was nervous or hiding something. "What if your parents go back and watch the footage after the party's over?"

"They won't," Alicia insisted.

"What if the cameras catch us lip-kissing?" Kristen gripped her armrest.

"We could end up on *Girls Gone Wild*!" Dylan panicked.

"Or worse!" Kristen said. "*America's Funniest Home Videos*!"

Dylan and Kristen dissolved into nervous giggles. Alicia and Claire just stared at each other.

"What's going on, Kuh-laire?" Alicia finally said when the girls' laughter had died down.

"Whaddaya mean?" Claire asked, flushing a deeper shade of pink.

"Claire." Alicia narrowed her eyes at Claire until she

could barely see, hoping this upped her intimidation factor. It worked for Massie. "Spill."

"Well . . ." Claire said slowly, her thumbnail instinctively flying to her mouth. "I was just thinking . . . maybe we could have the party at my house."

"Why would I want to have my dinner party at 'your house'?" Alicia air-quoted 'your house,' since Claire basically lived in Massie's backyard. Suddenly, the wood-paneled walls of the home theater felt like they were closing in on her. Why was Claire trying so hard to take over? Was she trying to steal Alicia's spot as alpha? For a millisecond, Alicia understood how Massie must have felt when Alicia wanted to co-lead the Socc-Hers. But then she reminded herself it wasn't the same thing at all. Alicia *was* an alpha in dance. She should have been heading up the squad. But since when did Claire have any expertise in party planning?

"Party stays at my house," she ruled, smacking her palm against the wooden podium.

"You sure?" Claire asked, getting bolder by the second. Alicia gripped the sides of the podium, hard. "Because if we had the party at *my* house, you could spy on Massie's party. You know what they say: Keep your friends close. . . ." Claire's voice trailed off.

Alicia froze. She hadn't thought of the spy potential. Her mind spun. What was she supposed to do? Give in, and let the girls think Claire was running the show? Or keep the party at her house, and be left completely in the dark about Massie's party? She stared at Claire, wondering if Claire and Massie were somehow conspiring against her.

"So whaddaya think?" Claire asked lightly, twirling a white blond strand around her index finger.

Dylan and Kristen leaned forward expectantly.

Alicia felt trapped. Backed into a corner. But as much as she didn't want Claire thinking she could call all the shots, she wanted to be able to spy on Massie more.

"Just to be clear?" Alicia said. "Even if we do have the party at your house, it's still my party. Not yours. Got it?"

"Got it." Claire speed-bobbed her head.

Alicia paused, pretending she was still thinking about it.

"Okay," she said finally. "The party's at Claire's."

The girls cheered.

Claire settled back in her seat contentedly, like she'd just finished a giant Thanksgiving dinner.

"We'll start tomorrow decorating after school," Alicia called over the slap of high fives. "Dean can take us straight to your house, Claire. In the meantime, you can start by getting rid of every LBR-ish item in your house."

"Like . . ." Claire crossed her arms over her chest, but she was still smiling.

Everything! Alicia wanted to say. Instead, she took a measured breath. "Well, your old T-shirt pillowcases, for one," she said slowly.

"And your Keds," Dylan added gleefully.

"And those little ceramic angel figurines on your shelves," Kristen said.

"Hey!" Claire protested. "Grandma Lyons gave me those!"

"Exactly," Dylan deadpanned.

While the girls chattered about the necessary guesthouse renovations, Alicia kept her eyes on Claire. She still had the feeling something was going on. Like Claire had an ulterior motive. But since she had no idea what that motive could be, Alicia was just going to have to trust her. For now, at least.

After she'd taken Bean and the actors for their nightly walk, Massie lit the Kobo Moon Wisteria soy candle on her bedside table and inhaled deeply. Usually, the sweet, soft scent of jasmine and honeysuckle calmed her. But not tonight. She took three more slow, deep breaths, and turned to face the mess in her room.

Clothing donations for the fashion show had been arriving at the Blocks' doorstep all week, and wardrobe boxes were stuffed end-to-end in Massie's usually pristine white and purple bedroom. Colorful silk, sequins, and satin littered her floor.

Everything was so chaotic that it seemed more appropriate than ever that she'd made the benefit circus-themed.

A quick knock sounded on the other side of Massie's door. Before Massie could shoo the intruder away, Kendra was standing in her room.

"Good. You're back," she said, before registering the disaster state in front of her. Her hand flew to her mouth as her eyes traveled over the wardrobe boxes barfing last season's threads.

"I knooow, Mom," Massie said, kneeling down to fish Bean from beneath a pile. A pink silk head wrap tumbled from the puppy's mouth like a long, shiny tongue. "And I don't need a lecture. It'll be cleaned up by tomorrow."

"I hope so," Kendra murmured, taking a step back toward the doorway as though the mess might attack her. "You can ask Inez for help if you need it."

"'Kay." Massie willed her mom to leave.

"Where are the models?" Kendra asked, leaning against Massie's doorframe and smoothing her short dark bob. "Finished with the walk-through already?"

"Yup," Massie said, gently wrestling the pink head wrap away from her puppy and tossing it on her bed. "They're back at the hotel." She'd told her parents that the MAC girls were models she'd hired from Peace's agency, and that their nightly walks were rehearsals for the show.

"How's everything going?" Kendra asked, her voice taking on her "I know something's going on, so you might as well tell me all about it" tone. "You seem a little stressed."

"I'm fine." Massie waved her away. "It's just a lot of planning, that's all." She pretended to rearrange the hangers in one of the wardrobe boxes so she wouldn't have to face her mom. One look in Kendra's wide brown eyes, and Massie worried she'd spill everything.

"Okay, then," Kendra said from the other side of the box. "Get to bed soon, okay?" She stepped over three mountainous piles of clothes and pulled Massie in for a hug.

"Okay," Massie murmured into her mom's navy silk blouse. She inhaled the remaining vapors of Kendra's D&G Light Blue perfume, but even that familiar scent couldn't calm her. The only thing that was going to make her feel better was getting organized. So she pulled away and ducked back into the wardrobe box. "'Night."

"'Night-night," Kendra said. A few seconds later, the door to Massie's room clicked shut.

Massie breathed a sigh of relief and reached for her iPhone.

HO HO HOMELESS GAME PLAN

MAC GIRL	RUNWAY OUTFIT	HAIR	MAKEUP	ISSUES/ CONCERNS	RUNWAY READY?
Massie	Hervé Léger strapless foil dress (fabric looks x-tra shimmery under runway lights!), Miu Miu gold strappy sandals	Side part, loose waves. (Think Gisele in Rampage campaign.)	SHIMMER, SHIMMER, and MORE SHIMMER!!!!	None. ☺	★★★★★
Layne	Gaultier trench dress, Prada jeweled slides	CONDITION, CONDITION, CONDITION!!! No scrunchies. No headbands. No barrettes. No nuh-thing.	Anything but Hello Kitty. Seriously. Anything.	Hasn't worn nice clothes in her entire life. What if she has an allergic reaction to expensive fabric? Solution: Philosophy Amazing Grace body butter. Will keep her skin smooth and rash free.	★★★★

MAC GIRL	RUNWAY OUTFIT	HAIR	MAKEUP	ISSUES/ CONCERNS	RUNWAY READY?
Lilah	Nanette Lepore teal sequin georgette minidress (color will look ah-mazing with her matching eyes!), Jimmy Choo T-strap sandals	Ojon deep condition; shine spray. (Think Selma Blair.)	Keep it neutral.	Haven't seen her in heels or a dress. Ever. What if she trips? Solution: Keep the heels low and hope for the best.	★★★★
Jasmin	Ralph Lauren Collection silk jersey halter dress, Zanotti jeweled thongs	Messy, sexy beach hair. (Think Rachel Bilson.)	Beachy bronze goddess (Bobbi Brown Bronze Shimmer Brick, MAC Lustreglass in Instant Gold.)	Claire thinks she looks familiar! ☹ Could make the Tampax commercial connection and blow MAC girls' cover. Solution: Keep Jasmin away from tampons and Claire.	★★★
Kaitlyn	Stella McCartney black silk bow-sleeve dress, vintage black Louboutin pumps	Sleek bob (Think Katie Holmes, only less mannish.)	Smoky eyes, neutral lip.	She's super tall. What if Chris Abeley only has short friends? If worse comes to worst, put her in flats.	★★★★
Cassidy	Kendra's vintage Chanel goddess dress (the one that looks like a muumuu). Not the cutest, but somebody's got to wear it!	If Jakkob has time.	Ditto.	Always looking for quote-unquote "motivation." What if she loses it halfway down the runway and doesn't finish her walk? Remind her preshow that her "motivation" is $$$$$.	★★★
Bean	Burberry plaid wool sweater.	Oscar Blandi Jasmine Shine Spray for a shimmering coat	A natural beauty!	She will steal the show. ☺	★★★★★

Massie felt better staring at the neat, organized columns in her Glam Plan spreadsheet. But then she felt a rush of panic again, remembering what she was still missing. Boys. What good were glammed-up girls if she couldn't provide cute boys to escort them down the runway?

Frantically, she speed-dialed Layne. The call went straight to voice mail.

Chucking the phone onto her bed, Massie collapsed onto her duvet, every muscle in her body tensed. Had she not told Layne to be available by cell 24/7, especially in the few days before the party? The ex–Pretty Committee *never* would have slacked off in the most crucial pre-party hours like this.

Sensing her stress, Bean scampered onto her bed and settled next to her. But not even the soothing scent of her soy candle or the scratchy warmth of Bean's tiny tongue could calm her.

Calm was nawt an option when her reputation was on the line.

Even after a Philosophy fudge cake–scented bubble bath, two Laura Mercier milk scrubs, and an extra-thick layer of Sephora coconut cream body butter, the stress of the afternoon's meeting still hadn't melted away. Alicia lay in the center of her bed, staring up at the ceiling and wondering how party planning could possibly be this stressful. It was the opposite of fun.

Massie had always emphasized the importance of organization when it came to event prep. And Alicia had tried to organize. In fact, she'd tried so hard that she'd gone through six stacks of pink Post-it notes and two pens. But somehow, all she'd ended up with was a pink-papered room, ink-stained hands, and no real game plan. She reached down and plucked four pink Post-its from her coconut-slicked thigh, slapping them on the wall next to her bed.

RED-CARPET PARTY MENU
Appetizer: Posh Spice-y Tuna Rolls
Main Course: Mini Corbin Bleu Cheese Burgers
Dessert: Vanilla Milk-Jakes w/ Reese's Pieces
Halle Berries w/ Crème Fraîche
Demi S'Moores
German chocolate Justin Timber-cake

PARTY PLAYLIST

"Paparazzi" (Lady Gaga)
"Hollywood" (Jonas Brothers)
"Picture Perfect" (Nelly Furtado)
"Smile" (Lily Allen)
"La La Land" (Demi Lovato)

CELEB CONVERSATION TOPICS

Which (celeb) would you rather (lip-kiss)?
Examples: Chace Crawford or Chuck Bass
          Kellan Lutz or Channing Tatum
          Selena Gomez or Miley Cyrus
          Emma Roberts or Taylor Swift

CELEB GOSSIP

Examples: Is Tony leaving Jess because she's gotten too fat?
          Brad & Angie: How many kids is too many?
          Paris: How many BFFs could one girl possibly need?
          Is guyliner EVER acceptable for the red carpet?

PARTY GAMES

Pin the tail on Ashlee Simpson's nose (the old one).
Red-carpet looks: Who wore it better?
    (Note: Get pics from Us Weekly.)
Red-carpet costume contest
    (Note: Figure out what A and J are wearing!!!!!!)

NOTHING MASSIE BLOCK-RELATED!!!!!!!!!!!!!!!!!!!!!!!!!!!!!!!!

Staring at the Post-its on her wall, Alicia felt her stress level starting to rise again. Somehow, writing down all the things she needed to do to get ready for Friday night was making her more anxious—not less. How was she supposed to get everything done in time, plus make Claire's house party acceptable, *plus* look rested and beautiful for Josh? One girl couldn't possibly be expected to pull all this off, could she?

Exhausted, Alicia reached for her Sleeping Diva silk sleep mask. She already knew the answer to that question. *One* girl she knew could have pulled this party off. But that girl wasn't Alicia Rivera.

That girl was Massie Block.

It looked like an actual circus had rolled into Westchester that morning and parked in the backyard between the Block estate and the guesthouse. Lighting engineers, fashion show producers, and a few of Layne's theater techie friends were hauling spotlights and yelling into wireless headsets as they rushed up and down the clear plastic runway that topped the Blocks' swimming pool. Performers in aqua unitards walked invisible tightropes overhead. Thanks to Massie's expired purple streak, she hadn't been able to get Cirque du Soleil performers. Instead, she'd had to settle for the less popular Cirque d'Olé!, a local Spanish troupe.

Massie headed for the white silk wardrobe tent that was connected to the catwalk with a long, white silk–covered carpet. She ducked past a herd of tuxedoed caterers carrying giant silver trays of sushi. Since the runway stretched over the pool, she'd decided at the last minute to lend an aquatic, underwater feel to the circus theme.

When she reached the opening of the tent, she paused to check her watch. Three point five hours until showtime. Thank Gawd Kendra had let her take a bad sushi day. There was no way she could have gotten everything done if she'd actually had to go to school. She lifted the tent flap and ducked inside.

The MAC girls, dressed in lavender tracksuits with *Mac* scripted across the shoulders in metallic silver, were rolling over-stuffed wardrobe racks into the tent while Inez steamed wrinkles from the silk flaps with an industrial-size steamer. Meanwhile, Jakkob's entire staff was frantically unpacking trunks of hair spray, flatirons, and giant rollers while the makeup artists tee-tered in heels across the grassy tent floor, dragging bulging suit-cases in their wake. Even though the tent was overflowing with people, some were obviously missing.

Boys.

The band.

"LAYNE!" she screeched.

"Huh?" She appeared from behind a rolling wardrobe rack. "What's up?" She adjusted the headset she'd been wearing for the past two hours.

Massie crossed her arms over her chest. "I gave you *two* jobs. Boys and a band. Where *are* they?"

"Would you relax?" Layne checked herself out in one of the four makeup mirrors Massie had moved from the MAC actor trailer to the center of the wardrobe tent. Bean was sit-ting in the next chair over, getting a blowout. "I told you I'd take care of it, and I did. Trust me."

Just then, Kendra popped her head through the tent flap. "Where are the male models?" she asked, texting frantically on her BlackBerry. "They were supposed to be in hair and makeup an hour ago."

Massie glared at Layne, jerking her thumb in the LBR's direction. "Ask her."

"They'll be here," Layne repeated. But she was starting to look a little worried.

"If the boys aren't here in twenty minutes, we'll have to cancel the show," Kendra said, still speed-texting. "And if the entertainment isn't here in thirty, we'll have to default to the original entertainment plan.

Massie's eyes widened in horror. "You wouldn't."

Kendra nodded gravely. "I still have that Irish dancing troupe booked. . . ." Her BlackBerry buzzed and she pressed it to her ear, ducking back out of the tent.

"They'll be here," Layne repeated, reaching for a tube of magenta glitter liner on the shelf beneath her mirror.

Massie glared at Layne and swiped the liner. Tonight, glitter was strictly off-limits. She stuffed the tube in her pocket.

Layne got the hint. Defeat-sighing, she slid from her chair. "Lemme call and check their ETA." Without waiting for an answer, she whipped out her cell and headed for the tent exit.

Massie needed some air. She grabbed a bottle of Chanel No. 19 off a nearby makeup table, spritzed a cloud in front of her, and spun around in it. *Ahhhhh.* When she opened her eyes, she was face-to-face with Lilah, Kaitlyn, Jasmin, and Cassidy, who were carrying swaying stacks of press packets and fashion show programs. Kaitlyn stumbled over her heels, and papers went flying in all directions, littering the tent floor.

"Oops," Kaitlyn shouted over the commotion. She knelt to pick them up.

"It's okay. You can leave it," Massie said, forcing a smile. She didn't want to stress the models out before the show, and it was time to test-drive the catwalk. Besides, staying trapped in an airless tent while Inez pumped the place full of wrinkle-releasing humidity would frizz her ends.

"You're sure?" Kaitlyn glanced up, crinkling her nose in uncertainty.

"Pos," Massie assured her. "You girls ready to try out your runway?"

The girls nodded, their heads bobbing excitedly.

"Okay, then. Let's go." Massie made a beeline for the tent exit, not caring who or what was in her way. "Come on, Bean," she called to her puppy, who leaped from the makeup chair to follow her. She strode past racks of clothing, stacks of chairs, and an acrobat getting body-painted to look like a mermaid. Ducking through the silk tent flaps, she hurried along the narrow covered walkway that led to the runway.

"This is the only run-through," she called to the line of girls sprint-walking behind her. "So let's make it count." It felt so good to have four beautiful—but not more beautiful than her—girls walking behind her, watching her every move. They were just as excited about walking the runway as she was. Despite all the chaos, she and the MAC girls were in sync—

"Hey, Massie," Jasmin chirped behind her. "Do you want to be president?"

"What?" Massie asked, confused. "No."

"Then why are you running?" Jasmin finished.

The MAC girls cracked up behind her. Even Massie had to smile a little at the wannabe comeback. It wasn't the best, but wasn't imitation the sincerest form of flattery? She relaxed slightly, slowing down. Bean slowed, too.

"Uh, Massie?" Lilah droned behind Jasmin. "It's way past time for our break."

Massie whirled around. "But this is the only time we can practice."

Jasmin crossed her arms over her chest. "But this is the only time we can have a break."

"Yeah, it's kind of a legal thing," Kaitlyn reminded Massie.

Massie's palms were starting to sweat, and she wiped them on the legs of her tracksuit. "A real friend wouldn't want to split at a time like this. A real friend would do anything to make sure the show was perfect." She stared down the line of girls in front of her. Bean lifted her tiny pug nose, staring down at the girls, too.

"Reality check. I'm an eend—employee friend," Lilah shot back, stabbing Massie in the heart with her words. "And you're my bend, remember?"

"Remind me," Massie said slowly. "Are you or are you not getting paid to be my friend?"

"Absolutely," Cassidy piped up, tucking her short, newly dyed platinum locks behind her ear. Even she'd had to admit the dye job was inspired.

"Then act like it!" Massie thundered, whirling back around and finishing her walk.

If this was nothing but a job to these girls, then fine. She'd treat them like employees, and nothing else. As long as they did their jobs and made the Soul-M8s jealous, she'd keep them on the payroll.

When she reached the end of the walkway, she sidestepped an electrician and reglossed for the tenth time in fifteen minutes. She'd been stress-biting her bottom lip all afternoon, which meant she would probably vom Chocolate Biscotti Glossip Girl if she didn't stop.

Taking a seat next to the runway, Massie surveyed the progress of the backyard. Order was slowing emerging out of the chaos, like an unfinished Michelangelo sculpture. Rows of clear Lucite chairs filled with blue water, sand, and glow-in-the-dark fish were arranged on either side of the catwalk, echoing the neon coral reef, fish, and tiny sea horses that swam under the runway in the Blocks' pool. Tuxedo-clad security guards were securing the perimeter, and across the lawn Massie could see Alicia and Claire inside the guesthouse. Their faces were strained with effort as they blew up gold star-shaped balloons.

"If we're not getting our break, can you at least count us off?" Lilah sighed. Massie ignored her.

Claire's balloon escaped from her lips, whizzing across the room. Both girls collapsed against the doors, their bodies shaking with laugher. Massie's shoulders slumped as she watched. That used to be *her* there. Laughing and joking with her BFFs in the hours before one of their parties. Now she was stuck on the outside, dragging around a bunch of whiny actors who needed pee breaks more often than Bean. Alicia and Claire stopped laughing, and when they caught their breath, Massie caught Alicia's eye. She was staring directly at her.

"Massie." Lilah said again, louder this time.

"Fine," she said, feeling Alicia's eyes boring into her, even from hundreds of feet away. Massie stood up and plastered a runway-ready smile on her face.

"Ah-five, and six, and sev-en, eight!" On the beat, she launched into a perfect runway walk, leading her girls and Bean toward the end of the pool. Cool night air tossed her locks as she relaxed into the moment.

"Don't forget to smile," Kendra called from the lawn at the end of the runway.

Rolling her eyes, Massie pivoted and then grin-walked back to the tent with the confidence of an alpha who knew exactly who she was and where she was going. Nothing could get in her way. No one could distract her. Not even Alic—

"Hey!"

Massie skidded to a stop at the sight of a boy in vintage wash AG jeans, and an intentionally wrinkled white collared shirt, standing at the beginning of the runway. He had Adrian Grenier's messy black waves, Chace Crawford's penetrating light blue eyes, and Zac Efron's relaxed swagger. Not to mention Massie Block's full attention. Four more guys were crowded around him.

In one swift movement, she lifted her right hand. The MACs came to a screeching halt behind her. The hollow sound of Bean's tiny toenails against the plastic runway ceased.

"Can I hump you?" asked Cassidy with a mischievous giggle. "I mean, *help* you?"

Massie couldn't help cracking up. A split second later, so did the boys. When the boy in front of her laughed, a single dimple appeared on the right side of his cheek.

The laughter faded but the dimple on his cheek remained, sending love waves through Massie's body.

"I'm looking for May-see Block," the guy finally said.

"Here." She raised her hand, too struck to correct his mispronunciation. The boy was so hawt, she could practically feel the gloss melting off her lips.

"Landon! Finally!" Layne was galloping alongside the runway toward the boy.

"Laynie!" He raised his palm to greet her.

Landon? Laynie? Had the freak finally done something right?

"Would you excuse me for a sec?" Massie said, flirt-batting her lashes at Landon.

"Sure." He shrugged.

Massie jumped off the runway, gripped Layne's arm, and dragged her out of earshot. "Ehmagawd, where did you get him?" she whisper-shouted.

Unfazed, Layne checked her clipboard. "He goes to ADD. I know you have public school issues, but the public boys tend to be more available than the privates, and with such short notice I—"

"So . . . they know Chris?" Massie asked.

"Yup." Layne removed her lensless glasses and breathe-cleaned the empty frames. "Prrrretty much."

"What grade, again?"

"Ninth."

Massie paused, her amber eyes darting while she processed the new information.

"Layne," she finally said. "Are you a hammer?"

"No." Layne tilted her head in a "what did I do *now*" kind of way. "Why?"

"Because you *nailed* it!"

Layne released a beef jerky–scented sigh of relief. "Told ya I would."

Massie longed for the Chanel No. 19 in the tent. She wanted to spray him and claim him right there and then. On a stage. In public. So there would be no question as to whom he belonged to. But all she had in her pocket was a half-used tube of Chocolate Biscotti Glossip Girl, the thought of which gave her an instant stomachache. She dragged Layne back to the runway.

"Sorry 'bout that," she said sweetly to Landon, trying hard not to stare. "Where were we?"

"Uh, I guess we were doing introductions." Landon stepped to the side, revealing his entourage. "This is Miles—"

"Hey." A shaggy blonde in track pants and a gray hoodie stepped forward.

"Ace—"

"What's up?" An olive-skinned hottie in cargos and a vintage Prince T-shirt nodded.

"And Scott," Landon finished.

"Call me Re-Quest," Scott grinned, waving his iTouch.

"I'm DJing." In dark wash jeans and a faded T-shirt that read I TOUCH, U FEEL, he definitely looked the part.

"Hey." Massie smile-nodded at the group. Something poked her in the back.

"Ach-HEM!" Cassidy cough-reminded her.

"Oh. Right. Meet the girls of Massie and Crew." Massie didn't bother moving out of the way.

"Heyyyyyyyyy," Kaitlyn cooed behind her.

"'Sup," Tampax Sport said.

"A-lo-ha," Lilah intoned.

Bean speed-rushed Landon, running circles around him and yipping her approval. Massie couldn't blame her.

"And this is Bean," she said, taking advantage of the fact that Landon was focusing on the puppy. That meant she was free to focus on his hair. How did he get it that shiny?

"I have a pug too." Landon knelt down to scratch Bean's head. "My boy puppy looks just like him."

Bean stiffened at being mistaken for a boy. But Massie didn't correct Landon.

"Really?" she grinned, kneeling too so she could smell Landon's cologne. It was spicy and woodsy. CK Eternity Summer, if she had to guess.

"Yup." Landon nodded. "His name's Bark Obama." He glanced into Massie's eyes, grinned, then looked away.

Bark Obama? Massie felt faint. Cute, good cologne, an animal lover, and smart? Was Landon too good to be true?

"Oh-kay. Introductions. Check." Layne announced, ruining the moment. She checked her clipboard for the billionth time and hit Landon with it. "I told you to be here half an hour ago."

"Sorry." Landon shrugged, sneaking another glance at Massie. She tried not to notice. The last time a guy looked at her like that, he'd ended up falling for Kristen.

"We came straight from practice. Coach kept us late," said Re-Quest.

Massie felt her chest collapse with disappointment. *Puh-lease, Gawd, not soccer again!*

"Oh, really? What do you play?" Massie managed with fake pep.

"Lacrosse." Landon shrugged like it was no big deal.

Massie's spirits nosedived. What was it with cute boys and sports? Couldn't they shop out their aggression like everyone else? As cute as Landon was, Massie wasn't sure she could spend another season on a cold bleacher pretending to care. Faking interest was for listening to people's dreams. Nawt sports. Nawt anymore.

"But I'm done for the season." Landon tapped his left shoulder and sighed. "Delt injury."

"Thank Gawd," Massie accidentally said aloud.

"Huh?" Landon squinted, like maybe he hadn't heard her properly.

"I mean, thank Gawd you stopped playing," she managed. "Too many athletes ignore their injuries and then they're done for life." A wisp of brown hair blew toward her face, tickling the side of her cheek. "So whaddaya think? You done for life?"

"Maybe." Landon half smiled, like maybe they weren't talking about lacrosse anymore.

Massie half smiled back. "Cool."

"Light check!" one of the engineers yelled.

Massie and Landon were suddenly bathed in the heavenly glow of twelve different spotlights.

The universe approved.

Layne checked her large-face Nike digital watch, which looked more like a microwave than a timepiece. "Curtain goes up in an hour," she announced. "Time to get fitted for—"

Massie clapped twice. "Everyone to the tent for H&M." She didn't need Landon thinking Layne was in charge.

"Are you kidding?" Lilah planted one hand on her jutted hip. "I thought the clothes were designer."

Massie rolled her eyes. "H&M is—"

"Hair and makeup," Landon offered. Then blush-shrugged. "My mom works in fashion."

"No way!" Massie smacked his shoulder. "That's awesome."

"Ahhhhhhhhh." Landon gripped his injured delt while the lacrosse boys winced on his behalf.

"Ehmagawd, I'm so sorry." Her hovercrafts instantly powered down. Who was she kidding, thinking she was ready for another crush? Losing Dempsey to Kristen had left her feeling like a teddy bear without stuffing. Was it too soon to love again?

Crush deactivated. Starting now.

But he was too cute! On one hand, she couldn't live the rest of her life afraid of true love. On the other hand, she'd sworn to herself that she'd never let another boy humiliate her like Chris Abeley, Derrington, and Dempsey Solomon had. So now what?

"You guys have an appointment with Jakkob." Massie smiled, getting back to business. Her heart would have to wait. "Girls, can you show them to the wardrobe tent?"

The MAC girls giggle-nodded, and Shaggy, Prince, and Re-Quest followed them down the runway toward the giant white tent. Landon stayed behind, digging his sneaker into the runway.

"Um . . . aren't you going into makeup?" Massie asked, pressing her hands against her hips. "Nawt that you need it or anything." No! Wait! She was coming on too strong. Start over. "But I mean, everybody else is getting it, so you prah-bly should too." No matter how hard she tried, she couldn't sound crush free. She pinched her left hip, reminding herself that hawt boys were like Chanel's stiletto lace-up gladiators: breathtaking, but painful to get wrapped up in.

"Thought maybe you could show me. I get lost pretty easy." Landon grinned, his dimple reaching canyon-deep proportions.

Massie's throat tightened. She looked at Layne, who was too busy flipping through her "to do's" to notice the magic happening right in front of her.

"Can't," Massie choked out the necessary words. "I have to supervise Layne."

"Heard that," Layne muttered, scribbling something on her clipboard.

Landon's dimple disappeared when the smile slipped from his lips.

"But give me your number and I'll text you when I'm ready to walk," she added quickly, crushed by the dimple's sudden departure. She reached for her phone and handed it to him.

"Cool." Landon smile-programmed his number into Massie's cell, then hurried to catch up with his friends in the wardrobe tent. "See ya, May-see," he called over his good shoulder.

It didn't even matter that he'd mispronounced her name. When Landon said "May-see," it just sounded right. If she had to change it legally, so be it.

Massie victory-glossed. Twice.

Still an hour left to showtime, and everything was falling into place. With one exception. The people she wanted to gossip about Landon with were inside the guesthouse. And from the way they were laughing without her, she knew they couldn't have cared less.

CURRENT STATE OF THE UNION

IN	OUT
ADD	OCD
Injured delts	Broken hearts
Crushing	Crushed

A blinding flash of light exploded in Alicia's face as she stepped nervously into guesthouse living room. She screamed and blinked away the stars that swam in front of her eyes.

"Say cheeeeese!" Todd, Claire's younger brother, sang in a British accent as Alicia regained her sight.

"Todd!" she screeched. "You almost blinded me!"

"That's the price of celebrity, baby." Todd shrugged, lifting a giant camera on a strap from around his neck. He was wearing too-short jeans that showcased his dingy white socks, a white T-shirt, and a leather jacket. A wool skullcap was pulled tight over his head, and dark sunglasses shaded his eyes.

"What's that thing on your face?" Claire called from the couch where she, Dylan, and Kristen were sitting stiffly in their formal gowns. The other girls had gotten to the party early to put a few last-minute touches on the decorations.

"Yeah, what *is* that?" Kristen squinted at the black scribble of eyeliner that ran from Todd's lower lip to his chin.

"It's a goatee." Todd looked offended. "Alicia said to dress up like the paparazzi, so I'm dressed like Adnan Ghalib."

Alicia rolled her eyes in disgust, temporarily forgetting her pre-party nerves. She'd paid Todd and his best friend a

205

hundred dollars to play the part of paparazzi for the party. "You mean that dirtbag Britney's dating?"

"Used to date," Todd corrected her. "They're not together anymore. Not since the lawsu—" He realized his mistake too late. "There was nothing good on ESPN, so I switched to E!" he muttered.

"Busted." Kristen laughed.

Just then, Todd's best friend, Tiny Nathan, came through the doorway. He wore a teased brunette wig and Claire's mom's long black satin bathrobe and heels. Todd doubled over, collapsing on the sofa next to the girls.

"Ehmagawd!" Kristen laughed until she cried. Alicia's cheeks hurt from smiling.

"And this," Todd gasped, "is Maria Menounos. She'll be doing the red-carpet interviews when the boys get here."

"This sucks," Tiny Nathan announced.

"You lost the coin toss fair and square." Todd snorted. "Say it."

Tiny Nathan dutifully pulled a cordless mic from the pocket of the robe. "I'm Maria, and you're watching *Entertainment Tonight,*" he muttered.

While Todd and the girls cracked up all over again, Alicia smoothed the shimmering champagne-colored evening gown she'd ordered from Barneys. She knew she looked ah-mazing. But still, she'd never felt this nervous before a party in her entire life. Maybe that was because Massie was usually the one who took care of the details.

"Your hair looks great, Leesh," Dylan called, patting her

own hair, which had been flatironed and hung just past her boobs. She was wearing a strapless black gown she'd borrowed from the wardrobe department of *The Daily Grind*, her mom's popular talk show.

"Love the earrings," Kristen added, crossing her magenta chiffon–covered legs.

"Thanks," Alicia said, trying to calm the nerves that were vibrating through her body at top speed. Her hair had been swept back in a loose, elegant chignon, and her mom had let her borrow a stunning pair of diamond chandelier earrings. The jewels pulled her earlobes, but knowing how hot she looked made the suffering worth it.

Diiiiiiiiiing-dong.

The guesthouse doorbell jolted Alicia back to reality.

"Ehmagawd, the boys are here!" Dylan squealed. Kristen and Claire jumped up, smoothing their dresses.

"Todd!" Alicia yelled, even though he was standing inches away.

"What?" he yelled back.

"Door!" Knowing Josh was only a few yards away made her even more nervous than she'd been just a few seconds ago.

"Right!" Todd grabbed his camera and scampered toward the front hall. Tiny Nathan lifted the hem of his black silk robe and click-clacked after Todd.

As quickly as possible in her skintight, floor-length gown, Alicia shuffle-waddled toward the dining room.

"Let's go," she whisper-hissed to the girls. "We don't want them to think we've been waiting."

"Right," the girls whispered back, teetering behind her in their bejeweled high heels.

When Alicia had arrived at Claire's yesterday after school, the Crate and Barrel white-and-blue dining room hadn't looked like much. But she had single-handedly transformed the space from tired to inspired. The white table had been polished and dusted with Dior Night Diamond finishing powder to give it extra sheen. Glowing vanilla-scented pillar candles of varying sizes composed the centerpiece, and star-shaped balloons littered the floor and hung from the lights. The flea market oil painting of a winter lake that hung behind the head of the table had been draped in one of Alicia's mom's shimmering gold scarves. And the crystal stemware, ivory and gold china, and sterling silver at each place setting had been buffed and polished to perfection. The room screamed elegance and class. And that was exactly what Alicia was going for. So why did she still feel nervous?

"I bet the boys'll look beyond cute in their tuxes," Kristen said, straightening a place card that didn't need to be straightened.

"I know," Claire giggle-agreed, tugging anxiously at the oversize canary yellow gown she'd had to borrow from Dylan. "It's a good thing we're all dressed up, too, in case we want to head over to Massie's later."

Alicia's head whipped toward Claire. But before she had a chance to ask her what *that* was supposed to mean, Derrington barreled through the door. He was dressed in jeans, a hoodie, and sneakers.

Alicia gripped the back of one of the dining room chairs, her nails digging into the antique wood, praying she was having a hunger-induced hallucination. Why wasn't Derrington wearing a tux? She'd texted Josh to tell the boys the dress code was red-carpet chic. So what had happened?

Dylan's glossed lips parted in shock. "What're you *wearing*?" she asked, wrinkling her nose at his jeans and rumpled blue button-down.

"Why's everybody on my case?" Derrington looked confused. "That weird little girl with the mic just asked me the same thing."

Alicia finally recovered from her initial shock. "You were supposed to dress for the red carpet," she snapped.

Dylan flushed. "Ehmagawd, Leesh, I'm so sorry," she whispered.

"I did dress for the red carpet!" Derrington protested. "Not everybody dresses up in a tux."

"Yes, they do!" Alicia huffed, crossing her arms over her B-cups.

"The Jonas Brothers don't!" Derrington said earnestly.

Just then, Dempsey, Cam, and Josh hurried through the door, Todd snapping shot after shot behind them.

"Who are you weeaaaaaring?" Tiny Nathan squealed from the living room.

"Would you lay off for a second, buddy?" Cam squinted, shielding his eyes from Todd's camera.

The girls stood speechless as the guys crowded into the

dining room. Cam and Dempsey were dressed in jeans too. Josh was the only guy wearing a tux.

"I can't believe you guys didn't have to dress up," Josh said. He shook off his jacket, balled it up, and launched it across the table.

Alicia's throat tightened. *Didn't have to?* Josh should *want* to dress up with her, just like he should *want* to watch her try on clothes at the mall. Anger churned in her empty stomach. In under five seconds, the boys (minus Josh, sort of) had ruined the elegant atmosphere she'd slaved for hours to create. Glancing at Kristen, Dylan, and Claire, she knew they felt exactly the same way.

"Goooooaaaaaaaalllll!" Josh's yell made the stemware on the table shake. He was cheering for Dempsey, who had folded one of the place cards into a paper football and was shooting it across the table.

"Maybe everybody should sit?" she said tersely, slipping into her chair at the head of the table. Josh sat at the other end, disappearing behind the centerpiece. Alicia was suddenly aware of her throbbing earlobes. How much longer they could possibly last under the pressure? How had Massie always played the part of hostess so incredibly coolly?

"So!" She took a deep breath, putting her ex-friend out of her mind, and forced herself to smile brightly. A Lily Allen song came on over the loudspeaker, and Alicia rang the tiny bell next to her dinner plate. "I have a little game for us to play. It's called: Which celeb would you rather lip-kiss?"

"Love it!" Dylan proclaimed.

"Wait for it. . . ." Derrington and Josh were holding a balloon over the candle centerpiece, lowering it closer and closer to the wavering flames.

POP!

"Niiiiiiiiiiiccce!" the guys cheered.

Kristen, Dylan, and Claire giggled, then stopped when they saw Alicia's face.

Alicia reached for her water goblet and chugged every last cooling drop to force back the flurry of angry reprimands creeping up her throat. "First question," she said. "This one's for the girls. Which celeb would you rather lip-kiss? Robert Pattinson, or—"

Suddenly, the opening beat of Britney's "Circus" blasted from outside. The boys whip-turned toward the window.

"The fashion show!" Claire squealed, jumping from her seat.

Dylan and Kristen fidgeted with their silverware, pretending they didn't care about what was going on outside. But Alicia could see Dylan unconsciously bobbing her head to the beat.

Giant white spotlights swung across the Blocks' lawn, temporarily blinding Alicia as they dipped past the guesthouse dining room.

"There's only two types of people in the world.
The ones that entertain, and the ones that observe.
Well, baby, I'm a put-on-a-show kind of girl.
Don't like the backseat, gotta be first."

"Here come the models!" Claire said excitedly.

That was enough for Dylan and Kristen to spring out of their seats and head for the window.

"ROBERT PATTINSON OR PENN BADGLEY?" Alicia shouted over the sound of Britney. But no one was listening.

The boys stampeded toward the window.

"Whoa." Derrington's jaw dropped as he stared out the window. "Isn't that Eli Manning, the Giants' quarterback?"

"Where?" Cam and Josh shoved for spots at the window.

"In the audience. I swear it's him."

Alicia twisted the gold silk napkin in her lap. *Think. What would Massie do to get everybody back?* But she already knew the answer: Massie wouldn't have lost control like this in the first place. *Stop thinking about Massie,* she reprimanded herself. *YOU are the alpha of this clique. YOU are the girl everybody looks up to now.* But no one was looking at her now. She reached for the bell and rang it nonstop until Todd appeared in the doorway.

"Appetizers!" Todd announced. He and Tiny Nathan carried heavy sterling trays filled with hand-rolled sushi.

Alicia nodded at Tiny Nathan.

"PoshSpice–ytunarollswithwasabi," Tiny Nathan squeaked, blushing as he lowered his tray to the table.

"Be right back with the main course," Todd said.

But no one moved from their post at the window.

"Are those *ninth*-grade boys?" Kristen asked, standing on tiptoe.

"Is that dress from Hervé Léger's new spring line?" Dylan sounded awestruck.

Claire tugged at her strapless gown and clamped her arms at her sides to keep them in place. "We should go check it out," she suggested, turning around.

"Kuh-laire, we haven't even had appetizers yet," Alicia snapped, picking at a sushi roll on the platter in front of her.

"But it's for a good cause . . ." Claire protested, fixing her gaze on Dempsey.

Josh and the boys turned around too, looking like little kids standing outside FAO Schwarz. Josh's big brown eyes begged her to let him go.

Suddenly, Alicia wanted them to leave, so she could go home, change into her silk pajamas, and sob herself to sleep. But she couldn't let them know how upset she was. And she definitely couldn't let her crush go to Massie's party and have more fun than he'd had at hers. She'd just have to go with him.

Alicia faked a smile so giant, it made her face throb. "I guess Todd and Tiny Nathan can serve the main course when we get back."

"Great!" Claire didn't even bother to look at her as she charged to the front door.

"Awesome." Josh grinned.

Alicia was too upset to notice that his smile looked especially bright in the glow of candlelight. For a second she stared up at the ceiling, blinking back tears. Massie had come out on top. Again. Why had she even bothered? Maybe Alicia should have stuck with what she knew best: being a beta.

She shuffled toward the door, where her friends were eagerly filing outside.

"Watch the plate!" she heard Todd yell from the kitchen. "I don't—"

The sound of glass shattering exploded. After a split second of silence, Todd and Tiny Nathan burst out laughing.

Alicia closed her eyes, knowing exactly how the plate felt.

Crushed into a million pieces.

Two minutes later, Claire and her friends were making their way across the yard. She could tell Alicia was beyond mad by the way she was smiling that toothy smile. When Alicia was angry, she pouted. And when she was really, really mad, she oversmiled. Claire had only seen her furious hypergrin once: last year, when Skye Hamilton had beat her out for the big solo at a Body Alive dance recital.

And this smile was ten times bigger.

But right now, Claire couldn't care less that Alicia was grinning like an idiot. She could patch things up with her later. Right now, all she cared about was getting the Pretty Committee back together. And she was so close.

In fact, she was closer than close. Just a few feet away, actually. Inches from where the Soul-M8s stood was a thick red velvet rope blocking off the Blocks' backyard. And just beyond the velvet rope, the party was in full swing. Hundreds of guests in haute couture filled the seats around the clear plastic over-the-pool runway, and waiters in wet suits weaved in and out of the standing crowd, serving sushi, calamari, and seaweed salad.

"Just so we're clear," Dylan said, fixing her gaze on the runway, "I'm doing this for Hervé. Not Massie."

"Point." Alicia's smile seemed slightly more genuine that time.

"And I'm doing it for Eli," Derrington said.

"Right on." Without looking away from the runway, Dylan lifted her palm, and Derrington smacked it.

Claire followed Dylan's gaze. On the pool-slash-catwalk, the pretty brunette Claire had recognized in the New Café sashayed toward them, dressed in a black silk jersey halter dress and jeweled sandals. Shimmering aqua and teal spotlights swung overhead, making her look like she was walking underwater. On either side of the runway, flashbulbs popped from the front row seats. Claire would have been totally mesmerized by the party's atmosphere if she hadn't been so busy trying to figure out where she'd seen the girl before. Last she checked, Claire didn't know any billionaires. So why did Massie's new IBS BFF look so familiar?

"Guess we have to go around front." She sighed, still staring at the model. *Orlando? Photography class? Candy store?* Nope, nope, and nope.

"Let's just cut through." Cam lifted the rope, in a ladies-first sort of way.

Claire shook her head. "We shouldn't. Let's just walk around."

"It's for charity," Dempsey protested good-naturedly. "Nobody'll care."

"Right?" Kristen nod-agreed, and the couple fist-bumped.

Claire shook her head *no* again. She was already nervous enough about trying to reunite the Pretty Committee, when the only plan she had was to get everybody in the same back-yard and hope for the best. She didn't need to worry about getting in trouble for sneaking in the back way, too.

"'Kay." Cam released the rope. "You're the boss."

"Opposite of true," Alicia muttered under her breath, pursing her glossy lips together.

Claire breathed a tiny sigh of relief. At least the faux smile was gone and the real Alicia was back. The Alicia who wanted to be in charge. But right now, if the Pretty Committee stood any chance of getting back together, it was up to Claire.

"Let's go, guys." Claire gripped the top of her gown to keep it from slipping and led the way around the perimeter of the Blocks' yard. As they neared the front of the house, guests turned and stared. Tired of feeling like a guest in her own home, Claire wanted to shout above the thumping music, "I live here!" But tonight, she couldn't blame them. In their poorly fitting evening wear, jeans, and hoodies, they didn't exactly fit the profile of VIP donors.

A reporter lingering behind the back row turned and snapped their picture.

"Leesh! *Real* paparazzi!" Dylan grinned.

Alicia rolled her eyes. "It's just local."

"I wonder if Eli signs autographs." Josh rolled up the sleeves of his dress shirt and untucked it. He squinted into the seated crowd beyond the rope, looking for the quarterback. "Lost him," he muttered.

Alicia huffed her annoyance.

At the Blocks' front door two men wearing tuxedos with

shimmering aqua bow ties, dark Dior shades, and tiny plastic earpieces stood like statues. The one on the left was holding a clipboard.

"Uh, hey," Claire said nervously, reaching for the door-knob. "'Scuze us."

"Name?" Clipboard stepped in front of the door, his mouth set in a thin, stern line. Claire took a step back.

"Nice shades," Derrington called from the back of the Soul-M8s huddle.

Dylan giggle-shushed him. Derrington giggle-shushed her back.

Clipboard's sidekick looked at them both. He was probably glaring, but the shades made it hard to tell.

"Name?" Clipboard repeated.

Claire took a shaky breath. She felt like she was being called to Principal Burns's office when she hadn't done any-thing wrong. "ClaireLyonsCamFisherDylanMarvilDerrick HerringtonorDerringtoneitheroneKristenGregoryDempsey SolomonandJoshHotz," she exhaled.

"Did you say Claire Lyons?" Clipboard asked.

Claire nodded.

"You're in. The rest of you . . ." He shook his head once to the left, once to the right.

"What?" Claire balked. "Can you check again?" Secretly, she wasn't surprised that Massie had left the others off the list, but she was hoping Clipboard would chalk it up to an oversight and let them all in.

"Don't need to," Clipboard said. "They're not on the list."

"This was a bad idea," Kristen muttered.

"But we're the Ho Ho Homeless?" Dylan tried, mussing her hair so it fell in front of her face. "This whole party is for us."

Claire and Cam couldn't help giggling.

Derrington held out his palm like he was begging for change.

Kristen rubbed her flat belly like she was hungry.

Josh squinted and looked around—mouth agape, expression dazed—like he had never seen a house with a roof before.

Dempsey, who volunteered to feed the homeless over Thanksgiving looked away, slightly amused, but mostly embarrassed.

"How tragic." Sidekick dropped a nickel in Derrington's palm.

"Thank you, seh," Derrington said with an Oliver Twist–inspired accent.

Claire giggled again.

"You're quite welcome." Sidekick's thin lips hinted at a smile. "But you're still not getting in." He opened the door for Claire.

She hesitated, not knowing the right thing to do. Part of her felt giddy that Massie had put her on the guest list. She'd probably never get to go to this kind of event again in her life (at least until the Blocks threw the next one). But leaving her friends and crush behind wouldn't get her any closer to reuniting her old group. Or bonding with her new one.

"Just go," Cam offered, as if he knew exactly what she was trying to do. "We'll go back to the dinner party and—"

"Uhhh, I don't think I can make it all the way back to the guesthouse," Derrington said, leaning against Dylan as if he was too weak to stand. "Haven't eaten in hours."

Dempsey nodded, obviously not wanting to be sentenced to return to the dinner party. "Honestly, that little girl with the mic creeps me out."

Josh laughed out loud. Alicia looked like she couldn't decide whether to join him or shush him.

Suddenly, Claire had an idea.

"'Kay," she told Clipboard. "I'm going in."

He nodded and crossed her off the list.

"Really?" Dylan started. "You're just gonna Tom?"

"What?" Cam jealousy-panicked.

"Cruise," Kristen explained.

Claire power-winked, signaling that she wasn't just cruising, she had a plan.

"What's up with your eye, Lyons?" Derrington snickered. He began imitating her wink but looked more like someone holding a knife in a light socket.

Dylan elbowed him.

"Oww-chh!"

Claire hurried through the door before the party police could change their minds. She kept her head down as she wove past pockets of maki-munching adults. The last thing she wanted was for her parents to see her and waste precious minutes talking to her. She had to get back outside before everyone returned to Alicia's dinner party. Once she got a good look at the backyard setup, she'd find a place for the

Soul-M8s to sneak in. The rest was up to fate.

Slipping through the back doors, she scanned the back-yard. Her eyes landed on the giant white tent across the yard. Red velvet rope surrounded it like a noose. She pulled her cell from her Anya Hindmarch for Target clutch and fired off a text to Dylan and Kristen.

Claire: Evry1 meet behind the white tent.

She hurried behind the rows of fish-filled chairs and made a wide arc around the catwalk, which stretched from the back of the main house into the yard. The crowd was clapping for a platinum blonde with choppy locks strutting down the cat-walk in vintage Dior.

Claire wished she could enjoy the scenery: the body-painted acrobats swinging from jewel-toned ribbons above the runway, the glowing lanterns hanging from the trees, the photographers huddled at the foot of the runway, snapping shots of the models. She paused for a second as a statuesque girl with a short, angled bob, escorted by a cute-in-a-quirky-sort-of-way blond guy, stepped into the spotlight. She was wearing a gorgeous, emerald green silk gown. It looked ex-actly like the one Massie's mom had worn to the Blocks' an-nual Christmas party. For the first time since Kendra and Massie had announced the event, Claire found herself wonder-ing what a homeless person would do with a gown like that. Why not donate food, or warm clothing, or something useful?

The model and her escort paused at the end of the catwalk.

Dylan would have rocked that gown. Plus, she would have had so much fun doing the fashion show. The whole Pretty Committee would have. Claire felt the beginnings of anger gnawing in the pit of her stomach, spurring her toward the tent. This whole fight was ridiculous. The Pretty Committee belonged together. So why was she the only one who seemed to get that?

"I NEED LANDON CRANE FOR A TOUCH-UP, NOW!" a bald guy wearing all black yelled the second Claire lifted the white silk flap and stepped inside the tent. "YOU WALK WITH MASSIE IN THREE!"

Claire jumped back as a pack of brush-wielding makeup artists crisscrossed the tent. All around her, girls were primping in front of makeup mirrors and changing behind giant white screens. Hairdryers were buzzing, flatirons were sizzling, and a massive, ozone-destroying cloud of hair spray made the air inside the tent hazy. It was chaos.

Perfect.

She slipped to the very back of the tent, ducked around a rolling rack of hand-me-down couture, and crouched. Suddenly, a hand clamped down on her shoulder.

Busted.

Claire's heart revved. She whipped around, ready to beg for mercy.

"Oh," she heaved, fanning away the sting of adrenaline. "You scared me."

"Sorry," said a cute, dark-haired guy in a perfectly fitted Armani tux. His untied lavender silk bow tie hung loosely around his neck. "Lose something?"

"Sort of." Claire sighed.

The boy smiled an adorable, one-dimpled grin. "I'm Landon."

"Landon Crane?" Claire smiled back. "The Landon Crane who's on in three?"

"More like one and a half now." Landon said to the screen on his black Samsung. "And you are?" His eyes were a sea blue-green. The colors swirled together, like a perfect storm. Claire had to remind herself that she had a crush who was waiting for her on the other side of the white canvas wall. And he had some pretty great eyes of his own, thank you very much.

"I'm Claire. I live in the Blocks' guesthouse. And I'm kind of trying to sneak the rest of my—" Claire stopped herself. "The rest of *Massie's* friends into the party." She crossed her fingers behind her back. "There was sort of a mix-up with the list and I know she's busy, so I thought I'd—"

"Oh, you know May-see?" Landon's smile deepened.

Claire giggled at his mispronunciation but decided to let it go uncorrected. It was obviously an inside joke they shared. Suddenly, envy nipped her behind the belly. It had taken Claire more than a year to feel comfortable in the Pretty Committee. How had Massie been able to slap together a new group of friends, a fashion show, and a had-to-be-there nickname with a cute-times-ten boy in less than a month?

"So could you, like, keep a lookout, for just a sec?" Claire asked, embarrassed to sound like she'd stepped off the set of a second-rate crime drama.

"Sure." Landon shrugged. "Better than getting my touch-up." He stood up and dragged the clothing rack a little to the left, shielding Claire from view.

Lifting up the bottom edge of the white wall, Claire stuck her head out the other side. "Dylan?" she whisper-yelled. "Kristen?" The thumping beat of the music coming from the runway swallowed her voice.

"Took you long enough," Dylan grumbled from behind the velvet rope that skimmed the back edge of the tent. The rest of the Soul-M8s were huddled behind her.

"Sorry," Claire whispered. She looked straight at Alicia when she said it, but Alicia refused to meet her gaze.

One by one, her friends ducked under the rope and into the tent. When everyone was inside, Claire released the fabric to the ground and stood up.

"Okay," she called over the sound of whining models and shouting makeup artists. "Now all we've gotta do is—"

"Hey, man, what're you doing?" Landon's voice rose over the commotion.

Suddenly, the rack of clothes that protected them was yanked out of the way.

Claire's heart leaped into her throat at the sight of the same two security guards who had manned the front door.

Clipboard hovered over them, pressing his earpiece into his ear. "We've got a code Soul-M8 on the south side of the tent, Massie. Repeat, code Soul-M8."

Through the hair spray haze, Claire spotted Massie on the other side of the tent. She was barking into a headset, but Claire couldn't hear what she was saying.

"Seriously?" Kristen scrunched her nose in disbelief.

"Should've stayed at my dinner party," Alicia sang.

"Copy that." Clipboard was saying. "All right. Miss Block says she wants everybody out."

"Run!" Dylan bellowed, red-rovering straight into the clothes rack. She bounced off the couture and landed on her butt.

Everybody cracked up as the clothes swung back and forth, shaking off the impact.

"At least I tried something," she mumbled.

"Okay, let's go." Clipboard glared down at Claire and Landon. "All of you."

"Me?" Claire's jaw dropped. "But I live here! And I'm on the list!"

"And I'm on in—" Landon checked his Samsung again. "Now!"

"The only thing you're on is my security report," Clipboard barked. "Now follow me."

The Soul-M8s and Landon tromped through the tent, escorted by the security guards. Claire's cheeks burned as everyone turned to stare. Behind her, Dylan, Kristen, and Alicia were cursing Massie to a lifetime of visible pores, static cling, and a few other things she couldn't quite make out. Claire tried to catch Massie's eye on her way out, so she could glance-beg for mercy. But Massie was getting her hair shellacked by Jakkob, and she didn't notice.

"May-see!" Landon called as the guards herded them outside. But Massie still didn't turn.

"I'm supposed to walk with her. I don't want her to have to go out alone." Landon's shoulders slumped as they followed the guards around the spotlit runway and toward the house. "Now what's she gonna do?"

"Beats me." Tears stung Claire's eyes. "This is all my fault," she told Landon. And it was. Her plan had backfired. Now everybody was mad. And the odds of getting the Pretty Committee back together ever again were getting slimmer and slimmer.

Kuh-laire. Kuh-laire.

Scrambling for her phone, Claire felt a glimmer of hope. Maybe Massie had realized she'd made a mistake. Maybe she was ready to make up and move on.

She checked her text.

Massie: told u u can't have both.

Then again, maybe not.

"MASSIE BLOCK! YOU'RE ON IN THIRTY SECONDS!" A voice rose over the frenzied pitch in the tent.

"'Kay," she yelled back, kicking off her Miu Mius and slipping into a pair of rhinestone-encrusted Manolos. She flip-tousled her loose curls, tucked Bean tightly under her arm, and rushed out of the tent.

Bean's tiny heart was fluttering with excitement, and Massie knew exactly how she felt. The idea of seeing Landon for the first time in his tux with the matching lavender silk Armani bow tie made her pulse vibrate faster than her iPhone. She picked up the pace.

"Okay. I'm here." She exhaled once she reached the runway entrance. A stagehand spritzed the left side of her face with Evian facial mist. She turned, and the stagehand spritzed her right. "Where's Landon?" she asked, but no one answered.

"Kaitlyn!" The stage manager yelled over the pulsing music. "Go!"

Kaitlyn and Prince glided onto the runway.

Cassidy, Jasmin, and Lilah took their places behind Massie with their escorts.

"Layne?" the stage manager called.

227

"Not coming," Cassidy clarified. "She ate too much beef jerky. Salt bloat!"

But Layne was the least of Massie's worries. She turned around and caught Lilah's eye.

"Have you seen Landon?" she asked hopefully. She released Bean to the ground, half hoping Bean would suddenly turn into one of those police dogs who could sniff out missing crushes. But Bean just pranced around the girls in circles, loving herself in her lavender silk sheath.

"I've been working for eighteen hours straight and I still haven't had a bathroom break," Lilah snapped. "I'm not seeing much of anything right now."

Massie recoiled at Lilah's tone. The PC had never talked to her like that. Not even when they really had to pee or were busy stealing her crushes.

"Landon?" The stage manager lifted her pierced brow. "Saw him leave a few minutes ago. But you know you're on in—"

Massie didn't hear the rest.

Ehmagawd. She'd been left at the runway.

Landon Crane, her soul m—her crush, had ditched her. Just like Dempsey. And Derrington.

Massie's head was screaming at her heart for being so stupid, and she fought the urge to crumple into a high-couture ball right there on the runway. How could she have believed that Landon was actually different from the others? Being in ninth, knowing a designer, not playing soccer . . . he'd had all the qualities she'd ever wanted in a guy. She should have known he was too good to be true.

She yanked Bean from the floor and tucked her under her bicep.

"IN THREE, TWO, ONE!" The stage manager shoved Massie and Bean into the spotlight, seconds behind Kaitlyn and Prince. "GO!"

On cue, the color-coordinated fireworks Massie had planned exploded overhead, making the acrobats look like they were swinging through showers of blue and gold fire. Massie blinked back tears, gripping Bean tight. She wanted to turn and run. But alphas didn't turn and run. Alphas held their heads high.

She took a shaky step onto the catwalk. Bean licked her hand reassuringly. As she took her second step, the sparkling crowd that stretched in front of her leaped to their feet in applause. Camera flashes blended with the fireworks, making the night sky light up around her. But Massie didn't care about any of it. All she wanted to do was bury her face in Bean's soft, shiny fur and have a good, waterproof-mascara-running-down-your-cheeks, snot-all-over-your-face-but-who-cares, heaving cr—

Crrrraaaaaaaaaaaaaaaaaackkkkkkkkkkkkkkkkkkkkkkkk!

Massie heard the splintering sound of the plastic runway just seconds before Kaitlyn's angled bob dip below her sight line. The crowd let out a collective gasp.

"Ehhhhhhhhhhhhhhhhhhhmagaaaaaaaaaaaaaaaaaaaawd!" Massie screamed, side-leaping to the front row of seats as the other models fell through the cracked runway into the fish-filled pool.

"Ahhhhhhhhhhhhhhhhhhhhhhhhhhhhhhhhhhhhhhhhhhhhh!" the girls shrieked, disappearing beneath the glowing blue surface.

The crowd exploded with a mixture of cheers, cries, and screams. Some of the neighborhood kids rushed the runway, cannonballing into the pool with giant splashes.

"Yeaaaaaah!" The male models paddled through the shards of splintered plastic to high-five each other.

"My hair!" cried Lilah, fingering the neon pink faux-seaweed wig that hung over her eyes.

"My makeup!" Cassidy sobbed, burying her streaked face in her hands.

"My Praaaaaaaaaaaaaadaaaaaaaaaaa!" Kaitlyn screamed, treading water.

The paparazzi pounced. Stampeding around Massie and Bean, reporters loomed over the pool, snapping photos and capturing live footage.

Winkie Porter crouched next to the water while her cameraman counted her down. "Winkie Porter here, with a Channel Five special report: What happens when fashion tanks?"

"There's a sea horse in my braaaaaaaa!" Jasmin yelped when she surfaced, thrashing wildly in the water.

"The big story at eleven." Winkie beamed.

"Aaaand, we're out," the cameraman called.

"Perfect," Winkie said, straightening up. "Call Joe and tell him we've got a lead story. We'll call it 'Capsized Couture.'" She giggled to herself. "Let's get some more B-roll of the backyard." They walked off to interview the soaked guests.

Massie jumped to her feet. She tried to hold on to Bean, but the puppy squirmed from her grip and made a break for the house. Massie didn't blame her. This was a disaster. All around them, stage managers were fishing models out of the pool, and guests were rushing around in a panic. Worst of all, the press was documenting every humiliating second.

Lilah, Jasmin, Kaitlyn, and Cassidy squish-stomped over to her the second they were pulled from the pool. Their ruined couture was painted to their sopping wet bodies. Bits of glow-in-the-dark coral stuck to their hair.

"Massie?" Jasmin snapped. "We have something to tell you."

"Yeah!" Cassidy yelled. "You ruined my makeup!"

Jasmin looked confused. "No. The other thing," she side-whispered.

Massie opened her mouth. Before she could respond, the girls took a collective breath.

"WE QUIT!" they yelled in union.

Massie balked. "You can't quit!" she hissed, crossing her arms tightly over her chest. If the MAC girls quit, she'd be friendless. The thought made her feel like she'd been dunked in a giant vat of ice water. Even though *she* hadn't. "You haven't finished the job!"

"Oh, yeah, we have," Lilah snapped. "And if you'll excuse us, we're going to the bathroom. Because we can!" She and Kaitlyn high-fived, then turned around and linked arms with the ninth-grade boys.

Massie took a shaky breath as they disappeared into the

crowd. "Fine!" she yelled. Goose bumps covered her arms and legs. But nobody was there to notice. Not even Bean. "YOU'RE FIRED!" she screamed at their retreating backs.

"LADIES AND GENTLEMEN!" The music from the DJ booth screeched to a halt, and Kendra's embarrassed voice came over the mic. "We're so sorry for the inconvenience, but due to . . . technical . . . difficulties, Ho Ho Homeless will be winding up early. Please feel free to take a gift bag with you on your way out. There are some fabulous goodies in there that we just know you'll love!" She laughed a little too loudly.

Even though she and Kendra were on opposite sides of the yard, with hundreds of people, a broken runway, and a pool between them, Massie could feel her mom's embarrassment.

"Massie Block?" Winkie tapped Massie on the shoulder. "As hostess of this charity event, the tragic end to the night must come as quite a shock." She flashed a megawatt smile.

Massie squinted into the bright light Winkie's cameraman was shining into her eyes, wanting nothing more than to strangle Winkie with her own mic cord.

"Tell us how this will affect Westchester's homeless," Winkie cooed victoriously, shoving the mic in Massie's face.

Massie stared tight-lipped into the camera. It wasn't the homeless she was worried about.

After a social disaster like this, it would be almost impossible to make a comeback. Which meant that Massie Block was just like her botched event.

Over.

CURRENT STATE OF THE UNION	
IN	**OUT**
Bean	Landon, Dempsey, Derrington, Kristen, Alicia, Dylan, Cassidy, Jasmin, Lilah, Kaitlyn
Catfights	Catwalks
Firing friends	Hiring friends

Claire coasted down Massie's street, gripping the handlebars on her bike so tightly her knuckles turned white. Her iPod nano was blasting her *Fired Up Femme!* mix (Beyoncé, Katy Perry, and the Cheetah Girls, with a splash of P!nk). But even with the mix, and the afternoon bike ride to clear her head, she was dragging. She wished she could talk to her friends. Just hearing their voices would cheer her up. But she'd tried and nobody was taking her calls.

She'd fought the urge to ride her bike over to Alicia's to apologize. But after she'd gotten everyone kicked out of Massie's party, with threats from security to have them arrested for trespassing, she wasn't sure she was ready to face any of the Soul-M8s in person just yet. Her plan to bring the Pretty Committee back together could've landed her best friends in the pokey. That would have been a total disaster. Everybody knew how the ex–Pretty Committee felt about horizontal stripes.

A lump hardened in the back of Claire's throat as she turned into Massie's driveway. Ever since the Pretty Committee had split, she'd just assumed everything would be okay, eventually. That someone would apologize and they'd be stronger than ever. Now it seemed like the only thing "stronger" was the rift between them, thanks to Claire. And now that Massie had a whole new group of friends (plus Layne, which Claire still didn't get), the PC would grow further and further apart. The situation was hopeless.

"Heads up!"

Claire sucked in a sharp breath, swerving to avoid the familiar brunette from IBS who was standing directly in her path. Yanking her earbuds out of her ears, Claire hopped off her bike and let it drop on the grass.

"I'm so sorry!" Claire rushed over to the girl, who was holding a thick black portfolio. "You okay?"

"I was hoping to run into you!" The girl flicked her chestnut layers out of her face. A flicker of admiration sparked her bright hazel eyes. "But this wasn't exactly what I had in mind. I guess you're my replacement, huh?" She smiled warmly. "Makes sense I guess, since you have way more experience and actually live here."

"Replacement?" Claire squinted like someone who couldn't hear.

The girl opened her portfolio and produced a glossy eight-by-ten headshot of herself, grinning at the camera from over her left shoulder. "Would you give this to her? My résumé's on the back," she said, tucking the folder under her arm.

"Your résumé?" Claire repeated, taking the headshot. She knew she was starting to sound like a clueless parrot. But she seriously had no idea what was going on. And if she didn't figure out how she knew this girl in the next sixty seconds . . .

"Jasmin Collins," she read aloud, hoping the name would ring a bell. It didn't.

Jasmin shrugged. "You know, in case anything else comes up." She looked down at the ground and smiled. "Sounds kind of stupid, but even with everything we had to go through, this job was kind of cool. Now it's back to commercials, day parts, and extras work."

Claire wasn't paying attention. She flipped the headshot over, scanning the back for clues. Actually, the résumé looked pretty good. Guest spots on *Ugly Betty* and *90210* . . .

"You have no idea what it's like to tell the world about your heavy flow days on national television," Jasmin was saying.

. . . plus background work on *Gossip Girl* and *Mad Men* . . .

"Anyway, this should be fun for you as long as you keep a few ground rules in mind," Jasmin continued. "Massie hates it when you leave the house in the morning without running your outfit by her. So do yourself a favor. Don't try any costume changes without checking first."

"Mhmmm," Claire murmured, still scanning Jasmin's stats. Commercial work for Tampax, Aquafresh, and Pringles . . .

"Also? She hates it when you go off-script. Definite no-no."

. . . and an extra on *Dial L for Loser*.

"Ohhhh!" Claire shrieked, dropping the headshot. "You were in *Dial L*! I *knew* I recognized you!" She was so relieved, she threw her arms around Jasmin and squeezed tight. "I'm Claire! Claire Lyons!"

"Yeah! I know!" Jasmin giggle-wheezed. "You were the lead!"

"Oh. Right." Despite the chilly afternoon air, warmth rose to Claire's cheeks. She released her hostage, embarrassed.

"Don't you remember? We were in that one scene together where we both had to cry 'cause our crushes dumped us, and my cell started ringing, right in the middle? And you told Rupert—"

Claire dissolved into giggles. "I told Rupert it was *my* phone!" she remembered. "And he said—"

"*Bloody 'ell, shut your cell!*" the girls squealed in unison, cracking up.

"You totally saved my arse." Jasmin snorted. "I owe you one."

"Forget it." Then Claire scrunched her nose. "Wait. You were working for—" In under a second, Claire's jaw hit the pavement. Suddenly, it all became clear. How Massie had made four new friends in less time than it took her to pick out an outfit. How they looked even more airbrushed than a *Cosmo* cover. How they always seemed to know exactly what to say, and wear, and do . . .

"Claire?" Jasmin looked worried. "You okay?"

"MASSIE HIRED YOU GUYS TO BE HER FRIENDS?" Claire screeched. She couldn't even believe the words as she said them out loud.

"Uh, yeah. Massie and Layne."

Claire smacked her palm to her forehead, collapsing onto the lawn next to the pavement. She *knew* Massie and Layne were up to something. They wouldn't just be friends for no reason. "Why—"

"I guess they were both trying to get back at their friends for stealing some guy? Dumpy, or something? I heard them talking about it in the trailer one day."

"Unbelievable." Claire breathed. No wonder Layne had been so quick to hang with Massie. And no wonder Massie had let her. It was all part of a master plan. A brilliant, totally botched master plan to get revenge.

And now, Claire needed to form a plan of her own.

"Claire?" Jasmin stood up, brushing grass and dirt from her Earnest Sewn denim mini. "Am I missing something here?"

"Yup." Claire jumped up too, yanking her bike off the lawn. "But I don't have time to explain. I need to cash in on that favor."

"That was quick," Jasmin teased.

"Can you get the other actors here by six tonight?" Claire hopped on her bike, riding figure eights around the driveway. Massie Block wasn't the only girl in the world who knew how to scheme to get what she wanted. Claire had been in the Pretty Committee long enough to pick up a few tricks of her own.

"No problem." Jasmin buttoned her plum corduroy blazer. "You want us to do a scene?"

Claire nodded. "But . . . I can't pay, so—"

Jasmin cut her off. "No worries. I'll just tell them it's an audition."

"Perfect!" Claire grinned. "I'll email you with the details in a few hours." She started pedaling back toward the guest-house, wondering how she was going to get all her friends together in one place in just a few hours. Especially since no one was taking her calls. But she'd figure something out. She had to.

"See ya tonight!" Jasmin called after her as Claire coasted through the gates.

The closer Claire got to the guesthouse, the faster she pedaled. She remembered back to her *Dial L* days, when the director, Rupert Mann, had once told her the key to a good script is three words: Drama, drama, and more drama.

Well, Claire had a fourth word to add: drama.

"Bean, my fingertips are starting to get wrinklier than your face," Massie observed, inhaling the steamy, lavender-infused air that hovered over the Jacuzzi. She sank lower and lower into the heated water, hundreds of surface bubbles popping just beneath her diamond-studded earlobes.

Bean yapped in agreement from the tiny, inflatable doggie raft that was dipping and rolling over the jet spray–fueled rapids.

Massie had sworn to herself that she wouldn't get out of the hot tub until every last bit of stress and disappointment had been kneaded, steamed, soaked, or aromatherapied from her body. But even she knew that was impossible. How could she relax? Sure, she had a twenty-foot ceiling over her head, but she was completely alone. Even the homeless had friends.

Massie replayed Friday night's events over and over in her mind. The cracking runway, the screaming models, the live reporting, and Crane flying the coop.

"Bean, didn't you think Landon was into me?" Massie sighed.

Bean yipped in agreement, jumping to her feet. Her raft shook unsteadily underneath her round body.

"Me too." Was her guydar busted? All signs pointed to *completely*.

Ninth grade or not, Landon Crane was no different from all the other boys she'd known. He'd led her on, then deserted her in her hour of need. He was Tom Brady to her Bridget Moynahan. Only without the unplanned pregnancy, or the younger, hotter Victoria's Secret model waiting on the other side of the split.

Massie closed her eyes, feeling bubbles burst beneath her earlobes. What would happen if she spent the rest of her days in the spa? It wouldn't matter how wrinkled she got, anyway. She was swearing off boys for the rest of her life. If she'd had anybody there to pinky-swear with, she would've done it in a heartbeat.

The familiar clinking of fresh ice cubes on crystal rose over the hum of the jets. Finally. Inez had brought the chilled cucumber water she'd asked for an hour ago. Or was it five minutes? Who knew anymore? Time traveled at the speed of an uncharged golf cart when one was living with heartache.

"Thanks," she moaned, her eyes still closed. "Can you just put it over there by the towels?"

"We thought we might find you in here," Kendra said.

Massie's eyes snapped open. Her mom and dad were standing next to the hot tub in jeans and matching white oxfords, looking like they were winding up for a good lecture. Kendra had her thin, Pilates-toned arms crossed over her chest, while William just looked exhausted. Massie knew exactly how he felt.

"Oh. Hey. I thought you were Inez." Massie braved a smile.

"How long have you been hiding out in here?" Kendra said softly.

It was the opposite of what Massie expected from her mom. In a weird way, Massie would have preferred that Kendra yell at her and get it over with. The softness in her voice made Massie's stomach churn with sadness.

She bit her lip and shrugged.

Kendra *tsk*ed. "You know, you can't stay in here forever," she said, sitting on the edge of the hot tub. A few splashes of lavender-scented water soaked her jeans, leaving teardrop-shaped stains. William settled into one of the lounge chairs nearby.

"Try me," Massie snapped. She instantly wished she could take it back. She knew her mom was only trying to help.

"I know last night was tough," Kendra continued without skipping a beat. "But believe me, a month from now nobody will remember what happened. Life goes on, and you have to, too." She leaned down to kiss Massie on the top of the head. The flowery notes of her perfume mixed with the lavender scent in the spa, surrounding Massie in a thick sweetness.

"But I *can't* go on," she said, her voice cracking a little. "It's impossible." She couldn't tell if the tiny beads of water on her cheeks came from her eyes, or the hot tub.

"Why not?" The lines in William's forehead deepened as he leaned forward in his chair.

"Because." Massie exhaled an unsteady breath. "My old

friends hate me 'cause I ditched them for the models, and after last night, the models hate me too."

"Why did you ditch your old friends?" Kendra asked quietly.

"Because," Massie said again. "They kept trying to take over." She almost told her parents about Dempsey, but decided at the last minute it was too embarrassing. "They were driving me crazy."

Kendra rested her hand on Massie's slippery shoulder. It was enough to make the tears that had been gathering in her eyes spill down her cheeks.

"Massie, friends can be like employees," William offered.

Even through her tears, Massie laughed and rolled her eyes. If only her dad knew what a terrible analogy that was.

"From time to time, they don't perform the way you'd like them to. They may even have a bad month. But that doesn't erase all the good things they've done. And when things start to go wrong, a good boss doesn't just fire everybody and start over."

"She doesn't?" Massie asked, confused. She wiped her cheeks with the back of her hands.

William shook his head. "A good boss asks what part she could have played in the problem. And then she asks herself what she can do better next time."

Massie frowned, letting her father's words sink in. Maybe he was right. Maybe there was something she could do better next time. If she ever had to hire friends again, she could give them more bathroom breaks . . . and even friends she didn't hire . . . she could probably treat them better, too. But what good would that do now? Her *real* friends would probably never speak to her again after she got them kicked out of her party.

Kendra seemed to sense her despair. "It's never too late to fix things with people you love, Massie," she said.

"That's true," William agreed.

Massie sighed, hoping they were right.

Kendra's BlackBerry buzzed in the croc-embossed holster fastened to her hip. She whipped out her phone as though it were a pistol and glared at the screen.

"It's the board president." She groaned. "Don't worry, I'll take care of it."

She pressed the phone to her ear.

"Kaaaren!" She beamed into the receiver. She rolled her eyes at Massie before standing and exiting the spa. William winked at Massie and Bean, and followed his wife.

As if taking a hint from Kendra's phone, Massie's vibrated. But who could it be?

She glanced at the screen.

LAYNE ABELEY.

Massie's spirits lifted slightly. She'd completely forgotten about Layne! She jammed her finger into the touch screen.

"Hey!" The echo of her voice in the spa sounded almost giddy. But she didn't care. Now that she'd had some time to recoup, she and Layne could get started assembling their new clique. And Massie would definitely work at treating her new friends better.

"Hey. Did I leave my Hello Kitty gloss in the wardrobe tent?" Layne said over a mouthful of something crunchy.

"Don't think so," Massie lied. She'd thrown the gloss out, but it had been for Layne's own good. It was the kind of thing Kendra liked to call "tough love."

"So when do you want to head back to the agency and pick our new girls?" She lifted her left foot from the water, wiggling her wrinkled toes. "Isaac could probably take us Monday after school. But don't worry, I'm gonna do it different this time." A rush of inspiration churned inside her brain. Ideas began frothing and bubbling like they were powered by Jacuzzi jets. "We can hire improv actors instead of the kind that need lines. And I'll have them live on my property. Right here in the spa! They should be foreign, but from a good place like France or Italy, and I can pretend they're fashion exchange students here to learn about—"

"Not happenin'," Layne muttered. "Peace is pissed."

"What?" Massie's foot plunked back into the water, sending a giant splash over Bean's raft and soaking the puppy. "Why?"

"She said if I wasn't family she'd have us sued for actor endangerment," Layne explained. "Besides, this arrangement totally didn't work for me."

"For *you*?" Massie smacked the water. Large droplets slid down the screen of her phone.

"That's right, for *me*." Layne mimicked Massie's indignant

tone. "This was supposed to be about me getting revenge on Kristen for stealing Dempsey. And Twitter update: I saw them last night and she didn't seem too bothered."

Massie's mind was racing. Without Layne and Peace, she couldn't hire new friends. Without new friends, she'd be completely and totally alone. And alone was only good for trying on bathing suits. "But it's not too late," she tried. "We can still get back at Kristen!"

"Over it." Layne sighed. "I've got it bad for Cody from my stage combat class."

"But what will you do without me?" The heat from the spa was starting to make Massie dizzy. "Who will you hang out with?" She knew she was asking herself more than she was asking Layne.

"Everybody, just like I used to."

Massie rolled her eyes, then hung up. She'd always known Layne was layme. But being friends with *everyone* was lazy. It was like buying clothes without checking the labels. Downloading a new album without sampling it. Buying moisturizer for all skin types. It didn't guarantee she would end up with the best. Then again, at least Layne would end up with *something*.

"Knock knock!" a loud whisper sounded behind her. It sounded like Lilah. Only not mad.

Massie flopped around in the Jacuzzi, craning her neck toward the doorway. Lilah, Jasmin, Kaitlyn, and Cassidy were all standing there, looking refreshed, relaxed, and dry. *Huh?*

"Didn't I fire you guys?" Massie asked softly, genuinely wanting to know.

Cassidy opened her mouth, but Jasmin elbowed her. "Just because we're not working for you anymore, that doesn't mean we can't be friends, right?" she cooed.

Funny. Massie had been under the impression that that was exactly what that meant. But she wasn't in a position to be shooing girls away.

"So did you see the news coverage of the event?" Lilah rolled up the bottoms of her wool trousers and stuck her feet in the boiling water. Her fair skin flushed immediately.

"Are you kidding me?" Massie scoffed. "I wouldn't watch Winkie Porter if I just had Lasik eye surgery and it was the only thing on in the recovery room." Nobody needed to know that she'd DVR'd the six o'clock news and watched it on repeat while she hate-ate an entire bag of chocolate-covered almonds.

"Me neither," agreed Kaitlyn. She squeezed onto the side of the Jacuzzi next to Lilah and blinked.

"Ditto," said Cassidy, doing the same.

"Uhn-uhn," said Jasmin, crowding next to the other girls.

They all leaned in at once. Massie scooted to the other side of the tub, trying not to think about how Kristen would have had a razor-sharp insult for Winkie, instead of a head nod and a blinking spasm.

These girls were pretty, sure. Pretty much total snuh-oooozers.

"Owch!" Jasmin yanked her feet from the water. "Hot!"

"Uh, yeah," Massie said. "That's kind of the point." Then she remembered her promise to be nicer, and smiled.

Jasmin swung her feet over the edge of the tub and headed for the lounge chair under the window. Before she could sit down, something caught her eye.

"It's Claire!" she said, pressing her nose against the window. "And Landon."

"What?" Massie screeched, jumping from the hot tub and sending Jacuzzi waves sloshing over the edge. Bean gripped her raft for dear life. The biting cold air nipped at Massie's skin as she ran toward the window, but she almost didn't feel it.

Claire and Landon were standing in plain view. Landon was straddling a black sticker-covered bike, and Claire kept resting her hand on the handlebars as they chatted easily, like they were BFFs. Every few seconds, Claire would tilt her head back and laugh like Landon had just said the most hilarious thing. Massie knew that laugh. That laugh was usually reserved for Cam's lame-o jokes.

"Ehmagawd." Massie's throat tightened. Were her ex-friends just taking turns tormenting her? How could Claire do this to her, after everything she'd done to make Claire feel at home in Westchester? It was official. She couldn't trust anyone. She wanted to pound on the window and scream at Claire all at once, but instead she just stood there, staring in disbelief.

"Looks like she stole your crush, huh?" Cassidy pouted, twirling a short lock of platinum hair around her finger.

"And your brain," Massie snapped.

Cassidy opened her mouth like she was about to fire off a comeback and said, "Yeah, maybe."

"We would never do that to you," Kaitlyn said in a monotone voice.

"Not ever." Jasmin shook her head.

"Nope," Lilah whispered. "Unless you wanted us to."

"True." Kaitlyn nodded. "If you wanted us to, we would."

"Yeah," Cassidy agreed. "But only if you wanted us to."

They rapid-blinked again, waiting for her response.

Okay, these girls were starting to freak her out. Without a script to follow, they were more bland than plain low-sodium rice cakes. Didn't they have minds of their own? Or did they just agree with everything Massie told them to? She considered asking them, but what was the point? They'd just yes her.

"I'll be right back," she barked. She reached for a towel next to the hot tub and raced outside. Bean scampered off her raft and to the floor, following close behind.

"We'll come with you!" called Jasmin.

Massie storm-stomped barefoot across the lawn, Bean at her heels. The towel she wrapped around her frame did nothing to protect her from the chilly air. The frigid wind cut through the towel and into her wet skin like a knife. The same knife Claire was using to stab her in the heart.

The slap of the actors' bare feet on the wet grass made Massie shiver even more. She wished they would just leave. But no. When she needed them, they couldn't do anything right. But now that she was all set to pick new friends, they were clingier than static-soaked jersey cotton.

"Oh. Hey!" Claire said as Massie stomped toward her. "We

were just about to come get you." She smile-squinted, holding her hand up to shield her face from the sun.

"I bet." Massie glared at Landon, not even caring that she was wearing last year's Pucci-print bikini. Landon didn't deserve to see her in anything from this year's line. "Claire, do you play football for Pittsburgh?" she asked.

"No?" For some reason, Claire was smiling.

"Then why are you such a *Steeler*?" Massie shouted. Tiny shivers ran up and down her spine. *Nawt* love shivers. It was freezing outside.

Landon laughed out loud. His one-dimpled smile would normally have filled her with more warmth than a heat lamp and a plush robe. But now it looked like a giant pit of despair.

Claire shook her head, tucking her hair behind her ear. "I'm not stealing anybody. Landon's here to see you."

"You're about twenty hours late," Massie snapped, folding her goose bump–covered arms across her half-naked chest. "Don't worry, though. Bean took your place on the runway. And she was ah-mazing."

The puppy licked her chlorine-covered calf.

"May-see, you don't get it." Landon ran a hand through his wavy black hair. "When you kicked your friends out of the party you kicked me out too."

What???? Massie hope-glared at Claire.

"It's true." Claire shrugged. "I asked him to keep a lookout while I sneaked everybody in, and when I got busted, he took the rap with me."

"Awwwwww," cooed the girls behind her.

"No awwwww." Massie stomped her foot on the cold grass. The actors were instantly silent.

"Why were you helping them sneak in when I didn't want them here?" she asked Landon, temporarily distracted by a tiny gift bag dangling from the handlebars of his bike.

"Um, my fault," Claire jumped in. She glanced back and forth between Landon and the bag. "Now," she muttered.

"Here." He extended the tiny black gift bag in Massie's direction. It was covered in gold paw prints.

"What's this?" Massie accepted with trepidation, and then parted the soft tissue paper like dressing room curtains. Afraid of what she'd find when she entered.

"What is it?" Lilah pressed, leaning over the bag.

"Do you like it?" Kaitlyn asked.

"If she does, I do." Jasmin grinned.

"Same," Cassidy agreed.

Massie fought the urge to gag them with the tissue and focused on the gift.

"Ehmacute!" She gasped at the purple silk necklace. Its tiny sterling silver dog bone charms clinked when she lifted it from the bag. "A puppy charm collar!"

Bean yapped her appreciation, running circles around Massie and Landon. Or were they hearts?

"Patience," Massie cooed. "A girl should never act too excited." She knelt to the ground, corralled Bean, and fastened the collar around her puppy's neck. Ah-dorable times ten dog years. "Thank you."

"No problem." Landon nodded, suddenly looking a little shy. He stared down at his handlebars for a few seconds, then glanced back up at Massie. "I wanted to call, but I thought it'd be better if I just came by in person. And yesterday I had to work at Bark Jacobs, soooo—"

"You work at Marc Jacobs?" Massie unfolded her arms.

"No, *Bark* Jacobs. It's a pet clothing and accessory store. My mom owns it."

Massie giggled. "Well, as long as we're clarifying, my name is Massie." She offered Landon her shriveled hot-tub hand. "Like sassy. Not say-see."

Landon took it and shook it. "Sorry." He flushed, his cheeks turning the perfect shade of pink. Usually Massie had to pinch her own cheeks hard to get that kind of color.

"Forgiven." Massie beamed, squeezing his hand a little more before finally letting go.

Landon's dimple was in full force. It was no longer a pit of despair. More like a second smile. "My mom is having a trunk show tonight—mostly dog wedding dresses and honeymoon loungewear—and well, Bark Obama, my pug, will be there, so . . ."

EH-MA-YES! Massie wanted to scream. Instead, she counted four Massie-sippis and then smiled. "Sure. Sounds fun," she managed, even though she was already mentally rifling through her closet for an acceptable outfit, not just for her, but also for Bean.

"I'm in." Lilah nodded.

"Me too." Jasmin grinned.

"Wouldn't miss it," Kaitlyn announced.

"Me either," Cassidy agreed.

Massie was about to decline on their behalf but quickly changed her mind. They looked good. And until she found replacements they would have to do.

"I'll text the address." Landon slapped the rectangle in the back pocket of his baggy True Religions. He hopped on the seat of his black sticker-covered bike and leaned over the handlebars. His blue-green eyes held her with the force of a rushing fire hydrant. "See you soon, then."

He jumped on the pedal as if starting a motorcycle and bolted toward the open gate.

"'Kay," Massie said, or maybe only mumbled.

Just like in the movies, her frigid black-and-white body turned Technicolor. It felt like wearing cashmere in a tanning booth. Sleeping in a giant Ugg boot. Or staring in at the Wizard of Oz. Only better.

The only things missing were some real friends to share it with.

The Bark Jacobs boutique was ten times the size of Claire's bedroom and twenty times nicer. As she entered the high-ceilinged store behind Massie and the actors, she let out an involuntary, awed gasp. Giant gold paw prints meandered across the white marble floors, leading to the row of oversize dog mansions that served as dressing rooms at the back of the store. Glowing glass display cases at pet-eye level showcased accessories from collars to leashes to tiny satchels designed to mimic couture handbags. Crystal bowls filled with treats were everywhere, to the delight of the dogs and cats sniffing out the store while their owners perused the racks of doggie wedding gowns.

But Claire could gawk later. Right now, it was time for the final phase of her plan. She told herself it was going to work. It had to.

Quickly, she ducked behind a colorful display of Swarovski-monogrammed cashmere doggie beds and reached for her phone. When she was sure she'd lost Massie and the actresses, she got ready to text the girls for the second time that afternoon. The first text had been offering to buy everyone an *I'm sorry I screwed everything up on Friday night* latte. Her treat. The girls had agreed, which meant they were together and should be arriving any second. Fingers trembling with anticipation, she composed the last text.

Claire: Found the cutest pet boutique ever! Bark Jacobs. Clothes for cats. Beckham will luv. Huge sale! Cute accessories for ppl, 2.

She sent the text to Kristen and waited. She knew the sale part was a low blow, but these were desperate times.

Kristen: Purrfect. ☺ on our way.

So far, so good. Claire stuffed her phone in her purse, mentally crossing her fingers. She ducked back into the crowd and spotted Massie, Landon, and the actors hovering over one of the glass display cases across the store. Trying not to step on any of the tiny dogs that scampered underfoot, Claire bobbed and weaved through the loud, milling crowd of enthusiastic pet lovers.

"Ehmagawd, Claire, can you believe this place?" Massie was bent over the glass display case, fogging it up with her breath. Landon was standing next to her. "Did you see this?" She held up a tiny silver dog bone charm. "It's got a miniature camera in it. You attach it to your dog's collar, and you can monitor what they're up to twenty-four seven. There's a Web site and everything."

"SnoopDawg." Landon ran his hand through his curls.

"Totally his idea." Massie giggled, smoothing her jade green Zac Posen ruffled minidress. "Isn't that adorable?"

Behind Massie, the MAC girls were nodding in sync. Claire giggled to herself. Massie had tried to ditch them four times on the way to the store, but they were sticking to her like hair extensions.

"Where's Bean?" Claire asked, plucking a napkin and a dog bone–shaped finger sandwich from a passing waiter's tray. She popped the sandwich in her mouth and gagged immediately, spitting the sandwich into her napkin.

"Guh-ross! Liver," she wheezed. When she looked up at Massie and Landon, their bodies were shaking with laughter.

"You just ate a dog treat, Kuh-laire," Massie managed, a tear slipping down her cheek. Claire wiped her tongue with the napkin, almost not minding that they were making fun of her. It was the first time she'd seen Massie this happy in weeks.

"Where's Bean?" Claire asked.

"Trying some things on with Bark Obama and her new personal puppy stylist," Massie said.

Immediately, Bean scampered out from one of the dressing rooms, followed by a nearly identical pug. The two puppies weaved in and out of the crowd, making their way toward Massie and Landon. Bean looked cuter than cute in her purple silk footie pajamas with matching sleep mask. Bark wore the same mask and a tiny purple nightcap.

"Bean!" Massie squealed with delight. "It's so you."

Bark chased Bean in circles around Massie and Landon. Then the puppies reversed and Bean chased Bark.

"I think they luh-v each other." Massie smiled conspiratorially at Landon. "And I think I luh-v those jammies."

"They're from my Dawg Tired line of luxury sleepwear," explained a smooth voice.

Claire and Massie turned around to see a tall, willowy woman with wild, dark curls and clear blue-green eyes. She wore a black silk maxi-dress that looked just like one Massie had seen Angelina wear on the pages of last week's *People*. The woman added her own dash of style with a diamond-studded paw print brooch.

"Celia Crane," Landon's mom said, flashing a brilliant white smile. "So glad you all could make it."

"Your store is ah-mazing," Massie said, stepping forward. She stuck out her hand. "Massie Block. I'm a friend of Landon's." She cradled Bean in the crook of her arm like a designer clutch. "And this is Bean."

"Lovely to meet you, Massie and Bean," Celia said. "Have you been upstairs?" She nodded at the escalator in the back corner, snaking up to the second floor. Alongside it, a tiny escalator carried a pack of black lab puppies. "We have a full-service puppy salon and day spa. Owners and pets get side-by-side treatments."

If Massie had had a tail, it would have been wagging at high speed.

"Um, 'scuze me?" Jasmin piped up in a lilting tone. She

was holding a pair of madras puppy swim trunks up to her waist. "Do you have these shorts in a larger size?'

Claire had to bite the inside of her lip to keep from laughing.

Celia looked confused. "No, I don't believe we do."

"Hot pants are so in this season," Lilah observed.

Cassidy and Kaitlyn nodded like a pair of bobblehead dolls.

"Oh." Celia stifled a laugh. "No. Those are for pets, girls."

"Ohhhhhhh. Nooooow I get it," said Jasmin. She smiled dumbly. "I'm Jasmin? Massie's bestie?"

Massie turned a brilliant shade of purple.

Celia side-glanced at Landon, her eyes dancing with amusement.

Claire almost leaped out and hugged Jasmin. Her acting was nothing short of brilliant. And she was obviously driving Massie insane. She checked her watch. Where was Kristen?

"Excuse me, Celia Crane?" A man in khaki slacks and a button-down tapped Celia on the shoulder. "I'm Martin Peterman, from the *Westchester Daily*. We spoke on the phone this morning?"

"Of course." Celia beamed. "The profile story. Why don't we sit down in my office where we can talk? You can ask my son a few questions, too, if you'd like." She touched Landon on the sleeve, and he apology-shrugged at Massie.

Be right back, he mouthed.

Okay, Massie mouthed back.

A tiny, electronic yip sounded, signaling that the front

door had just opened. The sight of Alicia, Dylan, and Kristen coming her way soothed Claire like a bag full of sours. *Finally.* All her best friends were together in one place.

But when Kristen, Dylan, and Alicia saw Massie, they veered off in the other direction.

Wait! Claire wanted to yell after them. *This isn't how it's supposed to go! You're supposed to apologize!* She glanced at Massie, who was adding a nightcap to Bean's ensemble while Bark Obama drooled over his new puppy love.

"Berightback," Claire said quickly, dashing after her friends. She found them clustered around a display case of pet jewelry.

"Heyyy." Claire tried to sound lighthearted. "Isn't this place awesome?"

"You didn't tell us *she'd* be here." Alicia's chocolate brown eyes darted in Massie's direction, and then quickly back to Claire. For a split second, Claire recognized Alicia's expression. She'd seen the same one when her friend had first laid eyes on the Jimmy Choo Lois bag.

Longing. Desperation. Fear of a wait list.

Claire bit her bitten thumbnail. "Don't you want to go over and say hey, at least?"

"Nah." Dylan was staring at Massie like she was a fat-free chocolate-glazed donut.

"If she wants to say hi, she can come talk to us," Kristen said, without shifting her gaze.

"Fine," Claire huffed. "Be right back." She crisscrossed the store to Massie. This was getting ridiculous. It was obvious the girls missed their alpha. And even more obvious that Massie wouldn't stand for the MAC girls much longer. So why weren't they forgiveness-hugging and planning next Friday's sleepover?

"Kuh-laire, do you think Bean can pull off yellow?" Massie was holding up a chic rainy day ensemble.

Bark nodded his approval.

Claire shrugged. "Beats me."

"Oh. Right." Massie's face fell. "Forgot who I was talking to."

Ordinarily, the remark would have stung. But tonight, Claire couldn't have been more thrilled. Maybe Massie was finally starting to realize what Claire had known all along: Nobody could stand in for Alicia, Dylan, or Kristen. Not even her.

"I saw some cute jewelry on the other side of the store," Claire offered. "Wanna check it out?"

"Sure," Massie agreed. "Especially if it gets me away from these LBRs." She didn't even bother to lower her voice.

"We'll come!" the MAC girls yelled in unison.

Massie rolled her eyes. "Ehmagawd," she muttered to Claire. "They're on me like spray tan."

"I know," Claire muttered back. "I hope no one thinks you're . . ." She paused. "You know. . . ." She paused again.

"What?"

"Like them."

Massie gulped. Loud.

Claire led Massie, Bean, Bark, and the MAC girls through the crowd. Massie stopped suddenly.

"What're *they* doing here?" she asked. But her tone wasn't mean. It was sad.

"Same thing you are." Claire shrugged, her fists clenching at her sides. *Please, please, please say something nice.*

But Massie didn't. She glared at Alicia, Dylan, and Kristen, who stood in a row in front of them, their arms crossed over their designer-clad chests. Behind her, the MAC girls were trying to squeeze into plaid puppy ponchos. "Are you dial-up Internet?"

"What? No," Jasmin said.

"'Cause you're super *slow,*" Massie shot back.

"Huh?" Jasmin crinkled her brows.

Claire covered her smile with her hand. The girl deserved an Academy Award.

"These clothes are for four-leggers only."

It wasn't her best. But Alicia lifted a finger anyway. "Point," she said.

Then Dylan snickered.

And Kristen giggled.

Claire snorted.

And Massie cracked a shy smile.

"Ehmagawd." Dylan groaned. "Are all billionaires this stupid?"

"It's because of all that money," Alicia said, reglossing her pink pout. "They're so spoiled, it's like they've never had to *do* anything for themselves." She whipped her AmEx from her purse and handed it to a passing salesperson. "I'll take a poncho in every color."

Massie rolled her eyes. "You don't even have a pet!"

"But I *could*," Alicia said with a smile.

The girls cracked up.

For a second, it was like everything was back to normal. But when the laughter stopped, everyone got quiet, shifting their gazes to the floor.

Massie spoke first. "So where are your crushes?" she asked suspiciously, lifting Bean up. Bark yipped his disapproval.

Dylan, Alicia, and Kristen exchanged glances.

"Home," Dylan said, chewing her bottom lip and staring at her Tory Burch clogs. After an awkward pause, she looked up at Massie. "Um . . . I'm really sorry I stole Derrington."

Massie's eyes widened in surprise. "You are?"

Dylan nodded. "I should have checked with you first."

"And I'm sorry about Dempsey," Kristen said, her voice trembling with nerves. "I should have been more hawnest."

Ah-greed, Massie's look seemed to say. But instead, she offered a sympathetic half-smile. "'S okay," she said to both girls. "Besides, I have a new crush now. Landon."

"Ehmagawd!" Dylan giggle-gasped.

"Have you lip-kissed yet?" Kristen asked.

"Nawt yet," Massie admitted. Then her gaze fell on Alicia.

"I'm sorry I tried to take over." Alicia sniffed, her brown eyes bright with apology tears.

Massie just stood there for a beat, her amber eyes flicking among her former betas. Claire held her breath.

"Forgiven," Massie said finally. She chewed her glossy

bottom lip. "And I'm gonna try not to be so Lycra from here on out. Even though sometimes, you totally need—"

"YAYYYYY!" Claire cut her off, throwing her arms wide.

"YAYYYYYY!" the girls echoed, coming in for a giant group hug.

Claire popped her head out from inside the squeal-huddle, and turned toward the MAC girls.

Thanks, she mouthed to Jasmin.

Jasmin grinned, making an *L* with her index finger and thumb and lifting it to her forehead. Then she pinched her index finger and thumb together and drew them across her lips.

Claire did the same and watched the MAC girls disappear into the crowd—forever.

International Billionaires School may not be real . . .
but Alpha Academy is.
What happens when THE CLIQUE's Skye Hamilton,
the original eighth-grade alpha,
gets an invite to this ultra-exclusive academy?

Turn the page for a sneak peek of #1 bestselling author
Lisi Harrison's hawt new series.

There were five Skye Hamiltons in the Body Alive Dance Studio. One on each mirrored wall and one in the flesh. As in-the-flesh Skye step-turn-step-plié-step-fan-step-ball-changed, the reflections followed. So did the eight other girls in Atelier No. 1. Or at least they tried.

A trickle of sweat slithered from the base of Skye's tightly bunned blond waves down the back of her pale blue leo. She drew her shoulder blades back (even more), trying to pinch the salty snake, not because she was embarrassed, but because she could. Her body always did what it was told. All she had to do crank up the music and ask.

"And one . . . twooo . . . thu-hree . . . fourrrr . . . five . . . six . . . seh-vuuuun . . . eight." Madame Prokofiev slow-clapped to the jazzy ooze of Michael Bublé's "Fever" while scanning her students for TICS (Timing, Incongruity, Care-lessness, and Smiles). As always, her scrutinizing brown eyes whizzed past Skye like two bullets aimed at someone else.

"Too wristy, Becca!" She clapped. "Less chin, Reese." Clap. "Rolllllllll the knee, Wendi. Don't poke." Clap. Clap. "And I swear on my tendons, Heidi, if you don't fix that posture, I'm going to use you as a throw pillow!"

Chignoned and clad in a no-nonsense black cami with matching flare dance pants, the aging brunette looked like a prima ballerina laced up tighter than a pair of toe shoes. Yet she moved like honey and stung like a bee.

Skye loved her.

Charged by Madame P's silent approval, Skye added a turn before the freeze, then came out of it with hands in prayer pose, or rather, a Bollywood Namaste Flower. The routine hadn't called for it—her instincts had. She'd downloaded the M.I.A. track from *Slumdog*, and like some people got songs stuck in their heads, Skye had this one stuck in her body.

"Enough." Madame P clapped sharply, the frown lines in her passion-wrinkled forehead bunched like loose leg warmers. Had she gone too far with her flower?

All nine dancers stop-panted. But Skye's heart kept hitch-kicking against her rib cage. Finally, she crossed her arms over her B-minus cups and ordered it to take five.

She lined up with her dance BFFs Missy Cambridge,

Becca Brie, Leslie Lynn Rubin, and Heidi Sprout. Like Skye, her besties were blond—two in braids, two with ponies—and wore identical pink balloon skirts over gray leotards and tights (BADS Anna Pavlova Collection). Skye had added her signature sleeves; today's were black mesh with five mini sterling silver locker keys dangling from the holes—one for each of her friends. Every time she moved they jingled, adding a little extra something to the otherwise humdrum musical score.

"Flair, ladies." Madame P heel-toed to the center of the room, clucking her tongue in disappointment. "Dance is not just knowing the steps. It's interpreting them." She winked at Skye, releasing her from the scold. "So please try to remember. We're doing Twyla, not *Twilight*, so stop sucking!"

Some of the girls gasped. Some giggled nervously. Skye pressed her thumb against the sharp grooves of her locker key. The pain kept her from gloat-smirking.

Madame Prokofiev snapped her fingers. "Again! And one . . . twooo . . . thu-hree . . . fourrrr . . . five . . . six . . . seh-vuuuun . . . eight."

This time, the girls responded like thoroughbreds at the starting bell. Their Capezio'd feet polished the shiny wood floor that the Hamilton family had owned for years. The force of their synchronized movements pumped Skye with energy and made her sweat pride. Not only for the girls who danced, but also for her parents, who gave them the place to do it.

A thunderous knock interrupted their flow. The door opened just enough for Madame P to see that someone wanted her in the hall. She gave Skye a nod, silently transferring power to her star pupil, and then slipped out.

Skye rolled her neck, then padded happily to the front of the class, pausing only to change songs. "Same routine in triple time." She grinned, her legs twitching, ready for some real dancing.

"*WhenIgrowupIwannabeastarIwannabefamous* . . ." the Pussycat Dolls meowed from the iPod deck.

"Ah-five, six, seven, eight . . ." Skye went hard. The midday light pouring in from the windows found her like a spotlight.

Tutting, waving, popping and locking, she moved faster to the pounding beat than the Tasmanian Devil on *So You Think You Can Dance*. With Madame P gone, she could let go of the traditional dance steps and express herself freely. Borrowing at will, she riffed on a few Bollywood moves, added the punch of Broadway, a dash of Beyoncé hip shaking, and a sprinkle of ballet scissors from *Romeo and Juliet*. She moved between more styles than a *Moulin Rouge* montage. At the end she executed a final glissé tour jeté, leaped up, and gave a little bow to the captivated audience that would be there one day. The keys on her sleeves clanged together. They sounded like applause.

Straightening, she turned to the two rows of four behind her and panted, "Again. Without me this time."

Skye had set the barre high. Just like it had been set for her by her mother years ago. Leslie Lynn attacked the moves with gusto, but that very same headbanging enthusiasm caused her bangs to wriggle free from her loose braid. Her attempt to sideswipe them during an axel turn dropped her one second behind the other dancers, and left her dragging like a piece of toilet paper on the back of a shoe.

Feet turned out in textbook first position—her power position—Skye pursed her lips and channeled her inner Russian dance dictator. "The mirrors are here for us to perfect our form, not our hair," she announced. Leslie picked up the pace with an embarrassed grimace.

"Chest out," Skye demanded of Heidi, whose posture had taken another dive. Heidi had sprouted B-plus cups this year, the pull of which she was obviously still having trouble adjusting to. "Own 'em, H!"

Heidi thrust out her boobs while her back arched in protest.

Note to self: Introduce H to the new line of Martha Graham bust minimizer tops. Give her the friends and family discount if she balks.

Next to her, Becca spiked up into a high, athletic half split that was about two centimeters short of a cheerleader hurkey. Skye pulled Becca's ponytail down to stop her overzealous bobbing. "Less bounce, more weight."

Becca sucked in her already concave stomach on hearing the word *weight*. Skye sighed. Becca wasn't the brightest beta on the barre, but she was sweeter than Splenda and shadowed Skye with the dedication of a choral swan in *Swan Lake*. Those who can't lead follow. And as long as they were following Skye, everything was perfect.

Next, she circled Missy. Each strand of her hair was in place, just like her steps. She strung together the exquisite sequences with technical perfection: Her toe was pointed at a forty-five-degree angle, her shoulders parallel to the floor, and her leaps timed to a millisecond of the driving beat. But she was full of more lead than a Chinese toy.

The song ended and the dancers stopped. Missy blinked up at her friend, eagerly awaiting her notes. It was like a sadist's Hallmark card; when you care enough to be insulted by the very best.

"Watch me." Skye launched into a perfect piksa turn, arms wide, hands clasped, as if hugging Kevin Fat-erline. "You want to be solid and liquid at the same time, like an unopened juice box on a whirling merry-go-round," she instructed, borrowing a line from her mother and passing it off as her own.

One . . . two . . . three . . .

After the third revolution, the door creaked open and Madame P glided back in.

On the fourth turn, Skye saw her parents, dressed in matching gray-and-white *après*-dance warm-ups, her mother waving a piece of gold paper over her head.

And on the fifth—wait, was that a camera crew? Skye slowed, then settled on the balls of her feet. Lithe waitresses dressed in white BADS unitards and silver tutus wheeled in tray after tray of dim sum followed by Skye's favorite dessert, Payard's *Pont-Neuf*. It was a veritable port-a-party. But why? Food was never allowed in the studio. Or the dancers, for that matter.

Miss and Leslie widened their glitter-dusted eyes at Skye, who shrugged in return.

"Congratulations, my darling!" Natasha shouted in her faint Russian accent. Her moonlit whitish-blond hair was clipped in a low ponytail. But the rest of her moved with uninhibited joy. "You have been accepted to Alpha Academy!"

The back eight squealed in envy-delight.

"What?" Skye's blue eyes searched her mom's identical ones for an explanation. A retraction. A punch line.

But the pride on her mother's face was as genuine as it was rare.

The last time Skye had seen it was seven years ago, when she'd told Natasha she wanted to become a professional ballerina, just like her. Months later the studio had been built, instructors had been imported, and training had begun. But, no matter how hard Skye danced for it, that proud expression had never returned. Until now.

Skye threw up her arms and spun in a perfect pirouette. "I'm in!" She tapped her toe on the floor, her breath caught in her throat. This was it. Her big break. The gateway to more stages, more solos, more standing ovations, more proud expressions, more chances to be in the center of everything.

A brunette reporter with a chin-butt that rivaled Demi Lovato's stood in front of a one-man camera crew. She cleared her throat and forced a wide grin on her powder pink lips. "This is Winkie Porter reporting from Body Alive Dance Studio in Westchester, New York?" Winkie's voice went up at the end of every sentence, making even her name sound like a question. "When eccentric billionaire entertainment mogul Shira Brazille announced the opening of Alpha Academy last spring, thousands of kids from all over the country applied. CEO of Brazille International, acclaimed entrepreneur, innovator, and tastemaker, the Australian expat founded the exclusive boarding school—whose location is top secret—to, and I quote, 'nurture the next generation of exceptional talent without distractions from our mediocre world.' And our very own fourteen-year-old Skye Hamilton, dance wunderkind, is one of the lucky one hundred to secure a coveted spot."

"You did it Skye-High!" Her dad scooped her up into a lift, and she giggled on the way down. Even though she landed perfectly, she still felt like she was floating.

"Are we getting this?" Winkie asked her stubbly-but-cute camera guy. When he shook his head no, she said, "Mr. Hamilton, could you do that again?"

The dancers scuttled behind Skye and her father, in an attempt to get on camera. They moved in a tight tangle, like a clump of hair coasting toward the shower drain.

Skye shrugged and nodded at her dad, whose hazel eyes moistened with pride as he whirled her again. He set her down gently, his full head of dark blond hair slightly tousled from the spinning. She patted it down like he was her very large obedient poodle.

"Did you ever think your daughter would be sought after by the most influential woman in the world?" Winkie stuck a microphone under his strong chin.

"Of course." Geoffrey winked at his daughter.

Like he was proud? Or like he was lying?

Then he hooked his hand around his wife's tiny waist and pulled her close. "Natasha and I always knew Skye would follow in her mother's dance steps. Because she—"

"No," Natasha interrupted, her accent slicing his words like a kindjal sword. "Skye won't be as good as I was. She will be better."

Her declaration was a pointe shoe to the gut. How could

Skye ever be better than a world-class ballerina when she wasn't even close to 'as good'? To be better than her mother she would have to train her body to be disciplined. Obedient. Exact. And for Skye, dancing was the opposite of that. It was liberating. Expressive. Fun. But as always, Skye buried the pressure in a mental locker and leaned against the door until it closed.

Winkie rested her frosty hand on Skye's shoulder. "We heard there was a little mishap with your essay and that it was lost in the mail. Did you stay up all night rewriting? Take us through your ordeal."

Skye adjusted her sleeves. How did Winkie know about that?

Over the summer, Skye had received word that the essay portion of her application had been misplaced. After a few minutes of deep contemplation she had decided not to write a new one. After all, applying to the academy had been her mother's idea, not hers. And she was about to go to high school. With boys. Boys who might love her the way her father loved Natasha. So why head off to another all-girls school? Why leave BADS when she was the best dancer they ever had? Why start over and risk losing it all?

The disappearing essay turned out to be a gift. One she couldn't dream of returning. So, really, the "ordeal" hadn't been an ordeal at all. Until now. Either her mother rewrote the essay for her or they found the original. But how did you explain that to *America*?

"It was really stressful." Skye cupped her hair bun. The jingle of keys made her homesick even though she was still there. "Let's just say I have calluses on my hands to match the ones on my feet."

Winkie laughed with her mouth closed.

Behind the camera, old instructors, school friends, and neighbors were starting to arrive. Greeting one another with hugs, they stuffed dumplings in their mouths and then chew-nodded their delight in this local success story.

Winkie stuck a microphone under Skye's barely glossed lips. "Tell us how it feels to be chosen by Shira Brazille, entertainment mogul. Icon. Alpha."

Skye reached up and pulled a silver chopstick from her artful bird's nest, releasing a cascade of blond wavelets for the camera. "Shira's a real hero of mine," she said confidently. "Her outback-to-riches story is such an inspiration. It shows what a girl can do when she applies herself. And now to give back in this way—wow!" Skye inflected as if all this had just occurred to her and she hadn't practiced a million times with her mother over the summer before the essay was lost.

"What is the most important thing your mother has taught you about dance?" Winkie's head tilted, heavy with interest.

Natasha's bony fingers reached for her daughter's hand. A cue to return to the script. "My mom taught me that success is like ballet. You work until your feet hurt, until your muscles ache, until your body knows the steps without thinking. So when the lights come on and the performance begins, it looks effortless."

Her mom's round mouth and full lips moved along with her own. After a career full of interviews and TV appearances, Natasha always knew what to say. But Skye could never put her feelings into words. She was the type who had to get on her feet and show them.

"Well, you're certainly ready." Winkie's voice didn't go up that time—there was no question about it. Skye was ready.

At least to those watching the show.

"Thanks for the party, Mom." Skye followed Natasha to a pair of chairs in the corner once everyone had gone. "And for rewriting my essay."

"I didn't write it." Natasha crunched down on a piece of celery. "I added a few lines here and there, but you did most of the work."

Skye studied her mother's pronounced jaw. It was pulsing from chewing, not tension.

"When are you going to start believing in yourself?"

Natasha swallowed, her long pale neck lengthening slightly. "You are going to Alpha Academy because of your talent, not mine."

"Really?" Skye searched her mother's eyes, giving her one last chance to blink-admit that she'd somehow gotten Skye in.

"Really." Natasha lifted a silver box out from under her chair.

"Hmmmm." Skye looked up at the track lights, wondering if the essay had been found after all.

"Time to stop doubting and start accepting your fate." Natasha handed her daughter the box. "You're going to be a bigger star than I was. Now stop being afraid to shine."

Skye slowly untied the white bow. She wasn't afraid to shine like a star. She was afraid to fall like one.

Skye lifted a lavender toe shoe from the box, its worn silver satin ribbons trailing behind like smoke from a blown-out candle. The pair had hung over her mother's vanity forever. Like stamps on a passport, the scuffs, scrapes, and frayed silk told the story of her mom's career: from the Mariinsky Theatre in St. Petersburg, to the Théâtre du Châtelet in Paris, and the Royal Opera House in London, where a grand jeté gone wrong had landed her in King's College Hospital with a torn meniscus and a fractured career.

"They're too big for me," Skye said, hoping for a new pair. Maybe something in a soft gold. "Besides . . ." She searched the box for the other shoe, but the tissue was empty. "There's only one." Skye furrowed her brow, not sure what she was supposed to do with one big used shoe.

"This slipper is special," Natasha whispered. "It will fit your hads."

"Huh?" Skye blinked. Her mom had been in the country for eighteen years, but every once in a while something got lost in translation.

"It will fit your HADS," her mom explained. "Your Hopes And Dreams." She flipped open the tip of the shoe. "You write what you dream for and hide it in the shoe. When the time is right, it comes true."

"Really?" Skye leaned in closer. Wanting desperately to believe in the magic. It was easier than believing in herself, especially where she was going. "What did you wish for?"

"Meeting your father," Natasha mused, untucking Skye's hair from behind her ears. Skye knew the story well. Her mom had come to America when she was seventeen to perform at Lincoln Center. After one dance onstage, she'd landed a marriage proposal from a Broadway choreographer and defected. "This dance studio," Natasha continued. "And you."

Her mom's words filled her muscles with the kind of warmth that comes after a good stretch. They softened and strengthened her at the same time. Who cared how her application had landed on Shira's desk? All that mattered was that it did. Which meant the time was right.

Skye glanced around at the place she'd learned to dance, suddenly feeling too big for the small studio. The leaded windows, the track lighting with special bulbs that flattered blondes, the nick in the doorjamb where she'd spun and whacked the frame with her Tinker Bell wand when she was six. They were part of her past now. Destined to shrink into wallet-size snapshots in her memory. Images that she'd flip through when she needed to remember where she came from.

Weaving the shoe's silk straps through her fingers, Skye glanced at her mom's cheekbones. Her pale skin covered them like white tights over smooth stones when she smiled. And she was smiling now.

Skye opened the secret compartment, discovering neatly folded squares of blank, lavender-scented paper. They smelled like her mother.

"What are you going to wish for first?" Natasha pulled her daughter close.

"I dunno," Skye lied. The truth was she knew exactly what she wanted. She had hoped and dreamed for it her entire life. HAD No. 1 was to live up to her mother's expectations.

Unfortunately, Natasha expected perfection.

And perfection was no fun at all.

2

ALPHA JET
SOMEWHERE
SUNDAY, SEPTEMBER 5TH
9:24 A.M.

At thirty-eight thousand feet, Allie Abbott tried to GPS her emotional state. It was somewhere between *wow* and *whoa, what have I done!?* Her emerald-colored contact lenses flitted around the womblike belly of the personal private plane. After two-plus hours of flying and crying, her eyes were finally dry enough to take in their surroundings.

Hammered silver coated the convex egg-shaped walls, reflecting prisms and rainbows all over the cabin.

"I'm made from sixty thousand recycled aluminum cans," the wall announced in a woman's British accent when she ran her fingers over its warped surface.

She Purelled immediately.

Still, Allie never would have known that she was flying "green" if the plane's automated voice didn't remind her every time she touched anything. But maybe that was because the only thing she saw lately was red.

"Refreshment?" asked a bamboo cup as it magically hovered above her hand.

"Sure." Allie sniffled. She reached for the drink and gulped it down. "Barf!" she choke-shouted and then dry-heaved. T⸺rt sludge clawed at her taste buds, and then her chee⸺ ⸺ked in.

"Pr⸺ ⸺ lemonade?" asked a smoot⸺ ⸺ the cockpit. It wa⸺ ⸺. The sam⸺ ⸺iscreet lo⸺ ⸺er there w⸺ ⸺unway in

⸺ed—a skill ⸺nething that ⸺nded. Because ⸺ a very different Allie ⸺. The girl power poet–slash–eco⸺ the heartbroken mall model who worship⸺ ⸺e, pop songs, and Pop-Tarts. No. No one wanted that ⸺ ⸺ie these days.

Thumbing away another tear, Allie nestled into her ergonomic recliner. It was made of what looked like bubble wrap filled with water and felt like a massage from a hundred different people at once. If her intestines weren't contracting from the shot of wheat-ass, it might have felt incredible.

"Movie," Allie told the U-shaped plasma screen inside the curved wall. The lights dimmed and an electric cart filled with organic popcorn pulled up beside her. A hemp blanket slid out of the armrest like a fax and wrapped around her entire body until she felt like a crab hand roll.

Leonardo DiCaprio's *Eleventh Hour* began immediately. "This film will be shown in high definition using patent-pending Smell-O-Vision, a feature that sprays a scent to match the image on-screen." Just then Leo appeared on screen, accompanied by the fresh aroma of jojoba and eucalyptus, the notes in Fletcher's Intense Therapy Lip Balm.

Allie's mouth began to involuntarily pucker, longing for the taste of her ex-boyfriend's kisses. Serious-leh? If flying on a talking personal jet to an unknown destination while committing identity theft didn't help her forget him, a lobotomy was the only remaining option.

Allie had first seen Fletcher Barton at the Riverside Palace Mall. They'd locked eyes on the north escalators—she was going up, he was going down. Her arms were full of bags. His were full of muscles. Goose bumps sprouted all over her spray-tanned body that had nothing to do with the frigid air-conditioning and everything to do with his leather jacket. He was tall and fit, with product-enhanced light-brown hair and narrow blue eyes. She was the same. For a second, Allie wondered if they were related. Maybe fraternal twins separated at birth. But their attraction had been too strong for something that creepy.

Allie wanted to race toward him. But she was too awe-struck. Like in those dreams where you run and run but never move, she remained frustrated and frozen.

"Wait!" he shouted, pushing past moms and their kids, taking the steps two at a time as he darted up the down escalator.

They met at the top.

"I'm Fletcher," he panted, holding out his hand.

Allie immediately put down her bags and stuffed her hands in the kangaroo pouch of her suede tunic. She pocket-pumped some Purell onto her palms and rubbed them together. Not because she thought he looked germy. In fact, he looked more sanitary that any boy she'd ever seen. But because he had been gripping the rubber rail for at least twenty seconds, and that was more than enough time for a virus to adhere to his fingertips.

"You want?" Allie extended the clear bottle.

"No, thanks." He smiled with his entire face. "I've got the wipes." He pulled a square package out of his back pocket, tore it open with his tartar-free teeth, and rubbed. With a swift toss, the used cloth soared straight in the trash can and Cupid's arrow straight into Allie's heart.

From then on they were inseparable, and quickly became known for their combined physical perfection and strong immune systems. Everyone joked that when they got married and had kids, they would be studied for advancing the human genome. Allie said it too, only she was serious.

And the best part was that her BFF, Trina, who was single, and much less attractive than them, never got jealous or made Allie choose. In fact, she seemed just as inspired by their beauty as everyone else. Always wanting to be around them and nibble on the by-product of their love. But what Trina lacked in beauty she made up for in artistic talent. She could create a portrait faster than Polaroid—and offered to tag along with the couple to Disneyland for their eleven-month anniversary. Her gift would be to sketch every moment of their enchanted day in charcoal and red pastel.

"Ha!" A bitter laugh escaped Allie's waxy Burt's Bees–coated lips, an unfortunate favorite of Allie J's.

"Everything okay back there?" the voice asked from the cockpit.

Um, if by okay you mean wanting to shove my bare unpedicured foot up my ex-friend's butt like a shish kebab skewer, then yes, everything is fine, Allie wanted to shout. But that would blow her cover faster than a DNA sample. So she simply nodded yes and forced a smile in case the omniscient voice could see her from behind the aluminum wall.

"Good," it replied, satisfied.

But it wasn't. Nothing was good. Not since the happy threesome had boarded the yellow-and-blue submarine on the *Finding Nemo* ride. Not since everything went dark when they had been "swallowed by a whale." Not since the lights flashed back on and Fletcher's neck was covered in charcoal fingerprints. And Trina's lips smelled like jojoba and eucalyptus. And they both looked more caught than Nemo.

Allie slammed her compact shut without the satisfying click. She just didn't get it. She was beautiful. And not just in her opinion. She had the pageant tiaras and tear sheets from local modeling jobs to prove it. With puffy O-shaped lips, narrow navy blue eyes, skin that looked lit from within, and a nose so perfectly sloped that a girl two towns over had requested it for her fifteenth birthday, Beauty was her backstage pass. It got her everything she ever wanted. So why hadn't it been enough to keep Fletcher? Or rather, how had she lost him to a girl who was a mere 6.5 out of 10 after Photoshop?

She'd asked him that one day after school.

"Alliecat, you're a hottie, no question." Fletch leaned back like there was a wall behind him, even though they were in the middle of the basketball court during practice. "But Trina's talent is more attractive than being a perfect ten." He caught the ball and began dribbling it down the court. Allie followed despite the angry coach and his threats to call the police. Fletcher shot and scored. His teammates smacked him high fives. In the empty stands, Trina speed-sketched the moment. Allie began to cry.

"I'm sorry." Fletcher wiped his sweaty forehead with the bottom of his jersey. "But it's not about looks for me."

"Since when?" Allie mumbled, eyeing Trina's witchy black bangs, asymmetrical brown eyes, and pressed-down nose with borderline envy. Maybe if she had been born ugly she would have had to develop a talent too. But she hadn't been. And that wasn't her fault! Yet here she was, paying the price.

"Since always," Fletcher insisted, obviously lying. Because for the last eleven months he'd had no problem posting her pictures on his Facebook page. "I want to be inspired. And she does that."

"Real-leh? How? By drawing pictures of you out of barbecue ash?" Allie felt the grip of his coach's meaty hands on her shoulder. "Her binder doodles are just another way for you to admire yourself. They're like mirrors or pictures—" The meaty hands tightened and began pushing her toward the exit. "Ow!" Allie squealed all the way to the double doors.

Once outside, she Purelled her shoulder until she heard eleven boys and one girl applauding. It sounded like a thousand tiny slaps.

Word spread quickly about the scandal, and even more quickly about their on-court battle. There was only one thing left to do.

Hide.

Allie retreated into her room with the intention of never leaving it again. Her mom came in frequently with all her favorites from the food court. But the pit in her stomach was too deep to fill, even with Hunan Pan's crispy fried wings and pot stickers. The family doctor came. And the family shrink called. But they both said the same thing. "Get over it!"

"But how?" she pleaded.

"Find something to take your mind off of it," said the family doctor.

"I agree," said the family shrink.

Thanks for sucking, thought Allie.

But two days later, that something was delivered in a heavy, gold package.

Allie sat up in bed and asked her mother to kindly close the door behind her.

It's about time! She sniffled, tearing through the vellum. She wondered if Fletcher would just apologize or actually grovel. A gold mobile device fell onto her duvet-covered lap along with a letter. *Huh?*

Dear Allie J,
We welcome you to the inaugural class of Alpha Academy . . .

Allie whipped the letter on the ground and beat her Tinker Bell pillowcase. It figured Allie J. would be hitting a high note when Allie was at her lowest.

Allie had been getting the songwriter's fan mail for years. But ever since she'd left on some save-the-melting-ice-caps mission in Antarctica, they had been coming more frequently. Allie could have notified the post office, but that would have involved forms and post office people. Both of which were boring and probably covered in germs. Besides, Allie J's songs had shown up on the sound tracks of three teen summer flicks, and according to a blind item in Page Six, a certain trio of Disney brothers were fighting over more than her body of work. And who knew what one of them might send. Maybe himself?

Allie lowered her head, succumbing to a new generation of tears. Through salty blurred vision the gold seal of the envelope had caught the light and winked at her from the floor. Like they shared a joke. Or a secret. Or the need to escape.

Allie raced to her laptop and Google-imaged Allie J. Only three pics came up:

A green eye behind a mess of black hair.

Her thin body photographed from behind. She was onstage, facing the audience at New York's famed spoken word Nuyorican Café in a white dress and bare feet.

A grainy camera-phone pic of her face with what appeared to be a very large mole.

And that was it.

It was perfect.

Allie raced to the mall for the first time in days.

Hours later, she had black hair, green contact lenses, and a kohl-mole on her left cheek. She told her parents the new look was part one of her "get over it" plan. Part two was applying to Alpha Academy. They couldn't quite understand the mole, or how "catalogue modeling and a vast knowledge of mall culture" were talents Shira Brazille valued, but they went with it anyway. At least she was eating pot stickers again.

Days later, Allie waved her acceptance letter around (after gold-outing the J) and said goodbye to her supportive parents.

And here she was, a green-eyed butterfly flying toward a new beginning on a top secret mission to Get Over It.

"Sixty seconds until we enter the communications-free zone. No texting, no phoning, no Internet," announced the British voice.

"For how long?" Allie asked the speaker above her head.

"Until you return."

"Serious-leh?"

"Fifty seconds."

What? Allie felt her stomach twirl like the food court's Jamba Juice machine. If she couldn't let Fletcher and Trina know how awesome her life was without them, what was the point? She whipped out her Samsung and began texting.

I'm on a private plane heading for Alpha Academy. This is the last time you will hear from me. Turns out I have talent after all.

Allie read it over. Did the message imply *I am fine without you? I have moved on? I have more talent than Trina?*

"Twenty seconds." A countdown appeared where Leo's face had been. It smelled like loneliness.

Allie's thumb hovered over the send button. It was missing something, something that stung like a thousand tiny slaps. Something that—

"Nine seconds."

"Got it!" Allie half smiled, mindful of smudging her mole, and then added one final line.

In this world there are artists and subjects. You know, the people worth drawing? Well, I am a subject. I always will be. Capture me if you can. —Allie

She hit send and dropped the obsolete phone on the lap of her secondhand white dress—apparently Emily Dickinson had worn something white every day, and so did Allie J. But even after dry-cleaning nine times and liberally spraying the dress with Clinique Happy, Allie still smelled dead people.

"We are now in a communications-free zone," announced

the voice. "And are beginning our descent to Alpha Island, where temperature on the ground is a perfect seventy-two degrees." She snickered softly. "For now."

The aluminum walls disappeared into the floor and the entire plane became one big window. Below, clear blue water stretched on for miles. Was it ocean? A lake? A giant collection of her tears? The round windows reminded Allie of the portholes on the *Finding Nemo* submarine. The bitter taste of wheatgrass returning to her mouth.

Suddenly a mass of land came into view. It was as if someone had taken a giant @-shaped cookie cutter and carved an island out of mirrors, or some other reflective surface that was probably good for the environment.

Without warning, the plane swooped down along with Allie's stomach, as she considered what she'd gotten herself into. Sticking an earbud in each ear, she let the words from Allie J's latest hit, "Global Heartwarming," coax her into character.

Reduce, reuse, and recycle my heart
Give it back to me
'Cause I want a fresh start
Now that I'm fine,
You're on your knees
Begging me please
To be your main squeeze

You're starting to panic
Calling me satanic
But I prefer organic
And hold the cheese!

Reduce, reuse, and recycle my heart
It's ready for a brand-new start

She'd never really liked Allie J's music—she was too folksy and message-y for Allie's aerobic taste. But the lyrics to this one were spot-on. She tapped her newly short nails and continued memorizing the words, which could have been written for her—or better yet, by her. Then she touched up her mole and cranked the volume.

The jet was starting to dip. It was showtime.

3

ALPHA ACADEMY
JETWAY
SUNDAY, SEPTEMBER 5TH
1:43 P.M.

The gold glitter-flakes on the tarmac suddenly started to liquefy.

"Mom, what's happening?" Charlie Deery loosened her metallic tie and began fanning her flushing cheeks. "The temperature just went from seventy-two degrees to three thousand!"

"Hyperbole, Chah-lie," Bee Deery corrected her Jersey-born daughter in a proper British accent, as if exaggeration was strictly an American trait. Bee quickly reached for the sagging silver material around her daughter's neck and retied it. Not even the familiar smell of her rose-scented body cream—the only constant in Charlie's life—could soothe her today.

"Hyperbo-leave-me-alone!" Charlie swatted her mother's fussing hands and then instantly regretted it. Aggression toward Bee was like beating on Bambi, only worse. "Sorry."

She avoided her mother's kind brown eyes. "But I can't breathe."

Bee quickly scanned the area and then refastened the tie with a once-and-for-all cinch. "This is no time for a uniform violation. Not on the first day. Shira has enough stress as it is."

"What about me?" Charlie stomped her foot in a gold puddle, forever frustrated by her mother's efforts to please her boss, at any cost, even familial asphyxiation. "I don't even go here. Who cares if I wear the stupid tie?"

"It's about respect," Bee insisted, patting her tightly wound updo. Was it held by hair spray or the power of positive thinking?

With a surrendering sigh, Bee aimed her A-pod at Charlie's uniform: a platinum vest, matching tie, pleated mini in shimmering pewter, champagne-colored blouse with oversize puffed sleeves, and clear knee-high gladiator sandals with massaging soles and no–tan line technology. "Here." She pushed a button. The microscopic crystals in Charlie's shirt turned icy cool. "Better?"

"Much." Charlie smile-thanked her.

Just then, a giant glass Twizzler-shaped tower rose up from the ground with the hushed hum of a passing golf cart. One hundred platforms jutted off the sides. One for each Personal Alpha Plane—or PAP as Charlie and her mother secretly joked—to park after landing.

Charlie lifted her brown eyes and searched the sun-soaked sky. Flecks of light flashed in the distance like copper-colored winks. They were getting closer.

Shira's ground team raced onto the tarmac wearing thick regulation jumpsuits in white patent leather. Apparently they absorbed the reflection of the gold dust on the runway so the pilots wouldn't be blinded during landing.

"Why don't you just get rid of the gold dust?" Charlie asked, imagining how hot the team must have been.

Bee smoothed her white pleather blazer and skirt. "Because Shira likes it."

And that was that.

Suddenly Bee turned away, curling her ear toward her shoulder. "Affirmative," she reported into her Bluetooth device, which had been remodeled to look like a diamond stud earring. Charlie knew for a sad fact that she never turned it off, even when going two in the loo. She hoped the loyalty stemmed from pride—Charlie had invented the fashion-forward device—but knew better. Being Shira's head assistant wasn't a job, it was lifestyle. Minus the life. And being out of reach was not an option.

"We're in position." She nodded, still cupping her ear. "Yes. We're on the welcome platform, above the tarmac, facing due south."

Bee's warm brown eyes zeroed in on the hem of Charlie's

skirt—a prototype that was being donated to the Smithsonian as soon as the real Alphas arrived and Charlie left for boarding school in Hoboken. Which was in exactly ninety minutes. The devastating reality made her stomach lurch. Or was that her heart?

"Ugh!" She wiggled, as if trying to slip out of her own skin.

"Stand still," her mom demanded, snapping an errant thread off the pleated pewter mini.

But Charlie couldn't stand still. Time was running out. In eighty-eight minutes she wouldn't just be leaving her mother. Or the island she'd secretly helped design. She would be leaving him.

The oppressive heat suddenly blew by like a bad smell in the wind. A gray cloud mass gathered overhead, and warm droplets, the temperature of tears, began to fall. Well past caring, she didn't bother to cover the precious uniform. Instead she slipped the A-pod prototype out of her pocket and checked her messages. There were three gold heart bubbles, all from Darwin, all asking when he could see her.

For the last ten months, while Bee oversaw the construction of Alpha Island, Charlie played *Blue Lagoon* with her fifteen-year-old boyfriend, Darwin Brazille, Shira's oldest son. She hung out with all five Brazille brothers but had loved Darwin ever since they first napped together, twelve years ago, in the nursery on Shira's private plane. Darwin, on the other hand, claimed he'd loved her even before they met. And Charlie believed him. He never gave her any reason not to.

Since then, they had traveled the world together, getting homeschooled by life experience and a tutor who was legally bound to make sure their education was up to conventional standards, should they ever choose to enter society. Once she turned twelve, the tutor resigned. They had successfully passed their tenth-grade finals and were given the green light to sit back and enjoy the ride. A ride, that thanks to their hardworking mothers, took them to the most exotic places on the planet and left them alone to explore. A ride that filled their digital cameras with more romantic shots than a season of *The Bachelor*. A ride that, thanks to Shira, was about to end in a devastating crash.

"She's doing it on purpose." Charlie dabbed the corner of her eye with her champagne-colored sleeve, a flulike ache pulsing thorough her entire body.

"I sincerely doubt she built all this to break you and Darwin up." Bee splayed her arms, indicating the acres of state of the art architecture, woman-made beaches, and advanced technology.

"Then why am I getting sent back east to some boarding school while Darwin stays here, with a pack of alpha females?"

Bee sighed, like she was tired of saying what she was about to say but would say it one last time. "Every girl at the academy has been hand-selected by Shira because of her outstanding abilities. And after giving it a lot of thought, she figured it wouldn't be fair to admit you based on family connections. Not fair to them and not fair to you."

Charlie clenched her fists, wanting to punch the fawn right out of Bambi.

"Besides, do you really think a few months apart is going to undo twelve years?" Bee raised her light, arched brows and shook her head in disbelief. "Since when are you insecure about Darwin?"

"I'm not insecure about Darwin," Charlie insisted. "I'm insecure about me."

Charlie, despite her advanced brain and waist-length locks, always saw herself as a medium. Medium brown hair. Medium texture between a wave and a curve. Medium-size brown eyes. Medium hotness—more Aniston than Angie.

"We Deery women have a quiet beauty that sneaks up on people. At least that's what your father used to say." Bee smiled fondly at his memory.

Charlie twisted the three silver bracelets on her wrist. "Mom, guys don't want beauty that creeps. They want beauty that comes up and slaps them across the face. And that's what's about to land here. One hundred times over."

The rain stopped suddenly. Bee squinted up at the sky. The copper-colored kisses were getting bigger. "You are more talented than any of those girls, and Darwin knows that."

"Yeah, but Shira doesn't," Charlie hissed. "She has no

idea that I took apart her robo dog when I was ten and reprogrammed it to act like a cat. Or that I used to take the engines out of Darwin's electric cars and put them in my Bratz dolls so they could braid each other's hair. Or that I put wings on her cell so it would fly back when she lost it. Or that I invented the digital-camo iPhone case that changed color to match her outfits. She doesn't know you gave my blueprints to the Alpha lab and that most of this place was designed by me. Maybe if she did, she'd let me stay here with you and Darwin. But she's too arrogant to see it and you're too afraid to tell her."

"Lower your voice," Bee whisper-snapped.

But Charlie couldn't. Her voice had been lowered for too long.

Suddenly, a warm wind blew their clothes dry instantly and restored the gold puddles to dust.

"Maybe if I showed her what I made for Darwin she'd see that I'm not useless and let me stay." Charlie pulled an electronic butterfly out of her wrist-pack and slowly opened her hand.

"What does it do?" Bee couldn't help smiling at the cute little iridescent creature that batted its heart-shaped wings in Charlie's palm.

Charlie lowered her head, thinking of her first kiss with Darwin at the Butterfly Botanical Garden in Costa Rica. She kissed the butterfly softly. All of a sudden it took flight.

"Oh, it's wonderful." Bee clapped her hands until it landed, then smiled sadly. "Now put it away, sweetie. She'll be here any minute."

"I'm gonna show her," Charlie decided, filling with hope.

"Impossible." Bee sighed. "You've used her resources without permission."

"So?"

"Remember when she arrested Assistant Seven for filling her canteen from the glacier springs? She accused her of stealing. Imagine what she'll do when she discovers how much of her lab has become your secret workshop?"

Charlie lowered her head. More droplets fell. This time from her eyes.

"I know it's hard, love. But your time will come. For now, try to remember that Shira has given us everything."

"No, she's given us everything she doesn't want."

Charlie's fingers immediately went to the three silver bracelets on her wrist. Both she and Darwin had DD's (Dead Dads) who had died in car accidents when they were babies. His had left him a roomful of vinyl records, explaining his love for music. And hers had left the bracelets, an heirloom he had inherited from his mother. Each bracelet had a cameo that opened; one held a picture of her mom, one of her dad, and one of Darwin. They were the only non-Shira-tainted thing she owned. Everything else had once been Shira's or bought by Shira or bought for Shira and never returned.

Suddenly, the sky darkened overhead and more storm clouds rolled in. Thunder crackled in the distance. The temperature dropped twenty degrees in an instant.

Bee pressed a button on her A-pod to warm her daughter's uniform and then rolled back her shoulders.

A clear platform, identical to the one they were standing on, rose up from the ground. Shira, hands resting on the railing like she was standing at the bow of a ship, gazed at the horizon until the platform locked into place. She turned to face them; her wavy auburn hair blew as if blasted by a wind machine while her navy off-the-shoulder Grecian dress remained perfectly still. As usual, dark round sunglasses concealed her eyes.

In twelve years, Charlie had never seen her without them. One rumor was that Shira had tried to lighten her green irises but something had gone wrong and they had turned yellow, like a snake's. Others swore she had bat sonar technology implanted in her eyeballs so she could out-see regular humans. But Charlie had her own theory. Which was: Shira just liked to freak people out.

"Unbelievable!" Shira's down-under accent was outback fresh, even though she'd been off the continent for nearly two decades.

A crack of thunder startled everyone but Shira.

"What is it?" Bee cooed with dutiful concern.

"I just lost a promising actress to a George Clooney

movie." Her jaw muscles twitched. "Bee, call the producer and have her removed from the picture."

The appropriate contact information appeared in Bee's A-pod.

"What time would you like her here?"

"Here?" Shira's lips tightened. "I don't want that no-hoper here. I want her working in a Chuck E. Cheese costume by sundown."

Bee turned away with a reluctant sigh and began dialing.

Charlie's fingers started tingling. They always did when she thought up a new invention. It was her body urging her to start building. Only this time her tongue tingled too, forcing her to speak.

"So does this mean you have an open spot?" she asked quickly, before her mother could get off the phone.

Shira slowly nodded yes.

"Maybe I could take it?" she asked meekly.

"You?" Another crack of thunder echoed across the campus.

Charlie's legs began tingling. They wanted to run.

"What can you do?" she laughed without smiling. "Besides distract my son?"

Charlie reached into her wrist pack. "I kind of make things." She opened her hand. The metal butterfly sat stiffly in her palm. "Look." She kissed it and it flew.

"What are you doing?" Bee snapped her phone shut and glared at her daughter.

"She's trying to convince me to give her the open spot," Shira checked her reflection in her silver mirrored nail polish. "But we all know that's impossible."

"Why?" Charlie blurted. "Because you want me away from Darwin? Because you don't think I'm good enough—"

"Charlie!" Bee hissed.

"Well, I do question your motives for wanting to attend the academy." Shira brushed a speck of glitter off her pale forearm. "I didn't build it for girls to get their C-R-U-S-H degrees."

Charlie narrowed her brown eyes, no longer fearing the woman she had feared for years. She was about to get exiled from Alpha Island—what did she have to lose? "I don't want to go to the academy for Darwin." *Only*, she added silently. "I want to go for me." *And him. For us!*

Shira turned to face her. "It's a moot point, Lollie," she stated with feigned disappointment. "The admissions committee has strict rules about nepotism. Stating that anyone related to an employee can't attend."

"But you are the committee!"

"That's enough, Charlotte!" Bee insisted. "It's settled." She turned to Shira, her scowl dissolving like Crystal Light in water. "The actress has been removed from the film. Clooney sends his deepest apologies. Will there be anything else or can I release the circle-hold on the planes and prepare the ground crew for arrival?"

Shira tapped her nails against the platform railing, and the sky cleared instantly. "Unless . . ."

The single word hung in the air. Bee's eyes widened in anticipation. Charlie held her breath.

"Unless"—Shira turned toward her longtime assistant—"you resigned. Then Charlie wouldn't be related to anyone." She grinned, clearly pleased with herself for having lowered the evil bar that much closer to hell.

"What?" Charlie locked eyes with her mother's, a barrage of sentiments passing silently between them.

Bee's fluttering lids seemed to ask if this was what she really wanted. If she would be okay without her. If this would make her happy.

"Very well." Bee stretched up to her full height of five foot two. "I quit."

"Are you kidding? Mom, you can't!" Charlie blurted. Ever since her dad died, Bee had worked birthdays, holidays, weekends—work was as much a part of her mother as afternoon tea. And as much as Charlie abhorred Shira, she wasn't sure Bee could cope without her. What would keep her from missing her husband now?

"It's okay." She reached for her daughter's hand. "I've been meaning to visit Mum and Dad in Manchester for twelve years. Don't you think I'm overdue?"

"Are you sure about this, Bee?"

Bee gave a nod.

"Very well." Shira nodded back.

It was a done deal.

A look flickered across Shira's face that Charlie had never seen before. The corners of her lips lifted. Her brows relaxed behind her glasses. Was that satisfaction or the release of gas?

Bee pulled her daughter close and whispered into her ear. "Chahlie, everything I did was for you. You have a gift. It's time you shared it."

"But Mom, I can't—" Charlie whispered back, unable to fully process what had just happened. Within minutes, the entire course of her mother's life had changed. And for what? A boy?

"Do we have a deal?" Shira extended her arm.

Bee elbowed her daughter in the ribs. Charlie surrendered and offered her right hand.

"No." Shira shooed it away. "The other one."

"Huh?" Charlie slowly held out her left.

Shira stepped to the edge of her platform, leaned forward, and slipped a bracelet off Charlie's arm. In a single motion she popped open the cameo and removed the round picture of her son. Pleased, she handed it back.

How did you know about the photo? How did you know which bracelet it was in? How can you just take that from me? Charlie wanted to shout. But she couldn't. Her stomach was in her throat.

The sky buzzed. A fleet of gold-tinted PAPs circled overhead, waiting for clearance to land. Shira nodded at Bee. Bee signaled the crew to bring the planes in. It was her final job for Brazille Enterprises.

"As long as you're here, you will focus on your studies," Shira stated, watching her protégés descend onto the runway and roll to a stop. "Darwin is off-limits. When you break up with him, leave this conversation out of it. A true alpha makes sacrifices for her goals. And he will be your first sacrifice." She made a fist around the photo and squeezed. "Understood?"

Charlie inhaled deeply, trying to steady herself with her breath. Could she really convince Darwin she was over him? Did she even have a choice? What was the alternative? Boarding school in New Jersey? A long-distance relationship with the two most important people in her life? At least now she'd be able to see one of them. And maybe in time, if she got the grades, Shira would see that she was good enough for her son. And her mom could get her job back and—

"Understood?" Shira pressed.

"Understood," Charlie managed.

Shira's lips curled back against her teeth. To the untrained eye, it might have looked like a smile. But Charlie knew better. It was the look of a predator preparing to devour her prey.

"Welcome to Alpha Academy."

MEET THE ALPHAS

08·25·09

Two Ah-mazing
New CLIQUE Books

Coming Fall 2009

Special
Hardcover
Edition

Once upon a time, four betas
were waiting for their alpha.

Find out how the CLIQUE met in
**HARMED AND DANGEROUS:
The Rise of the Pretty Commitee**

Available 10/27/09

When it comes to ah-dorable
clothes, lip-kissing, and comebacks,
the Pretty Committee is always
prepared. You can be too with the
CLIQUETIONARY—your source
for all things CLIQUE.

**Available November 2009...
Just in time for the *holla*-days!**

poppy

Five Spectacular Stories.
One Ah-mazing Summer.

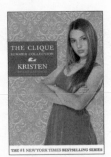

Fashion isn't everything.
It's the *only* thing. . . .

POSEUR

When four sophomores with a fierce passion for fashion are put in a class to create their own designer label, they Clash with a capital C. At LA's Winston Prep, survival of the fittest comes down to who fits in—and what fits.

POSEUR

The Good, the Fab and the Ugly

Petty in Pink

Welcome to Poppy.

A poppy is a beautiful blooming red flower
(like the one on the spine of this book). It is also
the name of the home of your favorite books.

Poppy takes the real world and makes it
a little funnier, a little more fabulous.

Poppy novels are wild, witty, and inspiring.
They were written just for you.

So sit back, get comfy, and pick a Poppy.

poppy

www.pickapoppy.com

THE A-LIST gossip girl THE CLIQUE

ALPHAS SECRETS OF MY
HOLLYWOOD LIFE POSEUR